FIELDS OF
WRATH

FIELDS OF WRATH

MARK WHEATON

Text copyright © 2016 Mark Wheaton

Published by Thomas & Mercer, Seattle

www.apub.com

Amazon, the Amazon logo, and Thomas & Mercer are trademarks of Amazon.com, Inc., or its affiliates.

ISBN-13: 9781503949966
ISBN-10: 1503949966

Cover design by Marc Cohen

Printed in the United States of America

For Lauren

PART I

/

I

The ocean came to him first. A breeze swept over the hills and cooled his skin. It arrived next as a taste, salt agitating his tongue and blistered lips. His water supply was long spent. Then it came as a sound, the tide crashing somewhere to the west. He didn't have far to go now.

Fifteen minutes later and he was looking at it, the undulating, black waters of the Pacific stretching to the horizon, where it met the cloudless field of stars.

It hadn't been so many years since the last time he'd trekked through unfamiliar territory to reach the sea. Like now, he'd done so to leave one life behind and begin another. He prayed he wouldn't have to do it again.

He moved to the edge of the ridge. The beach was a good eighty feet down at an incline that might as well have been ninety degrees. There was a highway between the cliff base and the beach. The headlights of the occasional passing vehicle were the first signs of civilization he'd seen for hours. He wondered if he'd have the energy to dash across the unlit road but then saw the narrow tunnel that ran under the highway.

He just had to get down the cliff.

With his feet cut, bleeding, and blistered, he knew he couldn't do it upright. Lowering himself onto his knees, he took a deep breath and started scaling down backwards. His hands grasped for every rock and root as he kept as little weight as possible on dubious toeholds. Any misstep could be fatal.

The sound of the ocean grew as he descended. It felt as if he were lowering himself straight into the water. He imagined finding a boat and sailing away, never to return.

When he finally reached the bottom, tears filled his eyes. His knees had taken the brunt of the damage, blood trickling down his shins from half a dozen nicks. But it was over.

He hurried into the tunnel. The walls and ceiling were impressively tagged for such an isolated location. He tried to read a few of the highly stylized scribblings, but in the dim light they were as unintelligible as hieroglyphs.

Local poseurs, he mused. *Not a lot of hard-core gangsters out in the Santa Ynez Mountains.*

He emerged from the tunnel to find the beach's parking lot was roped off by a heavy chain. A sign hanging from it read, "Refugio Canyon State Beach—Open Daily, Sunrise to Sunset. Violators Will Be Fined."

He checked his watch. It was five minutes until two. However unlikely, he'd made it with time to spare.

He stepped over the chain. The narrow strip of sand, bracketed on both sides by piles of boulders, wasn't much to look at. The break of the water suggested it wouldn't be much good for surfing, swimming, or fishing, and it was too far from LA for day-trippers, making it strangely romantic. He imagined bringing Odilia here when things calmed down. Annie had warned them that they'd probably be confined for the first few months at least, but maybe they could steal away for just an afternoon.

He considered kicking off his shoes and stepping in but knew the salt would burn in his wounds. He'd driven down to the cliffs at Point Mugu once with his sister and her son. He'd heard you could see migrating whales out in the ocean from there. They'd stood for hours convincing each other that every rise and cresting wave was a humpback, an orca, or a shark.

He'd see them again soon, too. There would be a long, difficult conversation. But then they'd be all right. Or so he hoped.

He was suddenly engulfed in light. A car emerged from the narrow tunnel and paused at the chain. It was a cab.

"Uh . . . Santiago Higuera?" The cabdriver sounded surprised. Prepaid fare or not, it didn't seem like he thought anyone would actually be in this spot at the appointed time.

Santiago jogged over. The driver was Indian or Pakistani, maybe in his fifties. By the way the cabbie eyed him, Santiago knew he must look pretty bad.

"I have an address in Morningside Park," the driver said as Santiago half climbed, half collapsed across the backseat. "Four thirty-one and a half, South Fourth."

"Sounds good," Santiago said breathlessly. "Can we just go?"

Catching a sidelong glance from the driver, Santiago wiped the fear from his face.

———

Annie Whittaker's watch said it was 2:50, her laptop 2:52. Either was bad news.

"He's probably still in the cab," she said into the phone.

"You don't sound confident."

"Two forty-five was our best guess, barring traffic," she said. "We knew there could be other variables."

"My guy's already been by the house twice. Knocked on the gate and the front door. I don't think we can get away with sending him back many more times. You don't have any way of communicating with him?"

"I don't," she said, fighting back panic. "But this was your suggestion, remember?"

"Annie, I know how hard you've worked on this. It's just as important to this office *and* me. But I told you from the beginning, if we don't handle this right, we can lose everything. We'll do our part, but I need your assurance that there won't be any surprises on your end."

Annie inhaled. "Have your guy circle back in half an hour. That's all I ask."

———

Santiago said nothing on the drive into the city. The driver nodded to the satellite radio on the dashboard.

"You want to listen to the game?"

Santiago had no idea what game the man was speaking about and gave a noncommittal shrug. He turned back to the window and peered at passing cars. He didn't think they'd been followed but couldn't help himself. The driver left the radio off.

The cab exited the highway. The address was in South Central, which Santiago knew was off-limits for some cabdrivers. This one didn't seem to mind. They reached Crenshaw and pulled off the main street. The GPS guided them into a residential neighborhood. When they reached Fourth, the driver slowed. Santiago scanned the curbside numbers for 432.

"This is it," he announced.

Santiago hopped out and waved to the driver.

"Gracias!"

Santiago felt the driver's eyes on him as he jogged up the driveway, eschewing the front door for a gate leading to the backyard. He remembered the instructions and reached over to unhook the latch. It was just within reach. He pushed the gate open and slipped inside. Only when he closed the gate did the cab pull away.

He went to the side door and put his hand on the knob. It was unlocked and turned with the slightest pressure. He entered, resisted the urge to turn on a light, and waited by the window to see if any other cars would appear.

The man had been stuck in the same position for hours. There was no wind or moon, the only scent that of the nearby hackberry and jacaranda trees. The houses within his zone of fire all shared the same silhouette, the only difference in floor plan being whether the garage was on the left side of the house or right. Beyond that, the roofs, brick color, lawn, and token sapling thrust into each front lawn were the same.

He aimed his scope into the other houses, hoping again for some kind of peep show. The best he could do was a middle-aged housewife watching television in a terry-cloth robe. He waited for it to open a little or ride up, but it never did.

Shit.

He checked his watch. Ten past three. He turned the scope back to the only house with lights ablaze in every room of the first floor. The woman there was still pacing. He sighted down the barrel, held his thumb over the safety release, and waited.

There was almost no furniture in the house on South Fourth. A bed was in the bedroom, a sofa and easy chair in the living room, a refrigerator in the kitchen, but that was it. If not for the fresh towels in the bathroom, it would've looked like a time-share, albeit in an unlikely location.

Santiago searched the kitchen cabinets for food but found only disposable cups and plates. A few plastic forks, chopsticks, packets of soy sauce, and a pile of takeout menus sat in the drawer. He finally found a packet of microwavable popcorn and tossed it in the microwave. When only half the bag had popped, he took it out, tore it open, and shoveled a few dozen kernels into his mouth without caring that they burned his tongue.

Temporarily sated, he went to take a shower.

The past week had been mad. He hadn't been able to relax since Annie, the legal aide, told him their plan was a go. He'd have preferred she waited until hours before rather than days. Less time to overthink. Fewer opportunities to fuck up.

As the dirt and grime sluiced down and away from his body, he finally relaxed. He wouldn't be staying long, but it'd be nice while it lasted. He had no idea what the next few days would be like, to say nothing of the next few months. It would all be different now. For him, for his family, and hopefully for many more.

Including Odilia. God, when she was finally in his arms, it would be paradise.

He heard a noise from the other room.

"I'm in the shower!" he called in Spanish.

As he squirted a dollop of shampoo into his hand, the door burst open.

"Hey, what . . . ?"

Before he could finish, two men in the uniforms of the Los Angeles County Sheriff's Department—one white, one Hispanic—yanked him out. He kicked and flailed, but two swift elbows to the temple and he was out like a light.

Annie's heart leapt when she saw the number from the LA district attorney's office on her caller ID.

"Do you have him?" she asked.

"No. My guy just left the house. Still nobody there. I had to send him home."

That's when Annie knew. Somebody had found out. Santiago had either been taken that evening or intercepted on the way. Either scenario was devastating.

"I'll find out what happened," she said evenly. "Will you be there when I call?"

The deputy DA on the other end of the line, Michael Story, didn't hide his exasperation.

"I'm sorry, Annie," he replied. "Not sure what more I can do for you, and I've got court in a few hours. If we've tipped our hand, we'll never get another chance at these guys. And the blowback's going to be killer."

"I won't let that happen. It's not over yet. Wait by the phone."

Annie hung up before Michael could respond. It was ten till four. She turned to the young woman who'd been sitting in the corner of the room throughout the evening. If she'd moved an inch, Annie hadn't noticed.

"I have to leave," Annie said, seeing the apprehension rise on the young woman's face. "I shouldn't be gone long."

The young woman nodded.

The statement was something of a lie. Annie had no idea how long she'd be gone. But she couldn't say that. She grabbed her keys and walked out.

The shooter exhaled, waited until the woman was three steps from the driver's door of her blue Civic, and pulled the trigger. The bullet took so long to reach her, he momentarily wondered if he'd missed.

Impossible, he thought.

Half a second later she was lifted off her feet and propelled forward into the car. He chambered a second round and fired again. This bullet, aimed at a nonmoving target, tore through her throat with such force it almost severed her head.

He considered a third shot but knew she was dead from the first bullet. A third round was not only unnecessary, it would add to the ballistics evidence. He cleared the chamber and was preparing to depart when he detected movement. He swung the barrel around, catching sight of a figure running through Annie's backyard. He turned the night vision back on as whoever it was flung open the back gate and emerged into the arroyo behind Annie's walled neighborhood.

It was another woman.

He yanked back the slide, drawing a third bullet from the magazine into the chamber. He sighted on her torso and slowed his breathing. He needed a clean shot. Anything else wasn't worth taking.

The woman ran along the back wall in a straight line. This told him she had no idea anyone was aiming at her. It wasn't even sporting.

He led her with the barrel a second longer, exhaled, and squeezed the trigger.

II

"I'm sorry, Mr. Chavez," the club's young assistant reception manager, Talya, said. "This is a private club. If you're not a member, your name has to be on the guest list."

Luis Chavez sighed. He wasn't here by choice.

"I was told to come here at this time," Luis replied.

"By whom?" Talya asked.

Luis watched her eyes weigh his appearance. He was in black pants, heavy black shoes, and wore a gray jacket zipped up to his Adam's apple even though it was almost summer. He was clean shaven with short black hair. That he wasn't representative of the club's regular clientele wasn't even a question.

"Mr. Alazraqui."

"I'm sorry. We don't have a member by that name or anyone on our guest list."

Luis nodded. His job was done. He could go home in good conscience.

"My mistake," Luis said, nodding to the young woman.

He turned and was almost out the door when a white Mercedes SUV rolled up to the valet stand just outside in the sublevel parking garage. Its driver was a large Hispanic man practically bursting through the seams of an off-white suit and mustard-yellow shirt. Even though he was only an inch or two taller than Luis's diminutive five foot three, his expansive girth caused him to dwarf Luis.

Talya stepped past Luis to open the door for him.

"Good morning, Mr. Mata!"

Mata nodded a greeting at her and stepped through the door. As soon as the big man was through, Talya jogged ahead to ring for an elevator. Though the club's entrance was in a parking garage, the club itself was an elevator ride up to the ninth floor.

"Have a good breakfast, sir."

Luis had just located the valet ticket in his pocket when he heard the older man's voice.

"Padre?"

Luis winced.

"Oh, is Mr. Chavez a guest of yours?" Talya asked.

"He's the priest. To deliver the benediction."

Luis caught the surprised look on Talya's face, then felt Mata's heavy hand on his shoulder.

"Come on, Padre. Let's get you upstairs."

As soon as they were inside the elevator, Mata nodded to the tiny strip of white peering over the top of Luis's jacket.

"Why didn't you flash the collar?" Mata asked.

"Waited too late," Luis admitted. "Would've felt like a jerk."

"Ah," Mata said, laughing. "Guess enough people out there think priests are assholes, huh?"

Luis didn't reply.

Luis's benediction had been short and sweet: "Lord, by the light of the Holy Spirit, inspire these men to be wise and visionary in their planning."

The fifty or so businessmen of the Los Angeles chapter of the Mexican American Business and Professional Association mumbled their amens like waking children. A photographer snapped a photo of Luis alongside the chapter's president, Juando Alazraqui. Then he was excused.

When Luis's car was pulled around, his offer of a dollar tip was refused by the valet.

"My aunt," the valet said, eyes averted.

"What's her name?" Luis asked.

"Vaitiare Oyervidez. She has ALS."

Luis nodded and climbed into the car.

Luis didn't relax until he was on his way back downtown to the parish. His car, an '84 Chevy Caprice that had been donated to the church a few years back, was hardly flashy. The air-conditioning didn't work and the taillights were spotty. But what mattered to Luis was that the radio worked perfectly. Though they weren't allowed such things in St. Augustine's rectory, he relished listening to it in the car, albeit with some guilt. Near-monastic solitude forced a person to confront himself as well as his relationship with the ever-present divine. Most of the time this was just fine for Luis. But he was an LA kid. Sometimes the voice of El Cucuy on AM 690 was all it took to make him feel more connected to his roots and less defined by the collar around his neck.

The Church of St. Augustine, established in 1908, and its associated parochial school, St. John's, were located just west of downtown. Luis had been in his fifth year at the St. Robert Bellarmine Seminary in upstate New York when he learned St. Augustine's was ready for him. Though they gave him the opportunity to stay at St. Bellarmine for up to another year, he made the move in six weeks.

"Is he in?" Luis asked as he entered the church's administrative office.

The church secretary, a seventy-year-old laywoman named Erna Dahlstrang, glanced up from the papers strewn across her desk to smile at Luis. He handed over boxes of church bulletins he'd picked up from the printer before heading to the breakfast.

"He is!" Erna said. "How'd it go?"

"I was a prop," Luis replied.

"They already called to see if you could come back next month."

Luis was about to offer a sarcastic response when a voice bellowed from the inner office.

"What, in ill thoughts again?" the voice said. "Men must endure. Their going hence, even as their coming hither."

Erna chuckled as she indicated the office door behind her.

"He's waiting for you."

Pastor Whillans's office was small, windowless, and ringed with floor-to-ceiling bookshelves. Luis used to believe the pastor was making a point in having such a humble space in which to greet guests. Then he saw Whillans only took meetings in the garden or the nave. The office was his sanctuary.

"Matthew 10:22?" Luis asked.

"*King Lear*, act five, scene two," the pastor replied, rising to his feet. "How are you, Father?"

Gregory Hamish Whillans was tall with broad shoulders, but the dimensions of the room made him seem downright giant. He was pale, with a few strands of red hair clinging to a mostly bald pate.

"If you're bothered about this morning," Whillans said when Luis remained silent, "let me assure you it wasn't my decision to send you. They're major donors and good friends of the archdiocese."

"They just want their picture in our bulletin. I didn't know access like that was for sale."

"If it keeps afloat our after-school meals programs, then yes, yes, it is," Whillans said. "It's hardly selling indulgences."

"You're right," Luis charged. "With indulgences, the only thing poisoned were the souls of the sinners who thought they could buy their way into heaven and the priests who took advantage. Here we've taken a more active role."

Whillans sank into his chair, clearly bemused by Luis's comparison.

"If you're judging the sinner and not seeing the man, maybe God really did have a reason to send you out there," Whillans suggested. "I'll pray on this and ask you do the same. Then we'll speak further. Good?"

"Yes, Father."

Before Whillans could dismiss him, there came a frantic knock on the door.

"It's one of the boys from the baseball team," Erna called out. "Says we need to call an ambulance immediately."

"Is one of the boys hurt?" Whillans asked, springing to his feet.

"No, but there's an injured woman in the dugout. They think she's been shot!"

III

Boys in their blue St. John's T-shirts and shorts ringed the visitor's dugout as their coach, Father Sigfrido Territo, squatted inside. The woman was propped up on the bench. Though she'd attempted to hide it with a blanket, Luis saw that the left side of her shirt was stained with blood. She looked pale.

"The field's at the back of the school," Whillans said into his cell phone as he jogged over. "Best access is on West Adams. You can enter through the parking lot."

He hung up and pushed his way through the students.

"An ambulance is on the way," he announced. "How is she?"

"Not sure," Father Territo replied. "I think she was asleep. When one of the boys woke her up, she started ranting in some other language. She's disoriented."

"It was Zapotec," one of the boys said. "My grandma speaks it."

Luis eyed the young woman. She was in her late teens or early twenties. Though she looked as if she'd spent the night on the streets, he didn't think she was homeless. Her clothes, while simple, were recently purchased. He checked her eyes for indications she might be an addict. The tough feral eyes that stared back showed no signs.

"I speak Zapotec," Luis said to Whillans. "My mother was from Ixtlan."

"Ixtlan?" Whillans asked.

"Southern Mexico. Still has a heavy Zapotec Indian population."

The woman looked up, recognizing the word.

"I'm Father Chavez," Luis said, shifting to his mother's native tongue. "You're at St. Augustine's Church in Los Angeles. Where are you hurt?"

She was reluctant to show him. He thought she was being modest. Then she leaned close and spoke in a whisper.

"No police," she said in Zapotec. "Please. No police."

He hesitated, then nodded. She moved the towel aside. The wound was only superficial but no less ugly. The bullet had grazed her shoulder, leaving a four-inch-long red and black furrow in its wake. The blood around it and down her arm had dried, but more still seeped from the wound.

"It needs to be stitched," Luis said. "How'd you get this?"

"I fell."

"No," Luis whispered. "I can see the burn markings. The paramedics will be obligated to call the police. If you need our help, you'll need to tell them something different. Do you understand?"

She agreed she did.

"All right. Let's get you inside."

She said her name was Odilia Garanzuay and she was originally from Santa Lucía del Camino. She'd been in the States for around eighteen months. She avoided Luis's question as to whether she was involved in a crime but reiterated that she didn't want to speak to the police. She also admitted she was undocumented.

Luis was selective in what he translated to Pastor Whillans. In the six months he'd been at St. Augustine's, he'd witnessed several incidents involving the vast community of undocumented aliens living and working in the city. These people—some parishioners, some not—saw the church as a place they could turn when going to the police could mean deportation. Luis understood this. In a new country, sometimes the only familiar topographical landmark was a church steeple.

Whillans's first call after the paramedics was to the archdiocese's Bureau of Hispanic Affairs. They handled most issues within the undocumented community by handing the person off to what they hoped was the right faith-based nonprofit organization. If the individual was looking for the church to take a more active position, they were reminded that the archdiocese would not take part in anything even tangentially illegal.

The paramedics arrived. Odilia told them she'd brushed into an electrified fence. After a questioning glance to Luis and determining that the patient would refuse treatment if they insisted on taking her to a hospital, they stitched her up without a word. They established that Odilia was also dehydrated and possibly a little malnourished, but she wouldn't let them check her out further. When they left, the priests brought Odilia to the rectory to await the arrival of the Bureau rep.

"Where did you come from?" Luis asked, resuming his questioning.

"Oaxaca."

"Most recently, I mean."

"I'm not sure," she replied.

"Can you give me an idea?" Luis pressed. "I want to help you, but I can't do that without more information."

Odilia hesitated.

"Why help me?"

"God brought you here. It's what we do."

"God?" she sniffed. "A truck brought me here."

"Maybe a truck brought you to Los Angeles, but God led you to probably one of the only priests in the city who speaks your language. Doesn't that mean something?"

She thought about this.

"My friend, she told the city lawyer that Santiago was missing," Odilia said. "She went out the door, and I heard shots. I went to the window and saw she was dead."

"Who?"

"Annie Whittaker."

"And who's Santiago?" Luis asked.

"A . . . friend," she said.

"Start at the beginning. Where were you?"

"Annie's house. We were waiting to hear from the lawyer that Santiago was safe. Then he disappeared. Annie went to look for him, but she was shot in her driveway."

"Did you see who shot her?"

"No. She was against the car, shot in the back of the head. No one was there. I got scared and ran out the back door. Somebody shot at me as well, but I got away. I kept running until I got to the highway. I met a truck driver at a gas station. I begged for a ride. He said he could take me as far as the city. He dropped me off nearby." She indicated over her shoulder. "I didn't know where to go. I saw the church and thought I'd be safe."

"Why no police?"

"Police? They killed Annie."

This was a shocker. Luis had met several immigrants who took the corruption of law enforcement for granted. But there was certainty in Odilia's voice. True or not, she believed it.

Before Luis could continue, voices came in from the hall. Luis recognized the tremulous baritone of Bishop Eloy Duenas, the elderly head of the Los Angeles Archdiocese's Bureau of Hispanic Affairs.

"I was on a home visit in Silver Lake when I got your call," Duenas was telling Pastor Whillans. "You know Bishop Osorio."

"Of course."

"Caught him on a good day. He's still all fire and brimstone. *This* is blasphemy, *that* smacks of polytheism."

They reached the doorway. Whillans indicated Luis.

"Bishop Duenas, this is Father Chavez. He comes to us from the St. Robert Bellarmine Seminary in New York."

"But from here, correct?" Duenas asked, already looking past Luis to Odilia.

"Yes, Your Grace," replied Luis.

"When I told Bishop Osorio I was coming to St. Augustine's, he said I should meet you," Duenas noted.

"He was my mentor before I went to divinity school."

"Small world," Duenas said, nodding. He turned to Odilia and switched to Spanish. "You seek sanctuary?"

Luis began to translate the question into Zapotec. Duenas raised a hand.

"I'm a little rusty, but I think it helps to do these interviews one-on-one," the bishop said authoritatively.

He switched to poorly accented Zapotec and repeated his question. Odilia nodded. Duenas shot Luis a look that told him he was dismissed and closed the door after him.

It took Luis thirty seconds to find multiple articles about a shooting in Ventura County on Erna's computer. As Odilia had stated, the woman, Anne Whittaker, had been shot twice in her driveway at point-blank range by a large caliber pistol in what was believed to be a robbery gone bad. Her purse was missing and her car stolen, though it had already been located in a Walgreens parking lot in Oakland.

Whittaker was described as a fifth-year associate at the Santa Barbara–based law firm of Shughart & Hofmeier. There was no mention of a Santiago, a Los Angeles city attorney, or the possibility that anyone else was in Whittaker's house at the time.

Luis went to his room on the second floor of the rectory. It was about the size of a university dorm room. Designed for efficiency— with cherrywood paneling, cheap commercial carpet, and a window that looked out over the church courtyard—it reminded him of a train compartment on good days, of a cell in the county jail on others.

Luis considered the differences between Odilia's description of the shooting and what he'd read online. She said she'd heard the shots, looked out the window, and seen her dead friend slumped against the car, but no shooter. He didn't know the geography of the neighborhood, but for her to exit a back gate and be shot at from behind the house by someone who'd just killed a woman in the driveway didn't make sense.

How could the shooter get around the house that fast? If the goal was the car or the purse, why the killing? If, as Odilia suggested, Annie was simply shot in the back of the head, had there even been time for a struggle?

Luis had been around his share of crime. This sounded like murder, not robbery.

The drive from Los Angeles to the Ventura County Medical Examiner's Office was the longest of Michael Story's life. He hadn't slept, having stayed in his office at the Criminal Justice Center until well past sunrise, waiting to hear back from Annie. When his phone finally rang, Annie's cell number on the caller ID, he was surprised to hear a man's voice on the other end of the line.

"Who is this?" Michael asked.

"Camarillo Police Detective Lawrence Fisher. Who am I speaking to?"

"LA Deputy District Attorney Michael Story. Why do you have Annie Whittaker's phone?"

Before he got to the end of his question, his heart sank. He called down to the bailiff and asked that the day's proceedings get pushed to the afternoon.

Though he was going to Ventura County to identify the body, the mention of an armed robbery had given rise to several questions of his own. Annie didn't live in the big city. He didn't know the crime statistics of her neighborhood but imagined they were more along the lines of noise complaints and the occasional report of teen vandalism than murder and attempted carjacking.

The media had the story before he was outside the city limits. Another hour and they had police quotes to go with it. A random homicide with the hook that the victim was a young white woman in an upscale neighborhood.

He'd warned Annie. The stakes were high. Even so, he hadn't believed he'd one day be standing over her ruined body, nodding to a detective and a coroner's assistant who hadn't quite mastered a look of solemn concern.

"For the record, you're identifying this person as Anne Whittaker?" Fisher asked.

"I am," he agreed, glancing away as quickly as he could.

"Looks fishy, right?" Michael said when he and the detective stepped into the hall to compare notes.

"How do you mean?"

"A carjacker just happened to be in her neighborhood that time of night?"

"We're operating on the theory that it was a day laborer. They've got those fields across the highway. It's the peak of the season. All it takes is one guy to get high and go looking for trouble."

"Has anything like this happened before?" Michael asked.

"Not a murder, but there's been drunk driving, fights, burglary. You'd better believe I'll be spending the next few weeks getting all kinds of calls from the upstanding white people of this city asking what's being done about the illegals who they rely on the other fifty weeks of the year."

"Did you find the gun?"

"No, but we're hopeful. The bullets were pistol rounds, which was how we figured it was close range. Markings suggested an automatic. We're not looking for a decades-old revolver in a haystack for once."

Fisher hit Michael with a few more questions. Michael asked, as a professional courtesy, to be kept in the loop. Then they went their separate ways.

As he got back into his car, Michael checked his phone. Annie's law firm had returned his call to say that they'd contacted Annie's sister out in Florida. Michael's wife, Helen, had called as well, knowing something about her husband's evening plans hadn't gone right. He stopped the message and tossed the phone aside.

This case was supposed to be the stepping stone that would take him to the next level. How the hell could it have gone so wrong?

IV

Growing up, Ernesto Quintanilla *hated* cops. They rolled through his hood staring through those mirrored shades, daring anyone for a reason to get out of the car. You *knew* a beatdown would make their day.

Come on, muchacho. You know you'll end up in the back of my car one day. Why not make it today?

But Ernesto kept his eyes down, moved along, and stayed out of trouble. When he graduated community college with a degree in criminal justice, he didn't wait before applying to the Los Angeles County Sheriff's Department. He flew through twenty weeks of departmental training and a few weeks later was a Los Angeles County sheriff.

Now with his own squad car, he never put on shades, never treated anyone with condescension, and introduced himself to residents and business owners, addressing them as "sir" and "ma'am."

You want respect? Treat others with respect.

At six foot four, he was an imposing presence. He was fair but by the book. The one law enforcement officer in the city who didn't talk on his cell while driving. His stony gaze alone ended arguments and turned liars into truth tellers.

"Sir?" the pharmacist said. "There's a problem."

The pharmacist eyed Ernesto as if fearing this news might lead to trouble.

"What's that?" Ernesto asked, putting his hands on the counter.

"Your father's insurance covers three refills, but he needs to go back to the doctor to re-up."

"Can't they call it in? It's hard for him to leave the house."

"No, it's a requirement of his provider."

Ernesto scanned the man's face for signs he was looking to fuck with a cop. Not seeing any, he paid for the other prescriptions and left.

Traffic was light out to Downey. He parked in front of his old man's apartment complex and headed in.

"Dad?" he asked, hauling the bags to the kitchen.

"Be right out, Nesto!" came a voice from the bedroom.

Ernesto unpacked the groceries, kicking himself for once again forgetting to bring over the most recent school photos of his boys. The ones on his dad's fridge were over a year old.

Next time.

Moises Quintanilla, a bent old man in his midseventies, emerged from the hall, an outsized smile on his face.

"How are you, *mijo?*"

"Good, *papi.* I picked up your prescriptions."

Moises limped over to check the pill bottles. He'd been as tall as his son once but had dropped inches as his spine weakened and bowed. When he'd had hip replacement surgery a few years back, he lost another couple of inches, as well as a step or two. Then came the incontinence, followed by the heart trouble, and finally the rheumatoid arthritis. At this point, getting from room to room in his apartment was about all Moises could manage.

There was a noise from the hallway. Ernesto glanced to his father, who waved the third party into the doorway.

"You remember Father Chavez," Moises said. "He dropped by to see if I needed anything."

Ernesto met Luis's gaze. He'd liked the priest when he met him. The priest was personable and genuinely cared about his parishioners. It was Luis who'd contacted Ernesto about home visits once Moises could no longer attend services, and from the first day Moises had raved about the priest.

It was when Ernesto found out Luis was from Los Angeles that things went south. As he did with everyone who entered his family circle, he'd typed Luis's name into the police criminal records database. He didn't like what came back. The city was rife with Chicanos trying to put a heavy street background behind them, but those guys weren't visiting his father for Bible study and prayer. Luis Chavez had run with some serious criminals.

To his surprise, when he'd confronted Luis about it, the priest copped to everything and even said he'd discussed it with Moises. Regardless, it had given Ernesto pause. If there was one truism in law enforcement, it was that those who broke the law were likely to do so again. Even those who joined the priesthood.

"I was telling Luis it's a shame you can't get to services anymore," Moises said. "One of the boys always has sports. When you were a kid, nobody scheduled anything on the Sabbath."

"Times change, Pop."

Ernesto turned to Luis, bracing himself for further chastisement.

"The Bible only tells us to keep the Sabbath holy." Luis shrugged. "It doesn't say anything about church. Exodus just tells us to do no work."

"Is a children's baseball game keeping the Sabbath holy?" teased Moises.

"In Leviticus, God intertwines the idea of family and the Sabbath," Luis offered. "So, if they're together . . . maybe."

Moises threw up his hands.

"If a priest leaps to the defense of my backsliding son, there's little I can say," Moises said, sighing. "But isn't Leviticus also the book that says cursing one's parents is punishable by death?"

Luis and Ernesto put away the groceries, while Moises downed his midday pills. After a few minutes Moises was ready for a nap. Ernesto helped him to his bed.

"Sometimes new medication makes him slur his speech," Ernesto said after returning to the living room. "On the phone it'll sound like he's had a stroke. They'll adjust the dosage, and maybe the next ones just knock him out. They're extending his life, but he's less lucid every time I see him."

Luis nodded. "I'll show up sometimes and I'll know he doesn't recognize me. Rather than admit it, he invites me in and keeps me talking until he figures out who I am. My worry is one day it won't be me he invites in."

This gave Ernesto pause. He hadn't considered this.

"I'll talk to him. I know he's grateful for your visits. The church means so much to Dad. Did you know he was reluctant when you first offered?"

"Really?"

"He thought he was unworthy of the time and attention."

"It's a privilege," Luis responded. "I hope I'm as strong in my faith when I'm his age."

Ernesto agreed and kept looking at Luis expectantly. He'd been surprised to see the priest still there when he came out of the bedroom and figured he wanted something. Sensing this, Luis dug a piece of paper from his pocket and passed it over. It was a newspaper story about the Annie Whittaker shooting.

"The church has been approached by a possible witness," Luis explained.

"You advised them to contact law enforcement?"

"Of course. As did the archdiocese. But they think the police are involved."

Ernesto sighed.

"The witness's version of events," Luis continued, "is very different from the one in the media. She was shot at as well."

"She?"

"She."

"You know this how?"

"I saw the wound. It's superficial, but it was definitely from a bullet."

"The witness was at the same location as the vic?" Ernesto asked with surprise.

Luis nodded. "She mentioned a third party, Santiago Higuera, who went missing at the same time. They were to meet up in Los Angeles the next day with somebody she referred to as a city attorney. I think she meant a prosecutor."

Ernesto shook his head in disbelief.

"If the witness has information relating to a capital case, withholding it is spoliation of evidence, no matter what the reason," he said. "They have to come in."

"I'm afraid she'd clam up. That's why I came to you. Annie Whittaker was a legal rights advocate. If they were meeting with a prosecutor, there's a good chance somebody in the DA's office is already looking for them. If they're afraid the witness might be targeted, too, they might be keeping the search quiet."

"Let me guess. You want me to ask around?" Ernesto suggested, annoyed.

"I didn't know who else to ask."

Ernesto already had an idea who to call. He just didn't like being in anyone's debt.

"I hope you and the archdiocese know this isn't a game. If this person is right and she was targeted the same as Whittaker, she may still be in danger. Have you considered that?"

"She's safe," Luis said. "Nobody knows she's there."

———

Maria Higuera fought the urge to look at the clock. Working in a flower shop had taught her time passed faster when ignored, but she hadn't heard from her brother since Friday afternoon. He'd told her something big was going on that weekend that would have serious implications for their whole family.

"Why are you being mysterious?" she'd asked. "It's harvest-time, right? You think you're going to make a big profit this year or something?"

"I can't talk about it on the phone," Santiago had replied. "I'll explain everything on Monday first thing. Okay?"

"Okay."

Monday morning came and went. Though the shop owner, Mrs. Ponce, had a strict no-cell-phone policy, Maria had managed to slip out and check her phone a couple of times in the parking lot.

Nothing.

Her brother was a farmer. He owned his own land, over a hundred acres up in Ventura County, and was the only family Maria had in the States other than her son, Miguel. He'd left home when he was a teenager, lured to La Norte with the promise of a job. The family didn't hear from him for a few years. Then, not long after Maria discovered she was pregnant, Santiago sent word that he wanted to bring her over the border.

That was almost fifteen years ago. It had seemed so daunting at the time, but now Maria regarded her brother as her savior. That he hadn't called after making such a point that he would deeply troubled her.

Why couldn't he have just said what was going on?

She finally glanced to the clock. It was five. Half an hour before she could knock off. She plucked another six lilies from the flower box next to her and added them to the arrangement she was finishing up.

"Mom?"

She turned to the back doorway. Miguel stood there. He was out of breath.

"What are you doing here?" she asked, afraid Mrs. Ponce could return any minute. "Why aren't you at Mrs. Leñero's? Did you take the bus?"

That's when she saw the look on his face. It was ashen and strained. He appeared much older than his fourteen years.

"Mom. You need to see this."

He pulled his iPad out of his backpack and opened the cover. The front page of a Mexican newspaper was up in a browser. When she read the headline, she wasn't sure what it meant. When she saw the photograph next to it, she screamed.

V

After he left Los Angeles for divinity school, Luis returned only once, for the funeral of his mother. He'd flown in, stayed the night on a cot at Sacred Heart, and flown back to New York after the service. She was interred next to Luis's brother, Nicolas, in a plot she'd purchased when she buried her oldest son. This was befitting. Luis believed his mother had left a lot of herself behind at the cemetery following Nicolas's funeral.

Luis's father hadn't attended his ex-wife's services. In fact, Luis hadn't seen him since they buried Nic. If a part of his mother had never left her first child's grave, an even bigger part of Luis's father believed he was responsible for digging it. The old man blamed himself for Nicolas's death, as well as Luis's trouble. Luis thought this was bullshit, the senior Chavez looking for another reason for self-pity.

When he returned to Los Angeles for good, Luis made no attempt to contact his father.

But he thought of his parents as he walked down South Alvarado Street. The sights and smells of the open markets were so familiar, the wave of nostalgia practically gave him a head rush.

Moving past MacArthur Park, Luis spotted what he'd been looking for on the other side of the street. Called a phone room, it was just
that—a retail space the walls of which were lined with a couple dozen
sit-down phone booths and nothing else. Everything about it looked
temporary, as if it had snuck in after the last business failed and could
be packed up and moved out the moment a new tenant came along.

Luis approached the bulletproof cashier's cage and took out his
wallet. Taped to the barrier were phone cards featuring the flags and
outlines of an array of countries. Luis tapped one with a cartoon man
wearing a sombrero.

"Where in Mexico you calling?" the skinny Latino behind the glass
asked.

"Ixtlan."

The clerk reached under the counter. Coming back with a stack of
cards rubber-banded together, he stripped one off the bottom and slid
it to Luis.

"Ten dollars gets you four hours, though I've had some customers
tell me they've gotten days out of these. You know the country code
and area code?"

Luis nodded, handing over a ten. He took the card, chose a chair,
and scratched off the latex backing. As he did so, the clerk took a cell
phone from his pocket and dialed.

"Bueno?"

Luis had expected Zapotec, so he was surprised to hear Spanish.

"Hello," he answered in Spanish. "My name is Luis Chavez. I'm a
priest in California. I—"

"Oh no!" the voice sputtered back. "Odilia?"

"No, she's okay," Luis said. "She's at my parish. She gave me your
number, asking me to call. She wanted you to know she's okay."

"Thank God. Is she coming home?"

"She wants to."

"Is she in trouble?"

"Yes," Luis replied. "I'll have her get in touch with you as soon as possible."

"You have no idea how worried we've been. You hear nothing for so long, hoping she's doing well, terrified she's not."

"When did you last speak to her?"

"Oh, it's been nine, maybe ten—"

"Months?"

"*Years.*"

Odilia couldn't have been more than twenty years old.

"Thank you for calling, Father. Please help my daughter get home. Promise me."

"I will."

After hanging up, Luis headed back to his car with even more questions now. He had a lot of things to go over with Odilia. He was halfway to his car when he heard his name. A heavily tattooed man emerged from a bright-orange Charger parked at the curb.

"Luis Chavez! It *is* you, isn't it? My God!"

The larger-than-life presence of Oscar Beristáin de Icaza hopped onto the sidewalk next to Luis. Over six feet, with a chiseled physique, Oscar enveloped him in a hug. Luis gasped. When they were coming up together, Oscar had been the first in the neighborhood to hit the weights hard. Now that Oscar was all grown up, his embrace was akin to being stuffed into a stack of tractor tires.

"I'd heard about the collar, but I didn't believe it," Oscar said, sizing Luis up. "Looks like it fits."

"How are you, Oscar?"

"Good, man! When'd you get back to town?"

"Six months ago."

"You couldn't call?" Oscar retorted, feigning offense.

"You think I didn't know who Remberto would call the second I walked in?" Luis jutted his chin in the clerk's direction as he stood in the doorway of the phone room, trying to look as unobtrusive as possible.

"I suppose not. Who *have* you seen?"

"Nobody," Luis said. "The archdiocese likes its priests to hit the ground running."

"What do you do? Other than fuck altar boys, I mean."

Luis knew Oscar wanted a tolerant sigh in return for his caustic remark and gave it to him.

"But seriously, do you give the sermon? I'd come see that."

"No. The first six months is for learning the ropes."

"Picking up the choir robes from the dry cleaner's?"

"Close," Luis chuckled. "We have members of the laity who do that, but I have to order new ones soon."

"*Wow.* They already trust you with that shit, huh?"

"That and preparing communion, replacing candles, helping the pastor organize the service and research passages, minor repairs, and upkeep of the nave."

"What about confession?" Oscar interrupted. "You listen to little old ladies' fantasies about fucking Carlos Ferro or something?"

A passerby grunted in disgust but then saw the large men who'd emerged from Oscar's car as well and hurried along, keeping further comments to himself.

"No confessions yet. A couple of home and hospital visits, a few counseling sessions, a few drop-bys on Bible study groups."

"The excitement never stops," Oscar scoffed, now meaning the insult.

"At the beginning it's about establishing yourself into the ritual and routine," Luis said, actively trying to make his vocation sound as boring as possible to avoid a repeat encounter. "Also, putting in the time to adjust your expectations to life in the parish. You're looking for how God is already operating in the lives of the people around you."

Oscar stared at Luis with a look equal parts horror and amusement.

"That's fucked up, man," Oscar said. "Sounds like you joined the army but agreed to rank specialist seventeenth class your whole life."

Luis laughed but wondered if there'd come a time either of them could step out of the roles they'd embraced—Oscar as likely criminal, and Luis as priest—to catch up for real.

"How are things with you?" Luis asked.

"Not without responsibilities, but I choose my path."

"Which has led you . . . ?"

"To my own shop on Lemoyne," Oscar boasted. "Started out doing oil changes and tires, moved into custom bodywork and rims. Now got a second shop on Pico, and we're looking at locations around Culver for store number three, Marina del Rey for store four."

Chop shops, Luis figured.

"That's great."

"Yeah, but it's just the beginning," Oscar continued. "I've got big plans. You should come by. I don't know what you're driving, but I'll bet we could do a number on it."

"I'll keep that in mind."

It was the moment when small talk ended and either a real conversation or a parting of ways came next. Luis offered his hand. Oscar opened his arms.

"Come on, man. Are we cousins? Or are we *brothers?*"

Luis returned the embrace but didn't reply.

———

The El Sauzal overpass a few miles north of Ensenada, Mexico, had hardly been used by the locals it had been built for, and was barely noticed by travelers who had passed under it for decades.

This might have continued if not for an accident of location. Though thousands passed under it every day on their way north to Tijuana or south to Ensenada, only a handful passed over the bridge. When the drug war engulfed Mexico around 2009, the bridge was adopted for a secondary purpose. The first incident happened in March of that year, when three bodies were found hanging over the highway, facing the southbound lanes. The second came only weeks later—this time just one body—but a pattern had been established. Over the next few years, sixteen bodies would be left hanging over the guardrails on nine different occasions.

The onetime lonely overpass had become notorious.

Today there was only one body. Like the others, the individual had been killed elsewhere and brought here to be displayed. The victim was bound at the wrists and had been lowered over the side. Unlike the others, there was no message attached to the body taking credit for the slaying.

The Servicio Médico Forense unit came out, pulled the body onto the bridge, and began what was often the impossible task of identifying the victim. Though the claims of credit often gave the forensics techs a starting point, the cartels usually mangled a body beyond recognition. Even the dead person's family would never know peace, only the fear their vanished loved one had suffered a horrible, dehumanizing death.

In the case of the El Sauzal victim, the SEMEFO techs worried only DNA testing could make a positive ID, a process still expensive and labor intensive in Mexico. It was a welcome surprise, then, when they found a partial denture in the back of the victim's mouth. Within an hour they had a manufacturer and serial number. A call to the Indiana-based manufacturer traced the piece to the office of a Dr. Butchart in Ventura County. After some wrangling over patient confidentiality, they got a name: Santiago Higuera.

When it was determined that the victim might have been a native of Mexico but was now a naturalized citizen of the United States, the US State Department was alerted. Someone voiced the fear that the press might get word of this before they were able to notify the family. One look to the Internet told them they were already too late.

Maybe if he hadn't been an American.

———

Maria stared at the pixilated camera-phone image alongside the story, looking for that one telling detail that would reveal this to be a case of mistaken identity. It had to be. What would Santiago be doing in Mexico? He *never* went back. It was hard enough to get him to leave his land during the regular part of the year, but at harvesttime? Impossible.

She recalled his cryptic phone call. They hadn't been the words of a man in fear for his life.

She didn't know how she made it home without falling apart. When she walked into the house, she expected the phone to be ringing off the hook, but it was silent.

"I unplugged it," Miguel admitted. "And I deleted all the voice mails from reporters. Also got on the computer and delisted us from the phone books."

You can do that? Maria thought, always marveling at what her son was able to do online.

"There was one call from some lawyer about the farm, but I wasn't sure what to do with it. I saved it as an audio file, if you want to listen to it later . . ."

The image of the unrecognizable corpse hanging lifeless from a bridge returned to Maria's mind's eye. Her body began to quake as she tried to connect it with her brother, so strong and so confident. New tears poured from her eyes as she collapsed on the floor in anguish.

"Ah, Mom," Miguel said, kneeling and putting his arms around her. "It's going to be okay."

They huddled together for the better part of the next hour, Maria crying intermittently, until the sun set and the house was dark.

VI

"Our role in this is complicated," Bishop Duenas said, his voice sounding exasperated as it came out of the speaker phone. "I accept that you feel we have a responsibility to the woman, but we also have one to our parishioners and our clergy. I don't understand how you can think having a woman under your parish roof, even for a night, would be acceptable to the archdiocese."

Luis held his tongue. Whillans had told him if he sat in on the call, he had to stay quiet. He watched as his pastor sighed and sank into his chair. When Duenas had been at St. Augustine's earlier in the day, he'd been more pliable. Luis figured this had changed once the bishop had informed the archdiocese that Whillans believed the young woman should stay at the parish.

"It's one night, Bishop," Whillans replied, leaning over the speaker. "Father Chavez has already been in contact with the Sheriff's Department. His fear, which I share, is that if she's taken away from here, she might run off. She's very, very scared."

"There's no private home you could put her in?" Duenas pressed. "A member of the laity's perhaps?"

"I'd be too afraid of endangering someone outside the church. My priests understand and accept there's a risk."

There was a long silence. Luis eyed Whillans with concern. Whillans waved this away.

"One night," Duenas finally agreed. "But I need a report in the morning."

"You'll get it."

Whillans hung up and turned to Luis.

"Let's hope your sheriff's deputy works fast," he said. "How's our guest?"

"She's all right," Luis reported. "Erna got her some clothes from the donation box. She got cleaned up. After that, well . . ."

Luis trailed off. Whillans raised an eyebrow.

"What is it?"

"I thought she'd make a break for it," Luis said. "But she hasn't moved from the room all day. Erna said she just sat in a corner for hours. I'll bet if we offered her a closet, she'd jump at it."

"When you feel like the whole world's waiting to strike, a defensible position can be all you want," Whillans suggested. "Just ask a mouse."

Luis nodded and headed out. He thought Odilia Garanzuay might be many things, but a mouse wasn't one of them.

He walked over to the rectory and found Erna sitting with Odilia. Erna knew barely any Spanish, much less Zapotec, but chatted along animatedly as Odilia listened. When Erna spied Luis in the doorway, she hopped up.

"How are you, Father?" she asked.

"Good, Erna."

"You need to speak to Odilia?" she asked.

"I do, but you're welcome to stay."

"No, no," Erna said, heading for the door. "Have a few things I need to finish up in the office before getting home, if that's all right."

"No problem," he said, realizing Erna was just giving them privacy.

Luis took a seat opposite Odilia. Odilia nodded toward the departing Erna.

"She's very kind," she said in Zapotec. "Will you tell her that?"

"I will. I just wanted you to know that I called your mother. She was very worried about you."

For a moment it looked to Luis like the young woman might burst into tears. Then she straightened, her face hardening as if in acceptance of this.

"Did you tell her I was all right?"

"Yes, but she said something surprising. You said you'd just got here. She said you'd been away for years."

"I've been away from home for some time," Odilia admitted carefully, "but have been at the Blocks only since last year."

"The Blocks?"

"There are many people there who are in my situation."

"Which is what?"

Odilia didn't respond. Luis switched tack.

"I spoke to a friend in the Sheriff's Department," Luis said. "He's willing to help."

"I said no police," Odilia exclaimed.

"He is a friend, and I haven't even told him your name. I'm trying to use him to find Annie's contact."

"The city lawyer?" Odilia asked skeptically.

"Yes. I'm asking you to trust me. Will you?"

When Odilia didn't respond, Luis leaned in.

"I'm not accustomed to siding with law enforcement either," he admitted. "But if you want to find out what happened to your friends, this might be the only way to do it. Okay?"

"Okay."

"All right," Luis said. "I know you've been cooped up in here all day. You want to come down to Mass?"

"I haven't been to Mass since I was a little girl."

"That's too long," Luis said, grinning.

———

Monday night Mass at St. Augustine's was strictly an *abuela y ruca* affair, the median age around sixty. While a handful might come to make up for missing Sunday services, others had nowhere better to be. Luis greeted familiar congregants as he led Odilia to a rear pew.

"Do you know most of your parishioners?" she asked.

"Not at all," Luis admitted. "We service a community of over ten thousand here. These are the ones who are here three or four times a week."

"We had people like that back home. Widows generally."

"People like the ritual," Luis offered. "As your days wind on, the church is a reminder that another world awaits. It can lend perspective. If you live in the knowledge that this world is a gateway to the next, it can be a comfort."

"Do they teach you that in seminary?" Odilia challenged.

"I saw it on a bumper sticker."

Odilia laughed. The elderly congregants turned to look, more in surprise that a young person was there than in offense. Pastor Whillans entered from the sacristy and made his way to the podium.

"All right, bingo's in an hour," Whillans announced. "Shall we get this under way?"

Now it was the congregants' turn to laugh as the organist, a laywoman named Provence Verdejo, moved to her bench.

"I think 'Lord of All Hopefulness' is appropriate for today, no?" Whillans continued, keeping with the informal tone. "It's a good one for a group of this size to sing. We can turn the nave into the echo chamber it was designed to be."

"He's funny," Odilia said after Luis translated.

"He believes the community part of communion is as important as everything else," Luis said. "You should see him on a Sunday. Even with hundreds, he makes everyone feel as if this is their church. He's warm and inclusive."

"You admire him."

"I do. He makes it look easy."

Odilia looked away. When Luis caught her gaze again, she had tears in her eyes.

"Are you all right?"

"Just thinking of Annie," she said. "I didn't know her well, but she was a good person. I keep seeing her body crumpled over her car. It's like I'm remembering a dream, not reality."

Though he hadn't been a witness to his brother's murder, Luis could picture the scene so perfectly in his mind that it felt like a memory.

"Who killed her?" he asked quietly.

Odilia stared straight ahead, saying nothing. The hymn ended and Whillans raised his hands.

"Let us pray."

When Luis had arrived at St. Augustine's, Pastor Whillans had indicated the tremendous number of ecclesiastical texts on his bookshelves and told him that everything he needed to know about the Kingdom of Heaven could be found within.

"But everything you need to know about man you can find in this," he'd said, handing Luis the thickest novel he'd ever seen, a copy of James Joyce's *Ulysses*. "I've read it three times myself, and each time it's a new book."

Luis had placed the tome on his shelf and forgotten about it. Tonight he picked it up, wanting something irreligious for a change. He flipped through it, finding a fat man waking to shave on the first page. Already bored, he scanned down and found a few Latin phrases, which he translated, happy he still could. When the next few pages were as impenetrable as the first, he looked for other instances of Latin.

Above a particularly difficult passage, however, he found a beautiful song lyric:

> I am the boy
> That can enjoy
> Invisibility.

Luis set the book aside to think about this. Sleep would not come easy. He contemplated the day's events, looking for evidence of the Hand of God. Nothing filled a priest with greater self-doubt than wondering if he allowed God to operate through him or if, in his pride, he had substituted his own will.

That's when he remembered the name the valet had passed to him.

Vaitiare Oyervidez.

He got down on his knees, closed his eyes, opened his mind, and prayed.

The rectory door creaked downstairs. Luis glanced to the clock on his nightstand. It was past midnight, the other priests long in bed. He waited to hear the door close, but it stayed open long enough for more than one person to enter.

Then came a crash, metal on wood.

Luis was out the door in a flash. He tore down the hall and down the stairs, not caring who he roused. He exited the stairwell on the first floor, only to run into two men pointing pistols at him.

"What do you want?" he asked.

As if he didn't know. The door to the communal room was already off its hinges. Odilia was screaming.

"The cops are on their way," he spat.

The gunmen didn't flinch. Two more emerged from the communal room, dragging Odilia between them. They glanced at Luis, took his measure, and then kept dragging Odilia toward the door.

Luis charged. The gunmen didn't react until Luis had already driven a fist into the nose of the closest man, sending him spinning into the wall. The man wore a mask, so Luis couldn't see his face, but he caught sight of a number of tattoos down the side of his neck. They weren't quite gangster ink, but they weren't quite something else, either.

Luis whipped around to continue his attack but was met by a pistol brought down hard against his face, nearly knocking out his upper teeth. Luis swung wildly, but the butt of the pistol slammed into his temple. He dropped like a stone. The last thing he heard were Odilia's cries fading as she disappeared into the night.

PART II

VII

Monks first brought wine to California. They came to establish missions in the then Spanish-held territory but were quickly without wine for communion. Vines were planted, grapes were grown, and it was discovered that the Central Coast was a perfect place to produce wine.

Young Walter Marshak came to the West Coast from Indiana to try his luck at farming in the twenties. He'd tried his hand at cotton, but after three bad harvests in a row, he switched to wine grapes. For this, growing a fruit that required careful and dedicated cultivation, he had a knack.

Then came Prohibition.

Though bootleggers slipping liquor across the Canadian border got all the headlines, California vintners were also busy keeping the country stocked with illegal wine. While the making of wine used in communion services was exempted by the Volstead Act, the rate at which California wineries kept producing would have been enough to stock churches well into the twenty-first century.

Government agents got wise and tried to shutter the renegade vineyards, but sympathetic Sheriff's Departments made it their civic duty to tip off the local farmers. Men like Walter thrived. And when Prohibition was repealed in 1933, the cozy relationship between vineyards and law enforcement continued.

Though he became something of a decent wine grape grower, Marshak was no visionary. He had a solid work ethic and enough discipline to break even almost every year, but expansion never entered his mind. For Walter's sons, Henry and Glenn, this was all they'd thought about since childhood.

The younger brother, Glenn, had the head for business. Twelve when he took over his father's books, he dove into the numbers with near-religious zeal. He saw only flaws in the way his father did things. He attacked these imperfections, working late into the night to prove his ways were more efficient and profitable. At best he'd receive a shrug or amused nod for his efforts, at worst an admonishment to stick to the task at hand.

The experience made Glenn first hate and then pity his father, but it didn't affect his relationship with Henry. Though firstborn and favored, Henry never lorded it over his younger sibling. Henry's gifts manifested themselves in the vineyards. He shared his brother's zeal to innovate and constantly experimented with new farming techniques. When his father frowned on this, Henry shrank his sample size but continued to work.

After Walter died, the brothers implemented their changes the very next season. They increased their profits and market share so quickly, even the press noticed, dubbing them an overnight success. Where their father had been content to partner with vintners, the brothers cut out the middlemen and established their own winery. They bought up land, vanquished the old notion that a winemaker's focus should be on creating the finest quality product, and entered the marketplace with a line of affordable table wines aimed at the American mass market.

While aficionados regarded them as apostates, by the midsixties the Marshaks were a household name, and wine was no longer something just for special occasions. Soon, Americans drank more wine from

Marshak vineyards than all European imports combined. As the brothers reached their fifties, their annual income was in the tens of millions.

They continued to expand, turning their attention to other big California produce, like strawberries and lettuce. Almost superstitiously avoiding cotton due to their father's early failed harvests, they moved into citrus, buying orchards up and down the state. They moved into nuts. They bought dairy farms. They established their own warehouses and systems of distribution.

Now in his eighties, Glenn ran the business from downtown Los Angeles, as well as the main administrative campus closer to the fields in Ventura County, a warren of offices nestled in the foothills of the Santa Ynez range.

Henry, however, had checked out almost three decades prior. He was still listed as his brother's partner but was semi-retired. After his wife, Robin, died, he took back control of a few select fields, on which he could experiment with new methods of irrigation, organic fertilization, or soil compositing—a farmer's version of tinkering in the garage. He partnered with the viticulture and enology program at the University of California at Santa Barbara and brought students to these fields as well. His earthy humor and unaffected humility soon made him a favorite of faculty and students alike.

Henry had one son, Jason, but the boy was born with his uncle's head for business, not his father's love of the fields. The heir apparent to the Marshak empire was often mistaken for Glenn's son rather than Henry's.

Henry didn't mind.

As he drove through the fields that had borne his family's name for almost a century, he inhaled every scent coming through his open window. It was the height of the strawberry harvest. The rows were peppered with workers, moving from plant to plant, carefully plucking the fruit. He smelled the berries, sure, but also the sweat of the workers, the scents released from the soil as they broke it up with their feet, and the occasional hint of green, likely from a broken stem the workers would then try to hide. It was backbreaking labor, as there was no easy or machine-driven way to bring in strawberries. He didn't begrudge them a couple of damaged plants.

After another mile or so, the Marshak campus appeared up ahead. It looked like any large-scale office park, albeit one dropped in the middle of endless farm fields. He had his own barely used parking space a few steps from the front door and slid his rumpled '85 Ford pickup into the spot.

Henry's one real contribution to the building of the campus was the landscaping. He'd asked that all plants inside and out be California natives—huckleberry shrubs, flannelbush, California poppies, cactus, and so on. He paused on his way up the sidewalk to admire a spectacular desert agave, its budding stalk rising from a porcupine of succulent leaves at its base. He inhaled and could smell the beginnings of the buds' acrid fragrance.

"Morning, Mr. Marshak," the front desk security guard said, as if Henry's appearance was a regular occurrence. "How are you today?"

"Can't complain," Henry said with a smile. "How are you?"

The guard extracted a key card from his pocket as he flanked Henry on his way to the elevator bank.

"Going all the way up?"

"Yes, sir. Thank you."

As the elevator ascended the four floors, Henry had his first moment of hesitation.

What am I doing here? It isn't too late to let this be. Going home would be the easiest thing in the world.

But since when do I do things the easy way?

"Good to see you, Henry," Marge Babbitt, the senior receptionist, said as Henry emerged from the elevator.

"Morning, Marge. Glenn in yet?"

Henry knew the answer. When he'd called the house, Glenn's wife, Charlene, told him where he was.

"He is. Does he know you're coming?"

"No, no," Henry said. "Just wanted to see if I might catch him."

Before Marge could reply, the door leading to Glenn's office swung open and its occupant appeared, arms outstretched.

"Henry! What a pleasant surprise."

Though the brothers had long been a study in contrast, the last couple of decades had made this more pronounced. At some point Henry's aging seemed to accelerate even as Glenn's appeared to slow. Henry's skin was tanned and weathered from years in the sun, his thinning hair an unkempt bristle brush atop his head to match the fuzzy gray mustache above his top lip. He wore thick wire-rimmed bifocals, and his clothes were pulled from the store-brand bins at Walmart.

Glenn, on the other hand, was rarely without a suit coat, or at least a sports jacket with a tailor-made dress shirt underneath. At one time he favored Barneys or Brooks Brothers, but these days he preferred a personal tailor. Now, almost every outer garment he owned had been made to his exact measurements. He was the best-dressed man on any occasion.

"Hope I'm not interrupting," Henry said, raising his palms.

"Not at all!" replied Glenn. "Come on back."

Henry caught a tone on the second sentence. Though he felt he'd conditioned Glenn to expect his irregular appearances at the office to concern eccentric nonsense that was easily handled, there was always a small part of his brother that braced for the worst.

"So, what can I do for you?" Glenn asked once they were out on the balcony off his office.

Henry stared out past the fields to the mountains beyond for a second before eyeing his brother.

"Santiago Higuera?"

The name hung in the air a few seconds before Glenn realized it was a question. "Friend of yours?"

"Of ours. Worked for us in the fields a few years back. Then we sold him a piece of land out off South Lewis Road. Grew strawberries."

"'Grew'?"

Henry handed the morning's paper to his brother, the front page folded around so that a story about the discovery of Santiago Higuera's body in Mexico was on top.

"That's unfortunate," Glenn said cautiously. "How does this relate to us? Are we mentioned in the story?"

He had expected a self-interested response. "Not at all," Henry replied.

"If you're worried the press might try and make hay from the connection, I should tell you it'll probably come to nothing. Not great given the Crown Foods contract, but a blip."

"I'm not worried about Crown Foods."

"No, I suppose you wouldn't be, would you?" Glenn sighed. "It's a big deal, though. It's the future of this company. Which makes it your son's future."

Henry said nothing. Glenn handed the paper back.

"Was this all you wanted to talk about?"

"I thought you might be concerned," Henry said. "A good man is dead, and no one knows who did it."

"Did it happen on our land?" Glenn asked.

"It doesn't look like it. But a friend of mine in the Sheriff's Office gave me the heads-up. They might send someone by the office to ask a few questions."

"Well, if they do, I'll tell them the same thing I just told you. Won't even be worth the gas."

Henry nodded. "Okay. Just putting it on your radar."

Henry felt Glenn's gaze all the way back to the elevator. He'd come expecting a denial. Why, once he'd received it, did it feel like a confession?

VIII

Ernesto's cell rang while he was dropping his kids off at school. His father's number appeared on the caller ID. As his father never called this early, he answered at once.

"Dad? Everything okay?"

"Turn on the radio," Moises said quietly. "There was a break-in at St. Augustine's Church last night. A priest got beat up. They're not saying who."

Ernesto didn't need to turn on the radio. He hung up with his dad and radioed his dispatcher, already angling his car in the direction of the parish.

"The padre got lucky," a patrolman told Ernesto when he arrived. "The men who came in were armed. They could've hurt him a lot worse. You a friend of his?"

"He knows my father."

"He'll be all right," the patrolman assured him. "Apparently he heard a noise, came downstairs, and there they were. There was a homeless woman with them who'd been at the church last night, maybe acting sick. We think she might have been some kind of scout, casing the place, then letting the others in after-hours. Chavez interrupted them, got his ass handed to him on a plate, but kept them from getting away with anything."

"Wow," Ernesto said, marveling at how off base this assessment probably was. "Can I see him?"

"It would probably help. The detectives aren't getting much out of him. Between you and me, the only reason it's even a full-court press is because the chief's tight with the cardinal."

Ernesto was directed to the administrative offices, where he found two detectives trying hard not to look bored. Luis sat, hands folded, in front of the bookshelves. Pastor Whillans leaned against his desk, surveying the scene with distaste.

"You all right, Father Chavez?" Ernesto asked, eyeing the bandage covering much of the priest's right cheek.

Luis nodded. Ernesto explained who he was to the detectives. Happy for the excuse to hand off the scene to a fellow member of law enforcement, the pair passed out business cards and admonitions to call if anything came up.

"Who were they?" Ernesto asked.

"It was dark. But they were well equipped and knew what they were doing."

"Well equipped?"

"They wore night-vision goggles. Like in the military. All four of them. Expensive tech."

"What were you thinking?" Ernesto said. "They could've killed you."

"First thing I said to him, too," Whillans chimed in.

"They were too smart for that," Luis said. "Then the cops would actually have to do something."

Ernesto was about to bite back, then held his tongue. "I should've insisted you bring her into custody."

"If cops really are involved in this, that might not have changed anything," Luis replied.

Ernesto hadn't thought of that.

"It may be too late, but I might've found your city attorney. I can't be a hundred percent sure, but there's a deputy DA who was keeping a case that sounds a little like this under wraps."

"Do you know where I can find him?"

———

Michael eyed the police officer, Peter Cubillas, on the witness stand. He'd only been sworn in five minutes before but already looked uncomfortable.

Just stay with me for five more minutes. That's all I ask.

"Where did you find Miss Mascarello?"

"Burger King parking lot. Near the pay phones."

"How'd she look?"

"Objection," the defense attorney, Laura McClain, said. "Asking the witness for an opinion."

The judge looked sleepily from the defense attorney to the police officer, then over to Michael at the prosecutor's table.

"Rephrase?" he asked.

"Did it appear she'd left her home in a hurry?" Michael tried.

"Objection," McClain repeated. "Same reason."

The judge gave Michael a look that said, *Work with me.*

"Was she dressed?" Michael asked.

"She was," responded the officer.

"Pants? Shirt?"

"I don't remember."

Goddammit.

"Would it help refresh your memory to see the police report?"

"Yes."

"May I approach the witness?" Michael asked.

"You may," said the judge.

He moved to the witness box and handed Cubillas his own police report, open to the page in question. The officer looked at it and handed it back.

"What was she wearing?" Michael asked.

"A T-shirt and shorts."

"Shoes?"

"No."

Michael glanced to the jury. It was only the third day of the trial, but they were already spent. He couldn't blame them. It was an ugly case. An eighteen-year-old woman had been repeatedly threatened with violence by her sometimes live-in, sometimes homeless boyfriend. On the night in question he came home high on drugs and attacked her with a carving knife. She grabbed her baby and ran out of the apartment.

This was bad enough, but the guy (a) had a history of violence, (b) was a registered sex offender, and (c) had possibly impregnated the victim when she was underage. Though he hadn't been charged with statutory rape, the insinuation hung over the proceedings like an ammonia cloud.

No one wanted to be there.

The courtroom door opened and Michael glanced back, figuring it was some kind of court business for the bailiff. He was therefore surprised to see a priest, one who looked like he'd taken a shot or two to the face, grab a seat in the gallery. He didn't recognize him and thought he must be someone invited by the defense.

What, a visual reminder of the defendant's redemption?

He caught a bemused glance from the defense attorney and realized she thought it was his doing. He glanced back and saw that the priest was looking over at him. He nodded casually in greeting, and the priest nodded back. He shifted his gaze to the jury. At least half had seen the exchange.

Why thank you, Father, whoever you are . . .

———

On the next stenographer's break, Luis exited the courtroom with the jury and waited for Michael Story. The deputy DA exited a couple of minutes later, head bent over a cell phone. When he saw Luis rising to speak to him, he moved aside as if to avoid him. Then he saw the various jury members glancing back their way.

"Can I help you, Father?" Michael asked. "I know I'm a bit lapsed, but I didn't expect a house call."

"I need to talk to you about Anne Whittaker."

Michael looked as if he'd been punched. He recovered quickly, but Luis hadn't missed his reaction.

"Did you work with Annie?" Michael asked.

"No, but I know Odilia Garanzuay."

"Who's that?"

"She was in Annie Whittaker's house the night Whittaker was killed," Luis explained. "She says she barely escaped herself."

"Of course. The other one," Michael said, nodding. "Annie didn't give me her name. If she was in the house, she's a potential witness. Has she spoken to law enforcement?"

"She was too scared. I was trying to get to you, but she didn't know your name."

"Where is she now?"

"She was kidnapped from the parish last night," Luis reported regretfully.

"The incident at St. Augustine's," Michael realized. "*Shit.* So she's gone?"

Luis said nothing. He already felt like a fool for allowing it to happen. Michael cursed under his breath.

"Something went wrong," Michael said. "I still don't know what. They got our other potential witness as well."

"Was it Santiago?" Luis asked. "She mentioned a Santiago."

"Santiago Higuera," Michael said. "He was coming in on his own Sunday night but vanished before we could get to him. They found him strung up in Mexico yesterday. I tracked down the taxi driver. He delivered Higuera to the safe house. You know how many people know the addresses of departmental safe houses? *Few.*"

Luis tensed. This time it was Michael who noticed.

"This Odilia told you something?" Michael asked, eyeing him closely. "Did she know who might have done this?"

"She thought the police were involved," Luis admitted before realizing Michael might be the wrong person to say this to. "Maybe that was why. Are they?"

"I don't know," Michael sighed. "Annie only gave me dribs and drabs to get me interested. She specialized in the abuse of migrant or illegal labor, so I knew it might've been something people were turning their backs to."

"There's a difference between cops turning their backs and cops leaking the address of a safe house or, worse, actively delivering a whistle-blower to their death."

"Is there? If there's anything I've learned in this office, it's that cops are masters of internal compromise and rationalization, and that comes from someone who is on their side. Still, I got the idea that it was much bigger than a couple of corrupt cops and bad-apple field hands. Annie made it sound like there were a number of players, a number of victims, and a great deal of money."

"And she couldn't have done that just to pique your interest?"

"I don't think so," Michael said, shaking his head. "Not given what I saw from her."

"Are you going to continue the investigation?" Luis asked.

"Based on what?" Michael cried, before lowering his voice after a few jury members looked his way. "Malfeasance in the fields? A couple of local police looking the other way? I don't even have jurisdiction. Annie promised there was an LA connection involving transport, but without evidence I've got nothing. And I even checked in with INS, the Border Patrol, even the Feds, looking for a connection between people stopped at the border and a Ventura County destination. Nada."

"What about Annie's files?" Luis said, grasping at straws.

"Oh, you hadn't heard? Her computer and backup drives didn't have a single file on them. At least if they'd been stolen, that'd be a robbery. But no, we're to believe she plugged in her brand-new computer, hooked it up to a printer, a scanner, and a backup drive, then promptly never used them for anything more than browsing CNN. As much as I hate letting the bad guys win this round, I have a dozen other open cases clamoring for my attention."

A feeling of calm came over Luis. He understood logically that getting the brush-off like this should have frustrated him. The calm, he decided, was from God. The course of action would follow.

The bailiff stepped out of the courtroom to call everyone back in.

"Are we done here?" Michael asked.

"It's that easy for you to walk away?" Luis snapped.

Michael whirled around.

"Pardon me for saying so, Father, but you don't know *shit* about me," Michael snarled. "This case I've got going on in there right now? Should be a slam dunk. The defendant's a repeat offender for the same crime, we've got cop witnesses, but the key witness—the victim—won't testify because the defendant wrote her all these jailhouse letters swearing up and down that he was a changed man, that he'd go to church every day if she didn't come to court."

Luis said nothing. He knew the type.

"Without a witness," Michael continued, "without somebody there to say, 'This is what I saw, this is how it happened,' the entire case hinges on the attention span of your jury when it comes to facts and figures. You want to guess how long that is? Not very fucking long."

A few jury members glanced their way upon hearing this last expletive. Michael sighed and finished up.

"Annie Whittaker was my friend. I'm the one who had to drive up there and identify her corpse. So you'll have to excuse me if less than twenty-four hours later I'm still conflicted about next steps on a case with zero leads."

Luis nodded but then took Michael by the wrist, leaning in close.

"You said you couldn't do anything without a witness. What if I went up there? What if got whatever they were going to bring you? Could you act on it?"

Michael fell silent. Luis waited to hear he'd be arrested for such a stunt. That he had no business involving himself in a criminal investigation. Him, a *priest*. Michael's eyes trailed up to the ceiling, though his face remained unreadable.

"Two people are dead and a third missing and probably dead as well," Michael finally said but then added, "You'd be on your own. I couldn't help you or direct anyone else to."

"That's not what I asked."

"You're serious about this?" Michael asked with genuine surprise.

"I am."

Michael looked the priest over again, eyeing his wounds while trying to comprehend Luis's angle.

"This isn't some atoning thing, is it? You're going it alone, putting yourself in mortal danger because this Odilia woman got stolen from under you."

Luis wanted to punch him for saying that. Not because of the accusation itself but for fear Michael might be right. Still, that was the old Luis. The calm returned.

"If you could see things from this side of the collar, you'd understand," Luis said. "And you're wrong. I'm never on my own. That's the point. You should understand that, lapsed or not."

Michael held Luis's gaze for a moment longer, then lowered his voice.

"All right," he said, now in little more than a whisper. "You go up there, you find out why somebody would want these three people dead—and I don't mean hearsay, I mean a clear, actionable motive—and I'll come at them with everything I got. Cool?"

"Cool," Luis answered.

"All right," Michael said. "But be careful. Hard to think that anyone who'd murder one person in their own driveway and string up another in a way that incriminates the cartels would have any qualms about killing a priest."

Luis didn't need the warning but nodded anyway.

When Luis returned to St. Augustine's, he found Pastor Whillans in the courtyard waiting for him. The older man had a weary look on his face.

"That bad?" Luis asked.

Whillans took a seat on a concrete bench and indicated for Luis to join him.

"The archdiocese is concerned about you," Whillans said. "They think your reaction to the break-in last night was rash and may necessitate some *reflection* on your part."

"I was just trying to protect her," Luis protested.

"Yes, but the archdiocese isn't accustomed to priests getting pistol-whipped in their own rectory. They want me to relieve you of your duties and confine you to the parish grounds."

"And here I was coming to tell you that I needed some time away," Luis explained. "I may have a line in to where they took Odilia."

Whillans went very still, his breath slowly whistling out through his lips. He placed his fingers together, as if seeking divine aid.

"I wish you'd said you needed time to recover from your injury or were gun-shy after the beating," Whillans replied softly. "I might be able to convince myself that was true. But as it is, you're asking me to lie for you."

"Father—" Luis said quietly.

"Don't 'Father' me," Whillans snapped back. "Listen to what you're asking. There's no room in the church for a prideful priest. Is your loyalty to yourself or God?"

"To God of course."

"Then don't lie to me, his servant," the pastor demanded. "What sins are you planning to commit while you're away?"

"None, Father."

"No violence? No retribution?"

"No, Father."

"Then what?" he asked.

Luis told the pastor what he'd learned from Michael Story. The more he spoke, the more Whillans turned inward, mulling over what he heard.

"You think you have a responsibility in this?"

"God brought Odilia here. Was that for no reason? I spoke her language. She took me into her confidence. It was a sign of my arrogance and pride that I thought I was in control of the situation. I should've handed her over to law enforcement right away."

"And it's not prideful and arrogant now to think you can get in the way of God's will?" Whillans said. "It sounds like you mean to do so as a man, not as a man of God."

"Absolutely not," Luis countered. "I am only the latter. God is tasking me. The easy thing would be to walk away. The same hand that guides me in all things is telling me this."

"Demanding it be done?"

"No. The world is demanding that, crying out as loud as my mind can take. The voice telling me not to walk away is a whisper."

Whillans stared into the middle for a moment before reaching into his pocket. He handed Luis a folded piece of pink paper.

"I was the first one in her room. Everything was knocked over. Maybe they were looking for something. They even broke a chair. But they didn't find this."

Luis looked it over.

"What is it?"

"Something she didn't want anyone to find. It was tucked behind the paneling." Whillans said nothing for a moment, then got to his feet and headed back inside. "I hope you know what you're doing."

IX

Whiiiiiiiiine . . . whiiiiiiine . . . whiiiiine . . .

Oscar keyed the ignition a second time. The owner of the minivan, Ramona Gomez, stared blankly ahead, as if her hope of a quick fix was draining away.

"I wish it was better news," Oscar said, climbing out from behind the wheel. "We've been patching your transmission for months, telling you all along it would eventually crap out. Eventually is today, *niña*. Whole thing has to be replaced, unless you want to use your van as a planter. It won't make it another mile."

Oscar knew the woman ran a daycare out of her home. She barely made enough to keep food on the table for herself and the three—yes, *three*—lazy-ass drunks she'd been cursed with for sons. She used the van to take the kids to local parks, pools, and even the zoo on occasion. For working parents who didn't want their kids plopped in front of a television set all day, she was a godsend. She was also known for giving freebies to mothers who needed a few hours to go to job interviews. The loss of her vehicle would put a serious dent in her business.

Oscar waited for this to sink in before raising a finger.

"But," he added, knifing through the tension, "you kept coming back to my garage. Loyalty means something to me. I know what you do for our community. You *care.* So do I."

"Ah," she said. "What do you want from me?"

It was the response of a woman shrewd enough to avoid being too deep in another's debt.

"Nothing much. I just want to be the mechanic you recommend."

"What?" she croaked in surprise.

"People in the neighborhood come to you for everything. A woman in here the other day was telling somebody on the phone who needed a plumber to 'Call Ramona. She'll have somebody.' I'm sure you've got a roof guy, an appliance guy, a guy with a truck . . . I want to be the car guy."

Ramona cocked her head. She liked being flattered.

"Okay."

"Great. I'll have the transmission in by the end of the day. One of my guys can drive you home now, and we'll bring it up to you when it's ready. Satisfactory?"

It was. Ramona thanked him and was taken home in one of the shop's tow trucks. Oscar moved on to the next vehicle, only to find Luis Chavez in the garage doorway, having watched the exchange.

"What happened to your face? You miss the life after all?"

"Did you really find a complete transmission in some junker car?" the priest asked, deflecting Oscar's question. When his old friend didn't respond either, Luis arched an eyebrow. "You didn't fuck with her car just so you could cash this in, did you?"

"No!" Oscar laughed. "And since when do priests say 'fuck'?"

"So, someone out there woke up to an empty driveway one morning."

"Somewhere in the middle," Oscar admitted. "Straight insurance scam. Transmission came from a fleet car at a funeral home. The owner wanted to upgrade, needed the insurance to do it, so I made sure it happened."

"By switching out their perfectly good transmission with a busted one," Luis surmised.

Oscar shrugged. Luis chuckled.

"That's . . . enterprising."

"Shouldn't you counsel me to turn my life around?"

"Given what I'm here to ask you, that'd be the height of hypocrisy."

———

Luis had three favors to ask of Oscar. All required discretion. The first was to locate an address in Ventura County. The second was a ride to that address. The third was for a new identity.

"A new *identity?*" Oscar asked. "How the hell am I supposed to manage that?"

"Come on," Luis chided. "Even I know what kind of side business Remberto's got going on in that phone room."

"I'm not all that accustomed to doing favors without getting something in return," Oscar countered. "What can you offer me? *Absolution?*"

Luis lowered his gaze. He hadn't wanted to go there.

"You want to talk about the sheer number of times I pulled your stupid ass out of the fire back in the day?" Luis asked. "That you wouldn't be able to offer free transmissions to the neighborhood *abuela*, much less have made it to adulthood without me?"

"You think I owe you a *debt*, motherfucker?" Oscar growled.

"I think you think that," Luis shot back. "I think that's why you wanted to check on me the second you heard I was back in town. I'm here to tell you that if you do this for me, there's nothing between us and never will be again, real or imagined. I won't be so much as a lingering thought taking up real estate in the back of your head. Cool?"

Luis quietly prayed his gambit would pay off. The Oscar in his late twenties might in no way be susceptible to the old notions of personal honor and debt instilled in them both when they were kids.

"There's no debt. I don't owe you, you don't owe me. Good?" Oscar said finally.

———

When Luis returned to St. Augustine's, he went to the same donation box Erna had taken Odilia's replacement clothes from and pulled out a pair of old jeans, an ill-fitting T-shirt, a work shirt to go over that, and boots. He loaded a backpack with a few supplies and removed the bandage from his battered face. When he checked himself out in the mirror, he looked every bit the part of a laborer seeking a new start.

Oscar was set to pick him up after dark. Luis spent the rest of the day doing chores around the parish and keeping out of sight. He didn't want parishioners asking questions about his injuries. When it came time to go, he looked for Pastor Whillans to say good-bye, but he was doing a home visit. He'd have to see him when he came back.

"I hope you know what you're in for," Oscar said as Luis climbed into his truck.

"I don't," Luis admitted.

"Aside from picking strawberries being the worst job under the sun, what happens if one of these guys recognizes you from the parish?" Oscar asked. "The only reason to string a guy up below the border like that is if you want it to look like the work of the cartels. That takes balls. Doubt they'd have a problem killing you, too."

"Since when have you ever picked a strawberry?" Luis shot back.

Oscar laughed. "You think God's going to protect you?"

"I think God wants me to protect myself," Luis stated.

Oscar eyed him for a moment. Luis could tell his childhood friend wasn't sure if he was bullshitting him or possibly crazy.

"But what happens if they kill you?" Oscar countered. "God'll congratulate you in the afterlife for doing your best, but you'll know he's actually disappointed."

"What do you think he'll do for you?"

"When I get there, I hope I've lived my life to the fullest, done every last damn thing I wanted to do on this earth so I don't give a fuck what God thinks."

Luis laughed at this and shook his head.

"Now's the part where you tell me to come to church, right?" Oscar asked.

"Starting to sound like you want me to."

Oscar scoffed. Luis chuckled. It really was like old times. Maybe when Oscar had welcomed him back not as just an old friend but a brother, he hadn't been exaggerating. Maybe he'd really missed Luis.

"Ten years, bro," Oscar said quietly, as if having read Luis's mind. "You been gone ten years."

It was more like fourteen, Luis thought. Fourteen years since the night Luis and Oscar had been brought to the dry riverbed under the Fourth Street Bridge and surrounded by the rank and file as well as the OGs of the Alacrán gang.

The pair had hit a convenience store the week before. Oscar had been the triggerman, Luis the lookout. They hadn't been out of the store ten seconds before a police cruiser pulled up behind them. They were both fast runners. Two cops pursued on foot, but only one had the lungs for it. The teens had made the turn from Reservoir onto Waterloo when a second cop car appeared at the top of the street.

"*Split!*" Oscar had hissed.

Like birds guided by primordial instinct, they raced off in different directions. The squad car followed Oscar. The one cop, still running, pursued Luis.

Luis could've run all night. He was scared but exhilarated. He didn't think it'd be long before the cop was gassed. Not when weighted down by twenty pounds of equipment, ten more years of living, and a healthy sense of self-preservation in one of the worst neighborhoods in the city. What Luis couldn't have known was that his pursuer, Domingo Dominguez, had been a basketball standout at Morningside High and took immense pride deflating the image of the doughnut-huffing, fat-assed cop.

It only took him half a block more to catch up to Luis, grab his arm, and wheel him onto the lawn of the nearest house.

"You got anything in your pockets I'm going to hurt myself on?" the officer asked as he cuffed Luis.

Fighting to catch his breath after landing on his stomach, Luis couldn't remember for the life of him what was in his pockets.

"No, sir," he said as the officer tossed his phone and keys into the grass.

"Those keys to your mama's place?" Domingo asked. "If she's anything like mine, she's going to be *pissed, mijo.*"

Luis's heart skipped a beat. The officer didn't know how right he was. Sandra Chavez was so furious, she didn't even come down to the station for two days. She finally arrived with a change of clothes and some toiletries to find her son exhausted and terrified. It wasn't like he hadn't had his share of run-ins with the authorities, but those had been school related. When it got so serious that he would have to be expelled, a representative from the disciplinary board had warned Luis there was an 80 percent chance he'd be behind bars within six months.

An overachiever for the first time in his life, Luis had accomplished this in four.

Luis was kept in the juvenile wing with several other prisoners who'd been in and out of state custodial care for most of their young lives. They treated Luis as if the beating of his life could come at any second. He lived in constant fear. The only relief came once a day when robbery-homicide detectives Ari Lin and Vincent Coai arrived to interview him. They asked about the robbery, his thus-far-unidentified cohort, and put out feelers about his connection to the Alacrán street gang.

"Feel free to lie to us and prove to no one that cares what a stand-up guy you are," Detective Coai said grimly. "Or give us a couple of yeses or nos and we'll get you home by supper time."

Luis did neither. He said nothing for three days, no matter what was offered or threatened. The jailer came for him at the seventy-second hour, and he was released into the custody of his mother.

"You'll wish they kept you," was all she said on the drive home.

Though confined to his room, Luis was finally able to relax. He slept. He read and reread his comics. He waited. His mother didn't talk to him even when she brought meals.

Then there was Nicolas.

About a year earlier the bishop from the local church—one regularly attended by Luis's mother and her eldest son, but not at all by Luis—had come by the house. He told Sandra that Nicolas had approached him about receiving private instruction, as Nicolas believed he had a calling to become a priest. His bishop, a pre-retirement Osorio, had asked Nicolas to pray about this for two weeks and come back to him. When he did and asked again to receive instruction, with the goal of one day entering the priesthood, Osorio agreed, pending Sandra's approval.

She was thrilled.

For the next twelve months Nicolas went to school, got even better grades than before, got a job working as a busboy to help pay for divinity school, and spent every other waking moment at church. He'd been a constant presence in his brother's life up until then. That changed overnight.

So when a knock came to Luis's door two days after he'd been home, he was surprised to see who it was.

"You okay?" Nicolas asked.

"'Course," Luis said, shrugging with as much disaffection as he could muster.

Nicolas looked around Luis's room, as if he might find the answer there. He finally pushed a few of Luis's comics aside and sat on the bed next to him.

"It's not about letting these people into your life, it's about letting them into your head," he said. "Once you hear their voices when you're about to make a decision instead of your own or, even better, God's, you're not living for yourself anymore. You're living for them. And you might as well be living for the devil."

Luis was momentarily struck dumb. Then he laughed in his brother's face. He didn't know it then, but Nicolas's words would be burned into his mind for the rest of his life.

At the time, though, Luis expected not much more than a pitying smile and a retreat. Instead, Nicolas hugged him.

"I love you. Mom loves you. You're already ten times the man Dad was. We're just waiting for you to see that."

Luis shoved his brother away. Nicolas left the room. Luis got a call from Oscar a second later saying he'd be picked up after midnight. He never saw his brother alive again.

When he slipped out that night, Luis found a car waiting for him at the end of the block with two guys up front. He got the sense they'd been there for hours and wondered if the Alacrán OGs thought he might try to run. The drive was less than ten minutes. They reached the edge of Boyle Heights, pulling to a curb alongside the wide concrete riverbed of the so-called Los Angeles River. The men climbed out first and led him to a break in the chain-link fence that crowned it.

When they reached the bottom of the dry waterway, Luis realized why it was appealing to gangbangers. The lights of the city dimmed to an almost-perfect darkness in the gully. It took Luis's eyes a few seconds to adjust, but soon he saw the large group of Alacrán gangbangers waiting for them under the Fourth Street Bridge.

They're going to make an example of me, he thought.

Conversations quieted as they approached. Luis could make out Oscar, Remberto, and a few of the younger guys he'd run with, but many faces were unfamiliar. He'd seen various OGs around the neighborhood just enough to know they were a different level of gangster from him. They had reputations. They'd been to prison. They were feared by other gangs. They had families. Some had jobs or businesses. They weren't just criminals, they were part of a criminal economy.

One of them—a tall, skinny man with a shaved head and big, gaucho-style facial hair—stepped forward. Luis had never seen him before.

"Get over here, Chavez," he said in Spanish.

Luis did so, seeing the vast number of tattoos crisscrossing his face, neck, and arms. They were of three familiar varieties: Catholic, Chicano, and criminal. Nobody with ink like that thought twice about working in the straight world.

Luis caught Oscar's gaze, but his friend quickly looked away.

It's gonna be bad, Luis thought.

"So, you fucked up a robbery, fucked up the getaway, and got thrown in jail," the OG said. "It's only because of our intervention that there aren't going to be charges."

This answered one of Luis's questions. He considered thanking the guy but figured he should keep quiet.

"Everybody goes in at one time or another," the OG continued. "It's how you do your time that is the measure of a man. You got your cherry popped, but you did it right. Even better than not talking, you didn't complain and you didn't make friends. A man like that—and that's what you are now, a man—can be relied on."

Luis was confused. He shot a look to Oscar for clarification. His friend still wouldn't meet his gaze.

"But to be a man, you still have to deal with all of us."

Luis waited for an explanation. He got a fist to the kidney instead. For the next thirty seconds, Luis was pummeled from all sides. Most of the blows were to the torso, though some made it to his arms and legs. A couple glanced off his head, but any that hit there or to his face felt like accidents. A rib cracked and he gasped as he felt it in his lungs. Blood trickled into his eyes from a cut to his forehead. He'd tried to stand after the first couple of hits but now balled up in a fetal position, the concrete cold through his thin shirt.

He knew what this was. More importantly, he knew he wasn't to fight back. If he did, the intensity of the beating would likely increase or, worse, the beating would get called off entirely. No one got a second chance to be jumped in. You had to just take it.

The beating stopped as suddenly as it began. Everyone stepped back, though it still felt to Luis as if someone were pressing on his chest, holding him down. He'd soon learn this was because his broken rib had deflated his left lung.

"Hospital," snapped the OG.

The men who'd brought Luis lifted him to his feet, causing such a tremendous spasm of pain throughout his body that he almost passed out. If they noticed, they didn't act like it. As they dragged him past Oscar, the one who Luis had seen delivering the rib-breaking kick, his friend leaned in.

"Fuck you," Oscar hissed, all malice.

For a second Luis wasn't sure where the rage was coming from. Then it hit him. Oscar had planned the robbery. He'd had the gun, which was the real risk when it came to the cops. This should've been his opportunity to prove himself. Instead, his peon had grabbed the glory.

Luis would get him back. It wasn't as if Oscar's anger or the violence of the attack would've gone unnoticed by others. He'd have to save face.

"Fuck that guy," Luis choked out as he was shoved into the back of the car.

Around that same moment, four bullets entered Nicolas's body a couple of miles away.

X

Oscar and Luis didn't say much of substance on the way up to Santiago's farm. They caught up on each other's families, Luis played a few rounds of "where are they now?" and Oscar asked about his path to the priesthood. When they spoke of their own combined past, both seemed to realize that staying away from their teen years was best.

"They used to do that pumpkin patch every year," Oscar was saying, "and they put in a haunted house. The Soriano family or something. You got in free if you were under three, so my dad always made us pretend we couldn't talk."

Luis laughed.

"I remember that. Nic and I went with you guys once. The guy at the ticket booth even pointed out that I was wearing my school shirt. But your dad made us be assholes and hold up our fingers all *'Tengo tres años, señor.'*"

Luis waited for Oscar to chuckle but realized the mention of Luis's brother had shut him up.

"Hey, I talk about him. It's cool."

"Always hard to tell how raw things are with people," Oscar said. "I mean, probably easier to be away from it."

"It's not like I forget. Your shop's maybe two blocks from where it happened."

"Yeah. You visit him?"

"Nah. There's nothing of him there. My mom, either. They're long with God."

They wound up the highway, cresting a few hills before the vast flat farmlands of Ventura County sprawled out beneath them. Oscar checked the map on his phone against a sign on an overpass and hit his blinker.

"Next exit."

Alongside the highway there was an outlet mall, a few business parks, and even homes in the distance. Five minutes west and they might as well have been on another planet, surrounded on both sides by dark, empty fields.

"You're sure we're in the right place?" Luis asked.

"My guy seemed sure. You have to remember these aren't farms, these are fields. Every square foot counts. You put up a house or a barn, that's a couple hundred square feet you're not using to plant."

They passed a mile marker. Oscar slowed and pulled off the road.

"We're here."

"Where?" Luis asked.

Oscar pointed to a dark strip between two of the neighboring fields.

"I don't see anybody," Luis said.

"Neither do the cops, but they're down there. They'll probably be accustomed to new faces, but keep your head down. Look for a boss tomorrow morning and say yes to everything. Yes, you've worked fields before. Yes, that includes strawberries. And much as you'll want to, don't ask questions your first day."

Luis extended a hand.

"We good?" Oscar asked.

Luis knew what he was asking and nodded. The way Oscar shook his hand made it clear the gangster thought it might be for the last time. Luis clambered out of the truck and waved.

"Vaya con Dios," Oscar said in a joking tone, then pulled away.

The culvert looked like a refugee camp. About a hundred people lined the dry channel's walls in tiny but well-defined stakes. A few had actual tents, but many made do under tarps, makeshift roofs of cardboard or wood, or were simply laid out on the hard ground. Most were asleep, but a handful registered Luis's arrival. The glances asked if he was a threat or merely a stranger. He tried smiling back but received nothing in response.

He reached the end of the line and lowered his pack. The rotund woman who'd anchored the row nodded warmly to Luis as he unrolled a blanket. It was the first look of kindness he'd received. He wondered if she was just happy to have a body between her and the unseen lions of the night.

He nodded and laid out his bedroll. Then he prayed.

"Café?"

Luis awoke to a cornucopia of smells. There was freshly brewed coffee, roasted pork, beans, tortillas, and corn. The woman to Luis's left indicated a makeshift stove she'd made from a coffee tin balanced on a Sterno can.

"Gracias," Luis replied.

The woman's name was Carmen. Luis played dumb as she told him about the recent and brutal murder down in Mexico of the man who ran the farm and how several of his workers had left immediately, fearing more trouble. The word went out that a handful would stay on out of loyalty. They would continue the harvest, hoping for a piece of the profits, but mostly because they thought letting the fruit of Santiago's labor go to waste added insult to injury.

Luis was about to ask a question when most of the camp rose to climb out of the culvert, as if roused by a silent bugle. Luis followed. Waiting for them at the top, his face barely visible in the dim light, was a large man in his midfifties with unlaced boots and gray, sunken eyes. The rough stubble on his face added to his grave expression.

"For those who don't know, I'm Alberto," he said, staring into his hands. "We *are* going to work. I spoke to a couple of our drivers, and they'll take in the stock at midday and sundown. I also heard late last night we may get some help from the other side of the hill. That may be in additional workers or a guarantor of pay. Those with papers on file, get to it. Those without, same rate. Twenty dollars an hour if you move. You don't, you're out."

Three-quarters of the group moved to the field. Those that remained looked confused. With the exception of Luis.

"For you guys, I'll need to see and copy your green cards. You'll get your paperwork by the end of the day. Anyone without a green card— well, it might be easier for you to try somewhere else."

Most of the remainders shuffled off. Luis stepped forward.

"I need a labor cert. I was told I could do that here."

Oscar had been surprised when his contact in Ventura County had informed him that as far as the state was concerned, Higuera's fields were aboveboard. They were incorporated as a small business; Santiago's workers were listed and paid as seasonal labor.

"Yeah, but that's probably bullshit," Oscar had said. "He's probably just a smarter criminal."

Luis hadn't said anything. They'd come up with a couple of fake IDs, making him out to be a Mexican national. They dummied up some residency paperwork as well that suggested he was on the road toward naturalization. An almost-legal illegal. He was just missing one thing: a business owner's confirmation that he was a skilled employee.

"Good chance they'll blow you off if you bring it up," Oscar had warned. "But if they're trying to avoid scrutiny, they'll at least have to make a show of helping you with your paperwork."

"The same week the boss is murdered?"

"Hey, it's your plan, not mine! But if you only need to be there a few days anyway, they might not ask at all, and you can get right to work. This is for contingencies."

Now facing Alberto, Luis was happy to have jumped through the right hoops.

"You need a labor cert?" Alberto asked incredulously. "On these fields?"

Luis handed over the pages Oscar had printed off the Internet.

"It's all I need. I have an apartment. My kids are in school. They were born here. I wasn't. But I'm almost there. Just need a labor cert."

"You've got to work somewhere two years for that," Alberto said.

"No," Luis countered. "I need to work in the same labor pool. It can be in different fields."

"Things are changing in this state," Alberto said, barely able to hide his exasperation. "Heck, even the country. You could probably wait it out a few years . . ."

"Would you do that to your kids?"

Alberto stiffened. Clearly he would not.

"Look, I have to be straight with you. I don't know what's going on with this farm in the short *or* long term. Yeah, Santiago was big on helping people navigate all this. He was undocumented for a while and knew what it was like. That doesn't mean the next owner will feel that way at all."

Luis indicated the fields, now filling with workers.

"Maybe. But it looks like you need workers now. All I'm asking is to do the work. If it doesn't work out, I'll try somewhere else. You just have to know how few places will give you the time of day. They want you legal or under the table. You try to split the difference, and they think you're going to cost them."

"But not you."

Luis fell silent. Alberto stared him down like a man accustomed to winning these battles. When Luis pushed the papers forward, Alberto relented.

"I'll do what I can," Alberto said. "'Cause Santiago's voice in my head is telling me that's what he'd do."

And that's what he did for you, Luis realized.

———

Though mortification of the flesh as a way to get a sense of Christ's suffering had been a central practice of the Catholic Church for centuries before falling out of favor in the twentieth century, Luis was always surprised to see with what reverence it was written of in earlier texts. In various accounts of the lives of saints, ecclesiastical scholars wrote with veneration about the gory details of the pain the canonized had endured:

> *When the feast of the saint arrived, Father Grijalva whipped himself until the skin of his back was in ribbons and blood cascaded down his legs.*

> *After receiving the compliment, Father Antonio went to an olive tree, took down a branch, and flagellated himself to chase out the sin of pride.*

> *Following the miracle, Sister Agatha took the leather strap and humbled herself to her Lord.*

It was like something out of a Stephen King novel. How could the writer know how joyful the priest felt with every lash, how much closer to the Lord?

Luis was glad it had fallen out of favor, as he could never envision flagellating himself bloody as a reflection of the Passion. It was too absurd. Which was why, as he suffered through the most backbreaking labor he'd ever endured in over-a-hundred-degree heat, he questioned whether any of those enthusiastic writers had done any mortifying of the flesh themselves.

Not that his injuries were anywhere near comparable to Christ's. His hands and fingers were rubbed raw by stiffening leaves, his fingertips by the sharp edges of the plastic clamshells he filled with berries. Every microlaceration or abrasion combined, until it looked like his skin had been boiled away. Worse were the burns seared into any bit of his skin exposed to the sun. The backs of his hands and neck, his face, and his ears had erupted into a blazing rash. As advised to do by Oscar, he'd worn long pants and sleeves into the fields. But his clothes soon stuck to him from constant sweat, irritating all areas beneath. His skin was in full revolt.

His muscles ached as well. The only efficient way to pick strawberries was to move down the row bent over, using two fingers to grip and gently twist the berries free from the stem. They were then placed in a clamshell container that would later arrive in the supermarket. The fewer hands that touched the berry, the less likely damage to its skin. The smallest abrasion could lead to rot within days.

This process was the reason there was so much turnover in the stoop-crop fields. Wrists went, hip joints went, legs went, but worse than everything, backs went. At the end of the first day, he was so stiff, he couldn't even stretch. He thought he'd be better in the morning. Instead, he could barely get out of bed, much less stand.

"You gotta give the plants their due before they'll give you yours," another worker said. "They bleed you a little. Get a taste. Your hands callous up, your skin thickens, and you come to an understanding. Only then will they give up the berries."

Luis kept at it. A few of the other new faces quit. He didn't have that luxury.

Another thing Oscar had said was proven right on that first day, too. If he'd asked any questions about Santiago, much less Odilia, he would've been shut down immediately. No one socialized during the day, and in the night folks stayed with their own, seemingly suspicious of overtures of friendship.

So he worked, kept his mouth closed, and patiently waited. To assuage the pain, he remained in an almost-constant state of prayer.

Dear Lord. Please . . . please guide me today as I try to do your will. Lend me the strength to endure this pain and guide me toward a way to avoid this fate tomorrow.

The other thing Luis waited on was his paperwork. He'd brought it up again to Alberto on the second day but mostly got the brush-off. Alberto's priority was continuing the harvest, answering the questions of the small number of investigators that came by, and getting his people paid.

At the end of the third day, Alberto came looking for him.

"You're in the system, amigo."

Alberto handed him a white sheet of paper. The name from Luis's fake ID was on it, as well as some cursory information about the property on which he was employed. The state seal was in the upper right.

"You use this to start the process," Alberto explained. "If you're missing any forms, they've got them at the library and the post office."

"Thank you," Luis said. "I really appreciate it."

"You're going to need one more signature."

"From who?"

"Maria Higuera. This was her brother's place. She'll be here the day after tomorrow, but go easy on her though. She buried him yesterday. Legally speaking, she's your employer now."

Luis looked at the sheet and froze. It was so unexpected, but there it was. He hurried back to his pack, digging into the lining, where he'd tucked the piece of paper Pastor Whillans had found in Odilia's room.

Besides the color, the two forms were a match. There were spaces for their alien registration and foreign passport numbers, employer verification information, and a space where the documents had been independently signed by someone at the county level. It seemed to indicate that Odilia had worked there. It also suggested that Santiago really did keep things on the up and up.

Maybe.

His mind raced. Could he ask Alberto about her?

His thoughts were interrupted by a conversation down the row.

"You hear what they said about Santiago?" someone said. "They think he was alive when they took him across the border, then they killed him down there."

Luis looked down to where the people were speaking. It was three of the old-timers, guys whose hands looked like they'd picked hundreds of thousands of berries and whose skin had spent countless hours baking under the sun.

"Why do that?" another asked. "He could've yelled out at the border. I think they probably did him right here, rolled him up, and drove him down inside a tank or something."

"Nah," said the third, who had a raspberry birthmark across the right side of his face. "I saw him take off."

More were listening now.

"The lights were still on in his house, so I thought he was going right back in. He didn't take his truck. I thought maybe he was going over to one of the other fields. But he went straight west."

"What's that way?" Luis asked before he could catch himself.

All eyes turned in his direction.

"There are no farms over there," raspberry birthmark said. "No roads, no stores, no nothing else, either. You've got the mountains, and then you've got the ocean on the other side of that. I think he was going somewhere. But somebody found him."

"Was he the only one who left?"

As soon as the question left his mouth, Luis knew he'd gone too far. The men eyed him with suspicion. The question hung in the air unanswered. Luis thought they were about to turn the interrogation on him when the first of the speakers shrugged.

"Just him. Why? Not enough for you?"

Luis didn't reply. He rolled onto his blanket and found sleep.

XI

A well-manicured nail slid a single sheet of paper across the polished wood conference room table, stopping it in front of Glenn Marshak.

"We hope this package tells you how important the Marshak family is to Crown Foods," the owner of the nail, Crown VP Connie Brickell, said, her voice warm and winning. "This has been a very fruitful partnership and we hope it continues. In the years since our last contract, we've expanded into Canada and the UK following our CostMart acquisition, and opened our first three stores in Australia. We also broke ground on our first space in Asia, a hundred-seventy-thousand-square-foot retail mart in the HarbourFront precinct of Singapore. As we thrive, you thrive."

Glenn eyed her nail polish. It was a pale pink that he knew must be available from Crown retail marts. That was her thing. The suit and blouse were likely just as affordable, from some off-the-rack line by an up-and-coming designer in the Crown universe. Her shoes—patent leather, pointed-toe midheeled pumps—looked expensive, but he'd be surprised if she paid more than thirty dollars for them. Did her brand loyalty extend to her shampoo or perfume, in the event a vendor had a particularly sharp nose?

Glenn had a sharp nose, but rather than lavender or eucalyptus, he smelled bullshit. He'd gotten a preview of the deal now in front of him from a well-placed friend the night before. He glanced over it once to confirm it was the same, then slid it over to his nephew, Jason, on his right.

"Something wrong?" Connie asked.

"Oh, I was just waiting to see if you were joking."

It was no small feat to suck the air out of a conference room.

"I don't understand," Connie said.

"You say this is a deal you'd offer a partner," Glenn began. "But if we were to accept the terms of this agreement, it would be akin to slitting our own throat."

Connie shot a look down the table to the other Crown executives. Glenn didn't wait before continuing.

"What you've presented in the short form is a series of milestones by which we're meant to increase our profit share over the next several years," Glenn explained, before pointing to a thicker contract to her right. "What's buried in the long form is a caveat that allows you to opt out, citing fluctuations in consumer demand."

"That's in all our contracts. It protects us in case—"

Glenn slammed his hand down on the table. Connie recoiled in surprise.

"Stop treating us like we're children," Glenn snapped. "Maybe at one time you meant it in good faith, but on ten different occasions in the past five years you've used that stipulation to bleed your 'partners' dry. Crown claims a drop-off in sales and invokes the clause, forcing the vendor to make all of the cuts on their end."

Glenn paused, making sure he had the room's attention.

"The following year, another visit from Crown, hat in hand. No talk of expanding into Canada or emporiums in Singapore. Only talk of how bad the competition's gotten and the fragility of the economy. This time the cuts you ask for are a lot deeper. The kind of belt-tightening that means layoffs. If a vendor balks, the unstated threat is that Crown can always go with the competition. They'd be willing to take the deal in return for shelf space in the eight thousand Crown retail outlets worldwide."

A gray-haired man, Crown CFO Andrew Roenningke, sat at the end of the table eyeing Glenn coolly. His suit suggested he didn't feel beholden to dress in only what Crown had on its hangers.

"Glenn, if this is your way of saying that the business between our companies is at an end, I'd appreciate you coming out and saying it. This grandstanding is poor form."

"Go fuck yourself, Andrew," Glenn shot back. "I'm trying to explain to you what being a partner's really about. If you look at my market share and how much of your profits come from my fields, I think you'll realize we're right at the tipping point of being too big to manipulate. Heck, maybe that's what this contract's about."

Andrew scowled. Glenn reached into his briefcase and slid a single sheet of paper of his own down to him.

"What's this?" Andrew asked.

"A list of exactly one hundred of your vendors who use Marshak crops in their product. Whether it's strawberry flavoring for gummy bears, cane for their wicker chairs, or honey for their organic sweeteners, they rely on us. I'm sure you recognize some of the bigger names."

Glenn had their attention.

"Imagine the reason I'm being such a dick about your offer is because, say, Target has offered us something better. And by imagine, I mean conjure the image of me on the phone with their CEO, Tom Schaffer, one hour ago, explaining that I had the power to not only go exclusive with them but to take one hundred popular brands with me. What do you think he said?"

Andrew gaped at Glenn.

"You're bluffing," the CFO decided. "This is bullshit. Theatrical bullshit, but bullshit all the same."

Glenn rose and indicated for Jason to follow him out the door. The Crown execs watched them go in mild horror as the impact of Glenn's threat dawned on them.

When the two Marshaks were safely in the elevator on the way down to the building's valet station, Jason glanced at his uncle.

"One phone call and they'll be onto you," he said.

"Oh, he knew I was full of it right then," Glenn replied with a shrug. "What I want him to wonder is whether I've gone crazy."

Jason shot him a look suggesting he was now wondering the same thing. Glenn scoffed.

"The one thing you can rely on with Andrew is the fact that he does nothing without fretting over what his father would do in the same situation," Glenn explained.

"But his dad's out of the company."

"Hah!" Glenn spat. "He won't really be out till he's dead. And for Andrew, Daddy's gaze is like a phantom limb. It's always there. That's especially true when he's sitting opposite someone his father told him to watch out for."

"What do you think they'll do?" Jason asked.

"At the end of the day, the most important thing for Andrew is to keep the status quo. If he loses us, his board will talk, even if he's right to let me go. It makes him look bad. I'd be willing to bet we'll get an offer that's three times the money, minus the offending clause, by the end of next week."

"And we reject that one, too?"

The elevator doors opened to the parking garage. Glenn snorted.

"Hell no. We sign that on the spot to let them know we beat them."

Jason laughed out loud. It was the kind of story he would recount as quintessential Glenn Marshak for months to come. Glenn smiled, having made his point.

"Where are you off to now?" Jason asked as Glenn's driver brought around his town car.

"Home. Elizabeth's coming by to go over last-minute party plans. You'll be there, right?"

"Of course."

Glenn nodded and was about to climb into the town car's open back door when he stopped.

"One more thing. Will you look in on your dad? He had a burr up his ass about something earlier this week, and we're going to need his vote on the Crown Foods thing. If he's unhappy, you know he'll drag his feet and make us look bad."

"Will do, Glenn," Jason said.

"Thanks. We're at the one-yard line here. I know I've said it before, but this is the big one, the contract that'll keep the company going for the next twenty years. Let's just get it in the end zone and spike the ball."

Jason nodded. "I know how much this contract means," he parroted.

Glenn clapped him on the shoulder. It was meant to be a reassuring gesture, but he used too much force, tipping it into condescension. He checked Jason's face for a sign that he'd detected this but saw none.

"Okay then," Glenn said, climbing into the car. "See you at the party."

———

"Jesus Christ, they're *children.*"

Though the comment came from Michael's wife, Helen, as she scanned the party guests, Michael had been thinking it himself. He understood the ones she was referring to were all college graduates at the very least midway through law school, but none looked older than sixteen or seventeen.

"Children being offered five-figure signing bonuses to agree to six-figure starting salaries," Michael replied as he watched another pair of the young law school students giggle their way to the bar.

Though it was a midday retirement party for a judge he barely knew, word had gotten round that it might be embarrassingly under-attended, so Michael had made the effort. Swedburg, Grega & Chernov appeared to have sent over two dozen of their prospective summer associates to liven things up as well. The students were in town at the invitation of the firm to consider coming back in a month to work as summer associates.

Work, Michael scoffed.

He remembered his own associateship as a three-month party on the firm's dime meant to convince them to sign with the firm upon graduation. Of course, as soon as the courtship ended and they returned as first-year associates, their lives were shit. Hundred-hour workweeks in document warehouses, endless abuse at the hands of the second- and third-years, and all without the slightest chance of advancement.

Michael considered saying something to a couple of them but then chuckled. It wasn't like he would've listened at their age. Better to sip his drink.

He glanced to his wife as she waved to an acquaintance across the room, her bright, easy smile framed by a gorgeous mane of blond hair. It was a shade found only on Southern California girls who grew up outdoors without a care in the world. He'd been like these kids, tempted by riches due to his lower-middle-class upbringing, but something told him even then it was a dead end. His real ambition was politics, but that required money. Enter Helen. Helen came from a filthy amount of money. Their five-bedroom Bel-Air home had been bought not on Michael's salary as a Los Angeles deputy district attorney, but by Helen's father. The expectation was that it would be filled with children and used for parties meant to elevate Michael's political standing. Three kids and an endless parade of political fund-raisers and charity dinners later, Michael felt they'd held up their end of the bargain.

"Michael Story!"

Judson Nichols, one of the retiring judge's oldest friends, appeared at Michael's side.

"How are you, Judson?" Michael said, shaking his hand.

"Good, good," he replied, planting a kiss on Helen's cheek. "It's a sad day for those of us who'll miss seeing Ron around the courthouse, but a great one for the people of California, who'll now have a powerful ally in the halls of Congress."

Ah, so he's off to be a lobbyist, Michael thought. He'd idly wondered where the well-connected but not incredibly bright judge would end up.

"Really? I always figured he'd end up in DC, but at the Supreme Court," Michael lied.

Judson twisted his mouth up at the compliment. Michael hoped his flattery wasn't over the top.

"What I really came over to talk about is your future, Michael," he said, before turning to Helen. "Mind if I pull him away for a brief bit of shoptalk?"

Helen smiled with rehearsed geniality.

"I'll leave you boys to it and say hi to Ron's wife."

Helen floated away as Judson and Michael watched. The old political hack shook his head.

"You don't deserve her, you know. A woman like that," Judson spat.

Michael was caught off guard. It didn't sound like a joke.

"I think you're out of line there, Judson," Michael said, hoping to keep it light in case he'd misread the man's tone.

"The Whittaker woman," Judson fumed.

Michael froze. *How the fuck does he know about that?*

"Was it worth it? Almost throwing away your career? And for what? *Pussy?*"

Michael's mind raced. If Judson knew, that meant others knew. Powerful others. He had to keep a lid on this but didn't know how. That Judson wasn't keeping his voice down didn't help things, either.

"I don't know what you're talking about," Michael replied lamely.

"Save it," Judson scoffed. "I'm not the interested party."

Michael's blood ran cold. He looked around the room, wondering who else could see right through him.

"Who is the interested party?" Michael managed.

"One that wants to be sure this investigation of yours is over," Judson explained, calmer now. "From what I can tell, it is, isn't it?"

"I don't think this is the time or place to discuss it."

Judson's hand shot forward, grabbing Michael by the wrist and stabbing a finger between the tendon and bone, until it pressed directly on the nerve. Michael would've laughed at such a crass attempt at intimidation if it didn't hurt so much. Part of that lifetime of self-restraint seemed to have provided Judson with an iron grip well into his sixties.

"This is twofold, Michael," Judson hissed, albeit with the slightest hint of frivolity. "You walk away, and your indiscretion remains buried. You *stay* away, and when the day comes that appointed offices are no longer good enough and you seek the mandate of the people, they'll make sure it happens."

Michael thought about Luis and his promise to resurrect the case. As his wrist throbbed, he realized he couldn't lose. Kill the investigation and earn a political war chest. Nail it and get carried to higher office by the press. If he could just play both sides long enough . . .

"Judson," he said, setting his teeth to betray more pain than he felt. "It occurs to me that I have too many cases as it is to pursue the same wild-goose chase twice."

Judson relaxed his grip on Michael's wrist and gently withdrew his hand.

"I knew you were smart," Judson said, already walking away.

———

Michael made it home early that night. The older children, Jillian and Denny, were getting ready for bed. The youngest, Marlo, was already under the covers. It was the first time he'd been home before lights-out in weeks.

"Two books!" Marlo demanded after Michael finished the first and got up to leave.

"Daddy has to get some work done," Michael protested. "My day's not over yet."

"*Please,*" Marlo insisted. A command more than a request.

Though the youngest, Marlo, had zeroed in on her father's absentee-father guilt faster than her siblings.

"Short book," Michael agreed.

After extracting himself from Marlo's room a few minutes later, he ran into Helen coming out of Denny's room down the hall.

"Are you working tonight?"

"I have to answer a bunch of e-mails, but I'll be down in a minute."

Helen headed downstairs to watch television as Michael went to his office. He pulled his laptop from his bag. He spent the first few minutes replying to the forty or so waiting e-mails but then moved to the doorway. He could hear the television drone on below, Helen watching a reality show about a group of obnoxious realtors, two of whom she'd worked with through her own budding agency.

Michael closed the door and returned to his laptop. He logged in to an account where three welcoming e-mails sat alone and unopened in the inbox. There were no sent messages or junk mail. In the drafts folder, however, sat 262 unsent messages.

He opened this and found a long stretch of e-mails differentiated only by date. They had nothing in their subject or address lines. He hit the date button and inverted the order so the oldest appeared on top.

He opened the first e-mail and found it as expected: all business. It was from Annie, as she had been the one who'd suggested using this method after hearing it was how terrorists communicated without leaving a trail. The e-mail went further in depth into the case she'd touched on when they first met, and she'd attached a handful of documents.

Michael looked it over, deleted it, and moved on.

The next few e-mails were a contrast in styles, Annie going on in depth about what she'd uncovered, while his replies were terse and off-putting. No matter what she offered up, he came back with requests for information he didn't think she could possibly uncover in hopes of dissuading her from continuing. Then there'd come a follow-up e-mail with precisely what he'd requested. Michael watched himself becoming invested.

He was almost halfway through when he came to a draft with only three words in the body: "Pics from yesterday." Attached were six cell phone photos of the two of them in postcoital amusement. The first showed Annie nude, smiling as she sat astride him. The second was of the two of them, the camera held over their heads, as they leaned close to one another.

Christ, she's beautiful, Michael thought.

The third was the keeper. Annie on her back alongside him, head on the pillow, eyes staring straight back at him. This one wasn't playful; it was all emotion. Her big brown eyes were imploring him, *Now that you've seen me at my most vulnerable, please don't hurt me.*

Michael tried to remember what had happened next. He'd probably put the camera aside and kissed her. More than any other woman he'd ever known, Annie Whittaker loved to be kissed. They'd make love for hours, lips locked the entire time. After years of dutiful married sex with Helen, a woman any man would say was far more beautiful than Annie, it was a godsend.

He stared at the photo for a long moment, committing it to memory, then deleted it. He went through the rest of the draft e-mails, deleting the ones sans attachments without a second glance. For the ones with photos, he'd give them a last look before deleting those as well.

"We NEED to find some time to hang out this week," said one message with a photo attached showing Annie, again nude, her favorite sex toy inserted in her vagina. Her mouth was open in orgasm. It was almost more crass than erotic, but that wasn't the point. She'd been thinking about him. That was turn-on enough.

He deleted it and moved on. He was almost done before he found a draft from only a couple of weeks back. When they met, it was almost always for either sex or case-related business. The four photos attached here were from one of their rare outings, a day they'd met on a beach north of Malibu. They were supposed to be arranging the transfer of Santiago into protective custody, but that had been handled in five minutes. As it was a beautiful day, they'd gone for a walk up the beach. He'd shown her a trick his grandmother taught him for counting birds. She'd sat on the sand and wrapped his arms around her as they watched the tide come in.

Two of the pictures were ones they'd taken of themselves, heads pressed together. The other two were of her walking close to the water. In that moment there'd been no case, no DA's office, no nonprofit legal aid office in Camarillo, and no Helen, Denny, Marlo, or Jillian.

God, he'd loved her.

He stared at her image for the last time, deleted the e-mail, and deactivated the account. He deleted the browser's history, then shut down the laptop, sinking into his chair, hot with guilt.

XII

For no reason he could divine, Luis's fourth day in the fields was comparatively easy. He was still in tremendous pain, but it was somehow more manageable. He felt his muscles strengthening. He learned when to drink water and when to sweat. He still wasn't exactly a fast picker, but his numbers improved.

Slowly he began to reach out to the other workers, drawing them into conversation about where they were from, where they'd worked, and who they'd met. This was where his priest training helped, as he'd never been naturally social. His schools growing up, though almost entirely Hispanic, were divided into two groups. There were Chicanos—those of Mexican descent born in Los Angeles, who were well on their way to assimilation. Then there were the more recent immigrants, those fresh off the boat, some of whom might've only been in the States for months if not weeks or days. To differentiate the two, the Chicanos borrowed slurs from the whites, calling the new arrivals beaners, spics, or wetbacks. This ensured that, despite appearances, they didn't have a goddamn thing in common with these dregs of society.

It had been important to him and his friends to speak English, dress well, listen to American hip-hop, and watch American television and movies so no one would think they were some fresh-off-the-boat beaners who still listened to cúmbia or *banda*. Felt like God's punishment that he was now walking in the shoes of those he once derided.

That evening the brother of one of the workers came by to offer a ride to anyone who wanted to go into town to get supplies. Seeing one more chance to be social, Luis asked to go, volunteering to pick up items for those who wanted to stay behind.

Eight men went, two squeezing in with the driver, while six ringed the truck bed. It was already cold, but in the back of the speeding truck it was downright frigid. Smiles of shared misery were passed around as the truck bounced its way toward the nearest town, eschewing main roads for fear of tickets. They passed a Walmart and two large chain grocery stores before the truck pulled into the parking lot of a smaller *mercado* that seemed more butcher's shop than supermarket.

There hadn't been much conversation on the way, but the experience gave those in the back a temporary sense of camaraderie. Sensing it was now or never, Luis turned to one of the workers who'd been around the fields the longest.

"Did Santiago have a girlfriend?"

Rather than suspicion, the question was met with a laugh.

"Why? You thinking of swooping in there?"

"Nah, nah. Alberto mentioned a sister. I wondered if he had a girl, too. Hadn't seen anybody around."

"He might've, but he never brought her out here. He did go off somewhere sometimes and came back looking like he'd had a piece. No idea, though."

"What about Odilia?" Luis tried.

"Odilia? Who's that?" the guy said without evasion.

"A girl who worked Santiago's fields."

The man laughed.

"Ain't nobody named Odilia worked these fields. I couldn't tell you the name of every man that worked the farm. I don't even know *your* name. But women? I can even tell you their eye color and if they got all their teeth. Front ones at least. And there's never been a picker named Odilia."

"You sure about that?" Luis pressed. "Twenties? Slender? Brown hair and eyes. Fairly pretty."

The man stopped cold, hand on the market's door.

"Oh, *Odilia*," he deadpanned. "The only hot chick who ever picked a strawberry. Yeah, forgot about her. Attitude for miles, wouldn't even talk to me, had a bunch of guys in food trucks deliver her lunch every day 'cause that's how rare a creature she was. Sorry, Charlie. No such monster."

He walked in, leaving Luis even more baffled than before. If Odilia hadn't worked at Santiago's farm, how did they know each other? More importantly, why did she have what appeared to be a form from the state saying she did?

He followed the others into the market, not seeing the group of men gathered around the checkout stand. The silence should've registered with him even subconsciously, but it didn't. In fact, he'd almost bumped into them when a hand shot out, grabbed his arm, and yanked him away.

"What the—?"

"Shut up, dumbfuck!" his friend from the truck ride whispered.

Luis looked back at the group buying cases of beer, bottles of water, and paper plates and was confused. There were six of them, all Hispanic, all well-built, all with tattoos. He thought they must be bikers or something until he saw the gun sticking out of the waistband of the one bringing up the rear.

"Oh shit," he said, following the other one back. "Are they about to rob the place?"

His companion gaped at him with incredulity. He gripped Luis's head and turned it to face in a different direction.

"I thought you were from Mexico," he said. "Must've been a long time ago, huh?"

"What do you mean?"

"Don't you know not to be looking at the guy with a gun no one notices? Those are the guys from the Manzana."

The Blocks, Luis translated. "Yeah, I feel you," he said.

He followed his friend down an aisle, but only so he could get a better glimpse of the men up front. He finally found a security mirror over a beer cooler and stared at their reflections.

That they all had tattoos wasn't a surprise if they were hard-asses. But what he found unusual was that a lot of their ink had been altered or covered up. A Virgin Mary became a tiger. The crossed *L* and *A* of the Los Angeles Dodgers was woven into an American flag. A large statue of Quetzalcoatl was turned into a sleeve of tribal art. The unaltered ones were mostly military. They were blended, marked over.

Like the ones on the men at the rectory. The ones who'd taken Odilia.

He remembered something. Tattoos were okay in the army, just not gang ones. So to join up, whether to get out of the life or at the *suggestion* of a judge, the tattoos had to be reinked. So what did that make these guys? Gangsters turned soldiers turned . . . what? Kidnappers? Field overseers? Armed enforcers?

He had to follow them.

After their leader, a sinewy fellow with sharp facial features and copper-colored eyes, paid the bill, the group left. Luis trailed after them, making it halfway to the check stand before the man who had driven him there and his brother intercepted him.

"Hey, excuse me," Luis said.

But the two men didn't budge. The man Luis had asked about Odilia stood nearby.

"Can't let you do that, man."

"Hey, I just wanted to have a word . . ."

When the driver looked like he might coldcock him, Luis backed down. Through the front window, he saw the gunmen climb into a pair of pickup trucks and drive away into the night.

Once they were gone, the driver's brother took Luis by the arm.

"You can come back with us tonight, even work another day tomorrow. But you're gone by sunset. Got it?"

Luis felt the eyes of the other workers on his back and knew there was no way around this. Amateur mistake. This might've been his one shot. How could he have been so stupid?

When the pickup returned to Santiago's farm an hour later, a blue Toyota Camry was parked outside the shack in the middle of the fields. A light was on inside. Luis thought he saw a woman through the window.

Maria Higuera, he realized.

It had been a week of fitful sleep for Maria. Following Santiago's death, there was the difficulty of transporting his body back to the States (a helpful mortician in Chatsworth who specialized in cross-border funerals eventually guided her through the necessary bribes), dealing with the police in two different countries, and then worrying the violence visited upon her brother might blow back on the rest of her family. She'd heard from a number of people in relation to Santiago's farm, but the only one she'd talked to was Alberto Ocampo. Her brother had mentioned him several times as one of his most trusted associates. So when he came down for Santiago's funeral, they'd spoken at length about what he needed from her in the short term to finish the harvest.

She'd understood her presence would be required soon but had put off driving up to the farm for the first part of the week. When Thursday rolled around and Alberto rang again to see when she might make it up, she packed Miguel off to a willing neighbor, got in her car, and made the drive. Though she knew Alberto and the other workers would be asleep by the time she arrived, she wanted to be there at first light to speak with him before he got too busy in the fields.

But when she awoke that morning, it was into a feeling of cold terror. The smells were unfamiliar, as were the sounds. The bed was not her own. The sun came in not only through the window but from the ceiling and the walls. Though wrapped in blankets, her body was covered in gooseflesh.

Her heart raced as panic set in. She stumbled out of bed, grabbing a table to steady herself, then remembered where she was.

"Jesus Christ," she muttered, getting to her feet.

She wanted to shower, but the tap in the bathroom brought only cold water. She settled on a change of clothes, ate a cereal bar she'd tucked in her purse, and emerged from the shack to find the fields already buzzing with activity.

As if this was what he had been waiting for, Alberto jogged over.

"Good morning," he said, wiping his hands on a pink handkerchief he pulled from his pocket. "How did you sleep?"

"Santiago told me how cold it could get even in the summer, but I never believed him."

"We'd invite him to our fires, but he stayed here. I think it was a matter of pride. If he slept cold, it gave him a reason to get up in the morning. Also, and you'd know him better than I did, I think he liked being alone."

He did, Maria recalled. "He considered you family," she said, and she meant it as a compliment. She was surprised to see the big man quake and tremble, until she realized he was holding back tears. She reached out to him, and he half embraced her, half collapsed on her shoulder.

"He didn't deserve this," Alberto whispered.

"No, he didn't," she sighed. "He wasn't perfect, but that just seemed to make him forgive the imperfections of others. He wanted to succeed, but it didn't mean anything to him if he couldn't bring all of you with him."

After Alberto recovered, he took her on a tour of the fields.

"As I told you on the phone, the morning after he was found, no one had any idea what to do. But the worst thing imaginable for all of us was to see his crops die, too. So we continued the harvest."

"Were you able to get the buyers to give you an advance on the harvest?"

"I wasn't," Alberto admitted. "But then we heard from Henry Marshak."

"Who's that?"

"He's a big wheel in this area. Well, a big wheel all over the place. His family owns the largest factory farms in the state. Santiago used to work for the Marshaks. Their company sold him this piece of land. When he found out what happened, he offered to help. First by sending some of his workers, and then by floating us a loan so we could keep going."

"I think one of his people called the house as well. I should thank him," she said, staring out over the rows. "How is the harvest going?"

"That's another tragic part of all this. The harvest is going well. Best in the years I've been here. All Santiago's hard work the past few seasons getting the field in shape was paying off this year. He knew it, too. It was all coming together."

———

Two hours later Maria sat at the shack's kitchen table, going through her brother's files. For someone who kept such meticulous records, she was surprised that he'd store them in a building so open to the elements.

What she found put her mind at ease. He'd always assured her that he kept an honest shop, didn't employ illegal labor, and didn't cut corners. Though her understanding of small businesses was little to none, the paperwork seemed to back this up.

"I'm sorry about your brother."

The voice startled Maria. She whirled around to see a young man standing just outside the doorway.

"Oh. Thank you," she said.

When he didn't move away, she turned back.

"Did you know him well?"

"I never met him. I've heard he was a good man."

Maria indicated the papers, one pink and one white, in his hand.

"Are those for me?"

He nodded and handed them over. She read them and looked back up in confusion.

"I don't understand. Are you"—she eyed the white sheet—"Luis Dedios?"

"Chavez," he corrected. "I'm a priest from Los Angeles."

"You're working here?"

"I came looking for information. The woman whose name is on the other sheet came to our parish the morning Santiago disappeared."

"He didn't disappear. Somebody came here and took him away."

"No," Luis said. "He was going to Los Angeles to meet with a deputy district attorney and be taken into protective custody. Only somebody got to him first. Maybe corrupt members of law enforcement. A woman named Odilia Garanzuay was to speak to the deputy DA as well, likely as part of the same case. The woman who was bringing them in was murdered the same night. Odilia escaped, only to be kidnapped a day later. I'm hoping to find her."

Maria's jaw dropped. How a priest—if he really was a priest—came across such information she couldn't guess.

"I don't understand. What *case*?"

"That's what no one can figure out. The murdered woman, Annie Whittaker, was a legal rights advocate. I think she'd stumbled across something pretty major. Odilia and Santiago were her witnesses."

"But you don't know what it was?"

"No. And neither did the deputy DA. Did your brother say anything to you?"

"He told me something was going on but that he'd get back to me on Monday," Maria said, angering. "Why are you telling me all of this now?"

"Because I'm hoping Odilia might still be alive. If whoever is behind this thinks they've shut down the investigation by killing Annie and your brother, maybe they won't do the same to her."

In her wallet, Maria had business cards for two FBI agents, two LAPD detectives, an official from the State Department, an officer from the Mexican Consulate, and half a dozen lawyers. There were any number of sources she could check Luis's story with the moment he left the shack.

"Sorry to be blunt, but what do you want from me? I knew nothing about this. If my brother really was some kind of crook—"

"I don't think he was," Luis interrupted. "Everybody here goes on about how he kept things on the up and up. All I'm asking is whether you have any kind of record of Odilia Garanzuay working here."

It took twenty minutes for Maria to come back with a definitive no. She'd been reluctant to get involved, unsure of where it could lead, but her own curiosity got in the way. And if there was a Los Angeles deputy DA on the other side of the priest, she wanted to have a word with him.

"There's nothing. The records go back to when he first started here. The number of workers goes up a little each year, but you see a lot of the same names. No Odilia Garanzuay."

"But that is his signature on the page, isn't it?"

"It is," Maria admitted. "Any other questions?"

"No," Luis said quietly. "I appreciate your assistance."

He turned to leave. Maria sighed.

"I'm sorry I can't be more help," she said. "I don't know you. You might be who you say you are, but you might not be. And I have my son to think about. He just lost one of the only positive influences in his life. If for some reason he lost me, he'd be on his own."

"I understand," Luis said. "I won't trouble you again."

He moved to exit, but then glanced back one more time.

"Did your brother ever mention something called the Blocks?"

"No, not that I recall."

Luis nodded.

"Thanks for your time."

———

She'd heard the trucks a good twenty minutes before they arrived. Though she was in darkness, the desert around her was so quiet it could never hold a secret. There was the roar of the engine, the chassis bouncing on its shocks, and the tires losing traction on the dusty dirt track leading to her hill. She'd heard spitting gravel next, once they'd reached the actual road leading to the summit. Then finally the squeal of brakes, the opening and slamming of doors, and the footsteps of those who'd left her here.

She was no longer afraid. Her body had proved so much stronger than she thought it would be. The deprivations meant to drive her mad had done their job when she'd had hope. Once that had vanished and her routine was one only of survival, she retreated inward.

She didn't know where she was exactly. They'd called it La Calavera, "the skull" in Spanish. She'd only seen the outside when they carried her from the truck to the metal shed, but she understood the name right away. It was a small flat-topped hill whose crest had been wind-polished and sandblasted into a smooth surface. There were no trees, but there was an old fire tower near the shed.

One of the men was up there now. She only heard him when he opened the door to piss off the balcony. Then the door would bang shut, and she'd almost forget she wasn't the only human for miles.

The narrow road to the hill's summit was treacherous. As she heard the first truck rev its engine to begin the climb, she silently prayed that it would take a turn too fast or hit a bad patch of gravel and tumble over the side. It would be a temporary reprieve, but the men would be dead.

She waited for God to answer her prayer. Waited for a sudden crash, the sound of crumpling metal, the screams of the wounded—or, better yet, dying—but they didn't come. All there was were the dual sounds of the two truck engines drawing near.

The door to the fire tower swung open and closed with a bang, and she heard the ping of the man's shoes on the metal ladder as he descended to meet the trucks. They arrived as he reached the bottom. Judging by the time between truck doors opening and closing, she estimated there were three men in each vehicle. She imagined *he* was with them, the only one whose name she knew, El Matachín.

She assumed he had a real name, but it was what all his men called him.

She heard Matachín now ask the tower man for the key. A second later she heard his footsteps reach the metal door of the shed, where he inserted the key in the padlock that hung between the chains connecting the handles. After popping the shackle, he stripped the lock and chain away before swinging open the door. Odilia closed her eyes at the last minute, the sheer amount of light coming in enough to blind her after so many hours in the dark.

But the air that came in with the light was cool and felt good against her blistering skin. She shivered a little, rattling the chains that kept her bound to the corner of the shed.

"How are we doing today?" Matachín asked.

Her captor was a tall man, a good three or four inches past six foot. His hair was dark and he kept it short. He was all muscle. But what she'd noticed first about him were his copper eyes. In a different situation she might have found them attractive. Here, she thought it gave him a reptilian appearance. It fit.

"How are we doing today?" Matachín asked again.

Odilia didn't reply. Her tongue was swollen, so she didn't know if she'd be able to formulate a sentence, even a sound, regardless. The man in the tower had brought her water every hour. But in this heat, which turned the metal into an oven, an ocean wouldn't have been enough.

"I've got good news," Matachín announced. "It's over. You're done here. You're getting out."

Odilia looked up sharply but instantly regretted it. If he'd been teasing her, she'd just made his day.

"I'm not kidding!" Matachín insisted. "You've done your time."

He reached for her chains, but she pulled away.

"Easy," he soothed. "It's not a trick."

She let him unchain her, then help her to her feet. She could barely stand. He practically took her whole weight as he led her out onto the sun-bleached summit of La Calavera. Her legs were like jelly, and the sun burned at her raw skin. She started walking to the trucks, but Matachín grabbed her arm.

"No, something I want you to see first," he said. "Come here."

He turned her body toward a flat-topped boulder beyond the fire tower. Unlike every other surface, this one hadn't been bleached white by the sun. It was stained with deep reds and dark browns, as if bathed in wine. Odilia knew what had painted it and why Matachín wanted her to see it.

Neither sun nor wind nor water can get blood from a stone.

Matachín kicked at the back of her knees, causing them to buckle. She slumped onto the stone, head bowed as if in front of an altar. She'd spent the week thinking death would come for her in the shed. She'd dehydrate. Her organs would fail. She'd slowly starve. Now this. A very small part of her was glad that instead of dying alone in the dark, the last thing she would ever see was this amazing vista of the endless desert.

"I hope it was worth it," Matachín said quietly, leveling a pistol at the back of her head.

So beautiful . . .

PART III

XIII

"I'm sorry it's not better news. We thought we had a real chance with this latest protocol."

Pastor Whillans buttoned up his shirt as the doctor, David Yapp, went over his chart.

"Me too," Whillans replied dryly. "But we knew from the beginning these were long shots."

"Not true," Yapp chided. "You can never tell how a patient will react to treatment."

"And we're beyond surgical options?"

"There's a primary site and a secondary site. If we'd caught either one of them earlier, perhaps there would've been a chance."

Whillans sighed. "What I've been most curious about was why it didn't show up during my annual physical six months ago."

"Some cancers don't show up on routine tests. Not right away anyway."

"But I had it then?"

"You did," Yapp admitted. "I'm sorry."

Whillans couldn't tell from the doctor's tone if he meant it or not. He seemed the type that wished his patients would accept Stage Four cancer for what it was, a death sentence, and prepare for that rather than treatment. Maybe this was why he worked in a strip mall urgent-care facility and not Cedars-Sinai.

"How much time do I have?"

"We don't like giving patients life-expectancy estimates. It can vary. All I can say is that you need to get your affairs in order."

"You think I can't go on the Internet?" Whillans said, buttoning his Roman collar back in place. "I'll just type in everything you put on my chart."

Dr. Yapp sighed and acquiesced.

"All I feel comfortable saying is that I've had two patients with diagnoses similar to yours. One lived three months, the other two weeks."

When Whillans left a couple of minutes later, he checked his phone on the way out. Three voice mails from the archdiocese, all from Bishop Duenas's office. An hour before, Whillans would've obediently rung back to receive more verbal lashes over how he handled the Odilia situation. Now he had no problem deleting all three unheard and shoving the phone back in his pocket.

How quickly things can change, he mused.

"Mom?"

When Miguel's cell phone rang, he'd already been nervous. After seeing that it was his mother, he paled.

"Hey, Mom. Where are you?"

"Not 'How are you doing?' or 'How'd it go today?'" she said.

"Sorry," Miguel replied quickly. "How'd it go today?"

"Not bad, all things considered. How was Mrs. Leñero's house?"

"Boring."

"Good," she replied. "Any calls?"

"Another one from a bank. I took the number. Guy said he'd work with you on the various loans, but if you were looking to wash your hands of the farm, they'd already had inquiries."

"Did you tell him that wasn't the kind of information he should be giving to a fourteen-year-old?"

"He probably thought I was your husband. Wait, are you in the car?"

"I am. I had a strange encounter with one of the workers. I packed up most of the files and started heading home. I'm just passing Woodland Hills."

Woodland Hills, Miguel thought. *I've got two hours.*

"Where are you, by the way?" Maria asked.

"Enrique's giving me a ride home from school. We're almost there."

"All right. See you in a little while."

She hung up. Miguel turned to Enrique in a panic.

"She's coming home. I'm so busted."

Enrique rolled his eyes.

"Are you serious with this?" he asked as he turned off the highway.

"We should turn around," Miguel insisted. "If we go back now, I'll be home in time, or maybe a block or two away. I can say I needed printer paper or something."

Enrique stopped the car at a red light and stared at Miguel.

"Dude. It's too late to back out on these guys. These aren't a bunch of high school assholes."

Miguel scowled. He hated getting boxed in.

"We'll be in and out," Enrique assured him. "I promise."

"Fine. But how'd they find out about us anyway? Nobody was supposed to know."

"When you've got skills, word travels."

Miguel didn't like this response.

Fields of Wrath

It had started the previous fall. Miguel bombed a test. *Bad.* He'd simply forgotten to study. It wasn't the first time, but he'd skated by previously and managed passing grades. Not this go-round. It was the kind of disaster that put his entire semester in jeopardy. But then he'd done the math and realized that a couple of points added to one test, a few more to his homework assignments, and a minute bump on a couple of quizzes earlier in the year and he'd pass.

Whereas most boys Miguel's age were playing sports, chasing girls, or tinkering with cars, Miguel was into computers. This had been the case since he was six and had taken apart his mother's cell phone to see what made it tick. His mother had initially been furious but then watched in amazement as he'd put it back together and even repaired a couple of bugs. She soon convinced a coworker to let her have a phone he'd planned to discard and gave it to Miguel. He repaired it within a week and soon began creating his own rudimentary games and apps for the thing. By the time he was a teenager, he knew more about coding than either of his school's computer science teachers.

All this to say, when it came time to hack into the computer program his school used to log grades, getting through the one-step authentication security software would be a snap. The real question was whether he should spread the discrepancies over several projects or give himself one A-plus.

He decided on the former, calling it "grade arbitrage," before learning that wasn't what arbitrage was at all. He passed and wasn't caught. Like any criminal who encounters early success, he began to wonder where else he might apply this matrix. Though the possibilities were endless, so were the risks. He settled on low-level bank fraud utilizing online checking accounts, a twenty-first-century version of check kiting, and enlisted his best friend, Enrique, to help out.

Things had run smoothly for the past three months. They'd seen enough gangster movies to know that the key to failure in an illegal enterprise was getting greedy, so they kept things small.

Two months in they'd made ten thousand dollars. Rather than expand, Miguel stopped things cold for a month. Enrique understood it wasn't his place to question this. When no one came after them, Miguel turned the works back on and they cleared another ten thousand dollars over the next ten weeks.

Enrique took a job bussing tables and padded his tips a few bucks every shift to ease his cut into circulation. Miguel wasn't old enough to work a job, so he didn't spend a dime.

Then last week Enrique got a phone call. The caller said he needed to meet with Enrique and Miguel to talk about their activities. Realizing it wasn't law enforcement, Enrique denied all knowledge. He was informed this wasn't a request and was given directions and a time. If they didn't show up, a meeting would be held at Miguel's mother's workplace.

Miguel hadn't been sure how to take the news. He initially believed the call must have come from a bank, possibly a security official. As the meeting drew near, he began to have doubts. What if it was a trap? What if he'd pissed off some other hacker out there?

When Santiago was killed, the meeting was the first thing he'd thought about. It gnawed at him for days. He ran every scenario. How could it *not* be related?

But then the instructions for the meeting arrived, indicating the boys were to be in Glendale one week later at a specific time. The route they were to take was laid out, as well as what they could and could not bring to the meeting. There was no mention of Santiago.

"That's it," Enrique said, pointing to an Armenian restaurant at the end of a block of shops. "We're supposed to park in back."

As they turned into the parking lot behind the strip, they saw two large men. One indicated which spot, and Enrique pulled in.

"Here we go," he whispered.

The two men led them into the restaurant, ushering them through a small kitchen to a dining room with no more than a dozen tables out front. The room was empty save for an older man alone at a table nearest the kitchen. A "Closed" sign hung in the front door.

The old man indicated for them to sit at his table. He was short with thinning gray-black hair and wore a rumpled light-gray suit. His face was lined and leathered. He didn't look particularly strong, but there was intensity behind his coal-black eyes.

As the boys sat, he produced an old-fashioned, ivory-handled ice pick and set it on the table.

"You get one chance at this," the man said. "You stole from me. Yes?"

"What?" Enrique said, scrunching his brow. "I don't know what you're talking about, man . . ."

The ice pick flashed and was driven into Enrique's left hand with such force, the point chipped the Formica below. Enrique opened his mouth to scream, but one of the men who'd brought them in stepped forward and slapped a length of duct tape over it, silencing him. The old man leaned forward, gripped the pick with both hands, and yanked it straight up and out.

Then he turned to Miguel.

"Yes, we stole from you," Miguel admitted quickly.

Though in agony, Enrique turned to Miguel in surprise. The old man nodded to his men, who lifted Enrique off his chair and dragged him into the kitchen. When they were gone, the man turned back to Miguel.

"That makes you the smart one."

Miguel knew better than to confirm or deny this.

"Do you know who I am?" the man continued.

"No."

"Good," he said. "That's the only thing that could explain such an error in judgment on your part."

"I'm sorry," Miguel added. "I'll return whatever I took."

The old man belched out a cackle that revealed a set of weathered and rotting teeth.

"Thank you, Mr. Higuera. Without your return of my forty dollars, I'm not sure my business could remain afloat another day."

Miguel thought fast. That it was forty dollars told him little. This was the amount he skimmed off most extremely low-volume corporate accounts. He selected accounts that were underutilized but maintained a high balance to avoid fees. These were the deep-sleep, single officer types that existed for individuals doing business as corporations to reap federal benefits. A small onetime extraction could go unnoticed or unaddressed for weeks, if not months.

"When I discovered the discrepancy and called the bank, do you know what they said?" the old man continued. "We'll replace the money immediately. They were so apologetic. I asked if they would go after the culprit, and they hesitated, saying they would if I filed a police report and gave them a copy. It was obvious that if I didn't the matter would drop. Forty dollars wasn't enough to make them care."

Miguel said nothing.

"I'm paying you a compliment," the old man scowled.

"Thank you, sir."

"Tell me. How did you come to this forty-dollar amount?"

"It wasn't scientific," Miguel admitted. "And I'm sure the actual number their fraud division lets slide is higher. But I figured the absolute minimum would be around fifty dollars, so forty felt safe."

"How did you identify my account as vulnerable? You could never have gotten away with this on the checking account of a little old lady on a fixed income. Was there some kind of activity that suggested I might not be one to go to the police?"

"It was the way the account was set up," Miguel explained. "It was one of several created by the same person."

"How could you tell that?"

"Not from anything you did. It's how the bank handles its batch processing. The temp PIN codes were sequential, and the PO boxes were copied and pasted. It creates a pattern."

The old man seemed satisfied by this. Until he peered back at Miguel.

"Don't spare my feelings."

"There was one thing you did. The amounts of money coming in and out felt randomized, not random, as if selected to prove they were irregular. Another reason I thought it was automated and therefore vulnerable."

The old man's gaze left Miguel's face. He picked a corner of the ceiling and eyed it thoughtfully for a moment before turning back.

"I have an old-fashioned approach to business," he said. "If I spend one dollar, I want to make three. That is easy for me to understand, and it keeps things manageable. But what you showed me is a way I can lose money from a direction I didn't know to look in. My thinking, perhaps, is outmoded. What I need is new thinking."

"What you need is me," Miguel offered.

"Is that what I said?" the old man barked, coming alive with a vengeance. "That I need you?"

Miguel waited for the ice pick to flash. When it didn't, he let out a sigh of relief.

"What I *want*," the old man began, "is to see if we might do some business together. If you can steal from me, so can others. More importantly, if you can find patterns in what are meant to be secret accounts, so can others. It will require time away from your current profession, but you will be compensated."

Current profession. Miguel found this funny but then considered the offer on the table. It meant an exponential increase in risk but might allow him to explore other weaknesses in electronic banking to exploit.

"You're taking a long time to make a decision, Mr. Higuera," the old man said.

"What are the terms of our agreement? I'd never agree to anything without all our cards on the table."

The old gangster's eyes widened. Miguel feared he'd crossed the line from useful to troublesome. But then the old man's hyena-like cackle returned, followed by a hand thrust across the table. *Sans* ice pick.

"Everything's gone the way you might have hoped thus far," the old man intoned. "Let's not ruin it by having you dictate my terms. A trial period, okay?"

Miguel shook the hand, hoping his own palm wasn't as sweat soaked as the rest of him.

"Sounds good to me, boss."

"Basmadjian," the old man said. "That is my name, and that is what you'll call me. Got it?"

Miguel did. Now he just had to get home before his mother did.

XIV

Luis finished his fifth day in the fields before slipping away at nightfall. It was Friday night, and a number of workers were trekking to the nearest gas station for a weekend liquor run. Luis joined this party, but not a one looked at him. Word of his ostracization had been fully disseminated.

He waved a good-bye to the others at the station before heading to the highway. No one waved back.

It took him the better part of an hour to reach the 101 freeway and another two to get to his destination eight miles away. He'd considered ringing Oscar for a ride even though they'd agreed they were square. It occurred to him that other than Pastor Whillans, Oscar might be the closest thing he had to a friend these days. That was a strange feeling indeed. He pushed this from his mind, however, needing to focus his thoughts on the task at hand.

Throughout the day he picked apart Odilia's story. She hadn't been at Santiago's fields, so why did she have a paper signed by Santiago saying she did work there? What exactly was her connection to Annie Whittaker? Had she even been present at the shooting as she claimed?

Could she have lied about more than that? Maybe even about how the shooting at Annie's house had gone down. Was there more to it than she wanted to let on?

The instincts he'd developed from his years on the streets led him to believe she was telling the truth. But he was a priest now, not a detective. What made him think he could get to the bottom of it all?

That said, he'd been able to work out Annie Whittaker's home address from cross-referencing a number of articles online. The neighborhood was mentioned in one report, and photos of Annie's house in another obscured her house number, painted on the curb, but not the one next to it. A few minutes on Google Earth and he had his destination.

When he reached her neighborhood, a walled-in but not gated community called Tierra Rejada, Luis fully realized the extent of the risk he was taking by being there. For him to step into this upper-class suburban enclave not even a week after the murder of one of its residents by, as the papers suggested, someone that probably looked a lot like him, was stupid bordering on dangerous.

He might as well have arrived on a parade float.

Rather than go in, Luis passed the front entrance and followed the brick wall that ringed the neighborhood until it reached the foothills. He circled Tierra Rejada twice, cutting in close only to glimpse street signs. He settled on the house he believed to be Annie's and approached from the rear. As Odilia had reported, there was a gate on the back wall that led into the arroyo behind the neighborhood. Judging from the pickets around where Luis stood, a second neighborhood was planned to abut Tierra Rejada. The gate would eventually open onto a new road or alley that would run between the two.

The exterior of Annie's beige-brick, two-story prefab house was as unremarkable as the others in the community. Luis stood back from the fence and ran Odilia's story against this backdrop. He imagined her inside as Annie went out the front door and onto the driveway. Then the first shots. It seemed immediately that if Odilia's tale was accurate, there would have had to be two shooters. There was no way someone could've shot Annie in the driveway and then made it over the fence, through the backyard, and over the back wall to get a shot at Odilia as she exited the gate.

She could've been wrong. The bullets she thought were coming from in front of her could have been fired from behind. Having just seen her friend killed and being targeted herself, was she a reliable witness?

What bothered him was the neighborhood itself. There were plenty of streetlights. He'd seen the silhouettes of security cameras hanging off every other house as he walked. Even if the police were involved in some kind of cover-up, it would be impossible to loop in the other residents. He speculated that every homeowner on the block had gone over their camera footage with a fine-tooth comb the next morning.

He felt sure Annie's murder was premeditated. But who would look at this well-lit and walled-in neighborhood and decide that of all the places Annie might go on any given day, this was the best place to stage an armed robbery turned murder?

He moved to the wall behind Annie's house. He didn't know if the police were watching it, but he knew it wouldn't be wise to stick around for long. Beginning at the gate, he ran his fingers up and down the frame and along the wall. Odilia had said that the first shot came once she was out of the gate. If she was right and it came from in front of her, there was a chance it had struck the wall.

After five minutes of finding nothing out of the ordinary, Luis did a cursory glance over the gate to see if a window was broken or something obviously chipped in the backyard.

Nothing again.

If the shot had come from behind her, it was a lost cause. The sand and scrub would've easily concealed a bullet. He'd need a metal detector. Even then he'd be there all night.

So he stuck with Odilia's story and moved down the wall in the direction she described. As he moved down the row of houses, he found the same exact thing. Stuccoed, cinder-block walls with degrees of slight water damage and solid redwood gates.

He was unsure why he kept going to the end of the row, but something egged him on. It was at this last house that he found a slight fringe of wood Mohawking up from the top of the gate. Six thin splinters extruded away from a groove. Luis ran his finger over them. They arrowed downward, as if pointing to something.

Luis kneeled alongside the gate's frame, lining up the cut with where a bullet would've completed its trajectory. He was rewarded with a crack in the stucco and a shallow dent in the concrete beneath. A pencil eraser couldn't have sunk much deeper in the hole. His fingers searched for a piece of sharp or twisted metal but found nothing. Instead, there were a number of cuts and grooves.

They collected their rounds, Luis realized. *Definitely premeditated.*

Something disturbed him about the angle. For the bullet to have nicked the top of the gate and then embedded itself in the frame, it would've had to come from somewhere up high. Could someone have been running along the top of the wall?

He kneeled back down, staring into the direction from which the bullet had to have come. There was nothing there but night sky.

Except . . .

Except when he looked harder, he saw a hill about 150 yards away. The articles had been unambiguous. The bullets found in Annie Whittaker were pistol rounds, suggesting the shooter was close. The police could lie all they wanted, but how easily could the medical examiner's office be roped in? If there was even a hint of a discrepancy, all the family would've had to do was request an independent autopsy. The discovery of a single rifle bullet, implying the shooter was far away and no kind of armed robber at all, would've unraveled the official story, and these guys seemed too good to make a mistake like that.

Luis started toward the top of the hill. Traversing the uneven ground was not easy in the moonlight, but his eyes had adjusted by the time he reached the hill and scrambled up the rocky face with ease.

And there it was.

Though it took him a minute to figure out which one of the houses back in Tierra Rejada was Annie Whittaker's, he saw that from this vantage point there was a perfect sightline to Annie's driveway, as well as to the back of her house. With night-vision capabilities, a good scope, and—Luis thought—military training, a sniper could shoot Annie and, without switching position, take a shot at Odilia as well.

The genius move was in using a pistol. With the pistol rounds recovered during the autopsy, they wouldn't need the whole police force in on it, just a single forensic tech, who could fudge the speed at which the bullet entered Annie's body. He'd heard of hunters dropping deer with a pistol at five hundred yards. How much would the tech even have to fudge?

He was wondering what Michael Story might be able to do with this when the hairs on the back of his neck stood up. He was being watched.

The first shot echoed across the hill as Luis dropped to the ground. He felt the gentle push of hot air as the bullet whistled past. He didn't wait for a second one. He pitched himself over the edge of the cliff, taking his chances with the rocks rather than the sniper. As he rolled, a bullet ricocheted off a rock inches from his face, sending sparks up around his eyes. He closed them tight as inertia carried him all the way down the hill.

He heard an engine roar to life, but he couldn't tell from which direction it came. More bullets whizzed past, though they missed by a wider margin. He reached the bottom of the hill, got to his feet, and ran.

O Lord, please guide me . . .

It had been a week since his last confession. At any second he might die and wouldn't be in a state of grace, absolved of his earthly sins. Maybe a priest would reach the hospital in time to deliver the last rites, but given that, the person firing at him might've been the same who'd killed a woman at five times the distance.

O Lord, please . . .

━━━

Maria awoke realizing she'd been dreaming about Miguel's father, the one man Santiago swore to kill if he ever saw him again. This was a surprise, but the bigger one was that she wasn't repulsed or annoyed with herself. The man was a lowlife, after all, who preyed on impressionable young girls who believed him when he used words like *amor* or *corazón* or *siempre*.

But this had been a nice dream, one that disregarded that his name was forbidden in her household and that he'd established a pattern for her of entering into abusive relationships. She allowed men who said the right things about family and were nice to Miguel to get her hopes up, until she'd withstand anything to keep the affair afloat.

Even if that meant looking the other way after catching her boyfriend with his tongue down the throat of a seventeen-year-old high school junior.

Come on, baby, that was for laughs. She just wanted to see what a real man was like.

━━━

So, why not a trip down memory lane with the kind of asshole she could see coming from a mile away these days? She'd been beautiful then. Everything about her body had been smooth, tight, new, and unused. No wonder Santiago had worried about her.

The dream was fading, but Maria wanted to luxuriate a little longer. She selected a memory to relive, a night when they'd gone to a small house party together. There was a lot of alcohol and a band set up in the backyard. The driveway and back patio were filled with dancing. She missed dancing.

They'd both been tired from the day and were doing big, silly Danzón-type moves in imitation of their elders, drawing disapproving looks from all sides. When the music suddenly changed to a merengue, he pressed into her. She answered by snaking her hips into his and pressing herself against his chest. He drew her in for a long kiss, and she remembered glimpsing an uncle or cousin she knew would report all this back to her mother, chapter and verse.

Christ, I was naïve.

Emerging from her reverie, she entered the kitchen a few minutes later. Miguel was looking out the front window, eating a bowl of cereal.

"What?"

"There's a truck out front," he said, pointing through the glass. "Guy behind the wheel hasn't taken his eyes off our house. You want me to go talk to him, or you want me to call the cops?"

Maria remembered Luis's words about corrupt law enforcement and shook her head.

"No, calling the police is the last thing I want you to do. Lock the doors and don't go back to the window. If they think parking a truck in front of our house is going to intimidate us, they've picked the wrong family to tussle with."

XV

Michael had been looking forward to an easy Saturday. Sure, he'd have to spend most of it working, but even though Helen had an open house to prep for, the kids all had playdates and activities.

But that's when he got the call from DA Rebenold to be in her office by nine sharp.

At least there'd be no traffic.

"Jesus, Story," she said when he stepped into her office. "You think I needed this today?"

He saw the open file folder on her desk. There was a single letter inside with the seal of the Federal Bureau of Investigation at the top.

"I ran into Judson Nichols this morning."

Shit.

"He said he felt it important to bring this to my attention directly before the bureau does so officially on Monday."

"What is it?" Michael asked.

She pushed the folder over to him but didn't wait for him to read it before launching in.

"Can you explain to me how it is that you contacted the Mexican federal police without first running it by me?" she asked. "More importantly, why you did so with regard to a murder investigation that, to my knowledge, has nothing to do with this office?"

Oh fuck, Michael thought. He'd debated telling her but knew it'd open a can of worms. When he'd called the Policía Federal about Santiago moments after it hit the papers, he hadn't even given his name, saying it was a routine call from the LA district attorney's office to see if they needed any assistance. He pumped them for information, they gave him even less than they gave the press, and that was it.

And here it was, biting him in the ass.

"Hello?" she asked. "This is a letter from the FBI chastising this department for circumventing them and potentially obstructing their own investigation into the murder of an American citizen named . . ."

She looked at him expectantly.

"Santiago Higuera."

"Bingo. Who is that? And if you choose to lie, make it a good one."

As it'll be your last, Michael filled in. He hesitated a moment, shifting his weight as if to bolster himself before revealing a confidence. "I was approached by a member of the Los Angeles archdiocese and asked to look into it. I said that I would. They asked for discretion. I'm sorry I didn't run it by you, but it seemed like such a small thing."

This was not what District Attorney Rebenold expected to hear. She stared at Michael as if waiting for him to admit the lie. When he did not, her features relaxed, until she seemed on the verge of a smile.

"Well, like it or not, these things do happen in this city," she said, bemused. "But men like Judson love stirring the pot, so discretion or not, loop me in. I probably would've told you to handle it the same way, but I wouldn't have brought us in on a Saturday. Okay?"

"Okay."

Michael was about to leave when he sensed Rebenold wasn't done with him.

"Did you learn anything?"

"The PF think they found the kill site a few yards from the bridge. They brought him into Mexico, took him to this isolated location, cut his throat, then strung him up even before all the blood had drained out."

"Jesus Christ. Every time I think we've got sick fucks up here in LA, I remember we've got nothing on the cartels."

Michael went to his office with the idea of getting something done before heading back home. He pulled out his iPhone as he turned on his office computer and found a single new e-mail, the subject line reading, "Whittaker Case."

The sender was listed as Rabbit's Foot. He wondered if it was from Luis. There were sixteen attachments, and he could see by the thumbnails that they were photographs. He opened the first and his heart skipped a beat. It was an image of him and Annie having sex.

For a half second he thought it was something he'd accidentally sent to himself the day before. Only he didn't recognize the snap. He opened the next few, until it came to him: he hadn't taken these pictures.

Panicking, he sorted through the rest until he remembered the day—actually days, as they were from two different sessions—they were taken. One was from her house and the second from a motel they favored, a few miles away.

They'd been watching her house even then?

He was pissed. Were these from the people who'd sent Judson to warn him off the case? Had they somehow found out about his meeting with the priest? This was amateur-hour bullshit.

He hit "Reply" to shoot back an aggressive and taunting response. That was when he saw the message had been cc'd to someone. The e-mail address was instantly familiar. It was his wife's.

He felt something akin to an electric shock racing through his body. The e-mail had been sent at 9:52. It was now 10:02. Helen's phone was never out of her hand for more than a few minutes at a time. His life flashed in front of him in an instant. There'd be a divorce. He'd be out of the house. The child support would be devastating.

And, of course, there'd be fallout at work.

Lasting fallout. The kind that affected advancement.

It was then he noticed the *m* had been dropped from the *.com* in his wife's e-mail address. Instead of showing up in her inbox, it would have bounced back, undelivered, to the sender.

Even as his pulse returned to something resembling normal, Michael knew this was a new ballgame. The message was clear: we can destroy you, so drop the case. He decided he would do just that. When the priest next made contact, he would beg off. End of story.

He turned back to the e-mail. Somehow Annie managed to look even more vulnerable when she didn't know she was being photographed than when she did. All she'd wanted was a little justice in the world.

He stared into her eyes a minute longer, then deleted the e-mail.

Luis awoke to the sound of leaf blowers. He put down the knives and peered out the closet door. It was—*Oh shit*—already light out. He'd meant to be up and out the door well before dawn.

Though he'd initially had qualms about going into Annie's house, it was the only place he knew for certain would be empty. Any other yard or house, he was sure to attract the attention of all those high-priced security systems. Annie's just put him at risk that the local cops might be watching it, and maybe that wasn't the worst thing with bullets flying over his head.

It had been nothing to vault Annie's back gate after finding it locked. He'd assumed her windows and back door would be locked and was right. He didn't want to go around front but had no other choice. He didn't think he'd have any better luck with the front door or windows there, so he went straight to the garage door. It wasn't locked, but it was an automatic. He could only raise it a few inches, but that proved to be enough. He slipped under, praying that the metallic crunch of the door wouldn't awaken the neighbors, and scurried to the back of the garage.

He waited, but no one came. He eyed the door leading into the house but feared that the moment he turned the knob an alarm would go off. As he looked for a corner to spend the night, he came across the fuse box on the back wall. He opened it, but despite finding switches conveniently labeled "washer/dryer" and "air conditioner," none were marked "alarm." He decided to chance it, trying the door leading to the house. He turned the knob and pushed it open. No alarm. He went in. There would be more places to hide.

He spent the first hour watching the street from an upstairs window. He'd seen the truck a couple of times. It had slow-rolled down the block but hadn't stopped. Other vehicles went by as well, but he could tell they were residents. No, the men who wanted to kill him pretended to have somewhere to go, but their eyes were everywhere at once.

When it was obvious no one was coming in, he stayed awake regardless, searching the house for anything related to the case. As expected, he came up dry. Annie's clothes, photos, keepsakes, appliances, books, and other personal items were in every room. Any files, notes, or directories were gone.

In one of the guest rooms, he found new clothes and a few unopened toiletries, suggesting it was Odilia's room. At some point, exhaustion had sent him to find a place to sleep. The closet in the guest bedroom seemed the best bet, particularly after he'd barricaded himself in with boxes. Still, he'd closed his eyes, believing the next thing he'd see would be a gun barrel aimed between his eyes.

He crept out of the closet and listened. The house was silent. The only sounds came from outside. His body was stiff, a result of sleeping propped up in a tight corner all night, muscles tense, as he waited to be discovered.

Deciding it was time to go, he went downstairs and slipped out the back door. Rather than head to the rear gate, which he thought might be watched, he hopped the wall into the backyard of the neighbor's house, where a team of gardeners was mowing the grass and trimming bushes. He nodded and walked through the house's side gate to the truck out front. The group's foreman was loading equipment back onto the truck. Luis asked him for a ride into town, and the man shrugged.

After being dropped at a bus stop, Luis used the last of his cash for the two-hour ride back into Los Angeles. Once there he considered taking a Metro bus to St. Augustine's but felt he needed some time to think and walked instead. When he reached the parish an hour later, it was well into the afternoon.

He wasn't sure what drew him to Whillans's office. He just wanted a shower and a change of clothes, which could be found in the rectory. Maybe it was because he wanted to feel retethered to the life he'd been away from for a few days.

Whatever the case, when he stepped past Erna's empty desk—she never worked Saturdays—he fully expected to find Whillans in his office but hadn't anticipated finding him in the arms of a parishioner.

Luis had seen the woman—Bridgette something; Gildea? Goldea?—around the church a number of times. She was active in a number of the women's groups and taught Sunday school. In her late forties or early fifties, she was seldom without an inviting smile on her face. He knew she was single but figured her for one of those matronly women who'd accepted it wasn't in the cards for her early on and had devoted herself to the church instead.

But here she was with her arms around the pastor's neck, pulling him tight as she buried her face in his shoulder. It was not a comforting embrace but one of intimacy. That Whillans's hands were low around her waist confirmed this.

Luis stepped back quickly, but the movement caught the pastor's eye. He was surprised, a deer in the headlights, until he saw that it was Luis. Then he relaxed.

"Come in, Luis," Whillans said softly.

Bridgette's eyes shot to the doorway as she pulled away. Any possibility that Luis had slipped upon an innocent encounter was erased by the guilt on her face. She gathered her purse, touched the pastor's hand in a grave gesture, then exited without looking at Luis.

Whillans sighed and flopped into his desk chair.

"You're back. Did you find what you were looking for?"

"I have more questions, few answers," Luis replied curtly, waiting for an answer to the unasked question.

"Yes," Whillans said, opening his palms.

"'Yes'?" Luis asked.

"Yes, Bridgette and I have been in a union, a sort of unorthodox marriage, for the better part of ten years."

Luis couldn't have been more surprised if Whillans said he'd set fire to the sacristy.

"I don't understand."

"My biggest regret is that this is how you're finding out. I am deeply sorry."

"I . . . I don't want your apology," Luis stammered. "You have to break it off with her. Beg God's forgiveness."

"What's wonderful about you is your first thought is of my eternal soul," Whillans said. "I understand my actions and accepted long ago that I will be judged by God, as we all are."

"That sounds like pride."

"I suppose it does," Whillans said. "Did you know that for centuries Catholic priests were allowed to be married? It was the First Lateran Council that changed that in the twelfth century. When there was push-back from the clergy, the Vatican began arresting and killing the wives. Some were even sold into slavery. To avoid this happening to their loved ones, the priests accepted the new rules. In a gracious touch, the surviving wives were allowed to be considered widows by the pope rather than divorcées. Lovely of him, don't you think?"

Luis didn't reply. He turned to leave, but Whillans raised a hand. "There's something else."

———

It wasn't that Maria hadn't believed her son's story about the waiting truck; she just wanted to see for herself. She'd fixed herself coffee and breakfast. Sure enough, when she returned to the front window, the truck was gone.

"He just took off," Miguel said. "Maybe he saw me watching."

Maria nodded and went back about her business. There were the usual weekend chores to tackle, but she also wanted to finish going through Santiago's files. It would be the easiest thing in the world to let them slide, as she didn't fully understand what she was looking at, but she had to keep trying.

"Let me know if he comes back," Maria said as she walked to the bedroom.

In the early afternoon she left the house to go to the grocery store. She'd just reached the parking lot when Miguel rang her cell.

"There're two of them now. They're just waiting there."

She peeled out of the parking lot and was home in under five minutes. As she pulled up, the two men climbed out of their truck and moved to follow her.

"Mom! Come inside!" Miguel said, leaning out the kitchen door.

But the men were already at the edge of the driveway. The last thing she wanted was to appear intimidated.

"Go to your room," she instructed Miguel.

"But *Mom*—"

"Now," she insisted.

Miguel shot a glance to the men, then sulked away. Once the door was closed, she turned to the men.

"Can I help you?" she asked in a tone she reserved for telemarketers.

The men were a study in contrasts. One was a young white guy she thought looked like Eminem, down to the snarl in his upper lip. The other was Hispanic and wore a suit. A pair of glasses perched on his nose giving him the appearance of a schoolteacher.

"Ms. Higuera?" the suited man inquired.

"What do you want?" she scowled, arms crossed over her chest.

"No need for that tone, Ms. Higuera," the man said. "I'm Benjamin Valencia. I work for the bank that holds the note on your late brother's mortgage. I know this is a difficult time—"

"Look, I'm going through his finances as quickly as I can. I'll get it done, and you'll get your money."

Valencia peered at her through his glasses.

"No, that's not an issue. No, no. We're legally bound to inform the landowner when outside parties make financial offers on the property. And we have to do so in a timely fashion. It hasn't been easy getting ahold of you."

"Someone wants to buy Santiago's farm?" she surmised.

"Yes. But they want to move fast. The deal is contingent on being able to complete this year's harvest."

"Who is it?"

"Are you familiar with the Marshaks?"

Ah, that's why they sent workers to help, Maria thought.

"They own everything up there, right?" Maria said. "My brother worked for them before he got his land."

"Correct," Valencia replied. "Santiago bought this plot of land from them, taking out a mortgage from my company."

"How much did he owe?"

"Forty thousand dollars of the original sixty-five-thousand-dollar purchase price."

"And the Marshaks are offering . . . ?"

"They'll settle the mortgage and pay you an additional fifty thousand dollars to cover improvements Santiago made over the years to enhance the property's value."

Every impulse in Maria's head told her to accept the money on the spot and walk away. It would mean a more comfortable future for her and Miguel. But it was too much. If they'd tossed on an additional ten grand or so, she could've accepted that as a condolence.

Fifty grand told her they were relying on her greed to keep her from asking questions. Fifty grand came through middlemen, so the giver didn't have to dirty their hands. Fifty grand was a payoff that put a number on exactly what they thought her brother's life was worth.

"Do you have a card, Mr. Valencia?" Maria asked. "I want to think about it for a day or two. I promise it won't be longer than that."

From the look on Valencia's face, it was anything but all right. He handed her a business card and a manila envelope with a thin sheaf of papers inside.

"Take all the time you need," Valencia said. "My cell is on the back. Feel free to call anytime."

"Thank you," Maria replied.

She watched them leave and climb into their truck. She even managed to keep it together as they went down the block. As soon as they turned the corner, she slapped her hand against the side of the house, fighting back tears of anger.

But then, staring at the manila envelope, she got an idea.

XVI

"I love you. I love you so much it hurts. I understand what it feels like to be driven mad by love. That's how I feel about you. When you were gone, no other thought entered my head. Every single thought was of you. Every. Single. One. Every dream, every memory. It was the most pain anyone has ever put me through. I couldn't believe how terrible I felt. I'm not a suicidal person, but I wanted to hurl myself off the nearest bridge. That's how bad it got."

Jason Marshak stood in the middle of the poorly air-conditioned motel room. He wore only boxers, his skin glistening with sweat, but now from the heat rather than his recent exertions.

"Trust me, I know how fucked up this situation is," he implored. "It's crazy. I didn't plan it to be like this. I'm figuring it out as I go along, too. All I know is that when I look at you, I see our lives together. I see happiness for the first time in my life, not just an endless parade of work and trying to live up to my family's expectations. I mean, I can see us—just the two of us—on a beach somewhere far away. And I don't mean just fucking. I mean walking down the beach, your hand in mine, the eyes of every last person we pass staring at us. They're all thinking,

'Wow, he's the luckiest guy in the world.' I mean eating dinner together. Visiting all the little shops. Me buying you anything and everything you want. Attending events, your hand in mine, my arm around your waist. Leaning over to kiss you."

Odilia stood silently in the bathroom doorway. She was soaking wet, a towel wrapped around her torso, her hair slicked down against her neck and shoulders. She'd taken a shower the evening before when they brought her back from La Calavera, but there was no water pressure at the Blocks and the temperature was barely lukewarm. This one had been enough to make her feel almost human.

"I mean, I think about our children. How fucked up is that?" Jason laughed, incredulous. "I've spent my whole life trying *not* to get chicks pregnant. But with you? I can't wait. I want to see your belly with our kid in it, whether it's the first one, the second, or the third. Heck, maybe a fourth? Why not? You, me, and our kids opening presents around the Christmas tree. Sitting around the table at Thanksgiving. Going on road trips during the summer. Out watching fireworks on the Fourth of July. Or, hey, Cinco de Mayo."

Cinco de Mayo, Odilia thought. *That strangely American drinking holiday somebody—probably a liquor company—decided to pretend was Mexican Independence Day. Maybe Jason's company was behind it.*

She stared back at the middle-aged executive as he searched her face for the hint of a smile or even tenderness somewhere behind her eyes. There was none. He pointed at the towel.

"Take that off. Let it drop to the ground."

She did. Despite the heat, goose bumps rose on her arms and legs as Jason moved to her. He was a good foot and a half taller than she was. She looked back at him, wondering if this time he'd have any reaction to her burned and blistered skin. When he'd stripped her before, he'd done so with such veraciousness, she thought he might not have even seen the burns and blisters. But as he smiled and lowered himself to his knees, she knew he wasn't going to say anything. They were right in front of his eyes, but he looked through them.

"Someday our baby will be in here," he emphasized, placing his hands gently on her hips and pulling her close to kiss her just above the belly button. "I'll kiss it just like this every single day. And there won't be a day you or it won't feel loved. I promise."

Odilia knew she was meant to be placated by this. She was supposed to remember how wonderful and understanding he was for letting her back into his life after she'd committed such an unthinkable offense against him. That he loved her more than anyone else ever would or could. That to know that and still do what she'd done was so cruel, so evil.

"I'm sorry," she whispered.

He looked up, eyes all gratitude. But she knew him. He needed more.

"I'm sorry I ran away," she repeated. "You were right to punish me."

His body relaxed as if for the first time in days. He moved his hands around to her ass, where he kneaded the soft flesh he found there. She could see he was getting aroused again.

"No, it was my fault," he sighed. "I wasn't paying enough attention. I didn't know who else you'd been talking to. Your acting out was a response to my failings. But I'm telling you. We are days away from all this changing for good. There's a contract that will mean no more hiding. No more going around my family's back. It will be worth it. I promise."

Half an hour later she was in an SUV on her way home.

There'd been no shower afterwards this time, as Jason had to get back and didn't want his driver to have to wait for her. He'd kissed her, told her again how much he loved her, and said he'd see her in a few days.

She wondered if he was crazy enough to believe what he said. He made such a big show out of trying to satisfy her both physically and emotionally with all his talk of their future together. Maybe going through those motions allowed him to sleep at night, knowing that after he was done with her she was being sent back to squalid conditions to perform the exact same services on dozens of other men.

Or maybe the irony was lost on him.

Given her treatment out in the desert, she'd determined he was a psychopath. One with enough pull to keep a smart woman like Annie Whittaker from authoring her salvation. She'd promised Odilia she'd be safe with her. That no one in the States was above the law. How could she have been so foolish to believe that? Anyone who'd managed to accomplish what the Marshak family had hadn't done so without knowing all the angles, legal and otherwise. She'd witnessed the breadth of it firsthand. She should've known.

It was a fifteen-minute drive from the motel back to the Blocks, but it always felt like she crossed borders to get there. Her home was on the inland side of one of the wealthiest enclaves in the state. It was a spot where multimillionaires could spread out their wealth, draping their compounds over rolling hills.

But only a few miles and a turn down a gravel road away was a compound of a different kind, one much larger than even the largest of the lavish estates. Rather than housing an elite family, this one had been constructed to house over a thousand workers.

Odilia found it hard to believe that no one had ever taken a wrong turn and found themselves in front of this great wall of cinder-block apartments tucked within the neighboring hills. Had no one seen the doors with sliding locks on the outside or convoys of trucks arriving at dawn or returning at dusk to transport the workers to and from the fields like cattle?

Odilia decided they all knew. It was the theory that upset her the most but felt the most likely. She'd seen how locals stared right through them.

The SUV turned off the main road and bounced along the gravel path that bisected the fenced-in graze land. A barbed wire fence ran along either side, with "No Trespassing" signs every few dozen yards. A few head of cattle roamed free but seemed only for show. After rolling over a cattle guard, the SUV stopped at an unmanned metal gate. The driver hopped out, unlocked the chain, pulled the SUV through, then relocked it behind them. Half a mile later the road became paved again, widening into two lanes.

A hundred yards past that was the Blocks.

To Odilia, the Blocks looked like images she'd seen of Pueblo Indian villages carved out of the sides of mountains. There didn't seem to be much of a plan, new units built on top of old when they needed room for more workers. After an entire second level had been added, a third level sprang up just as randomly. Steps ran up the sides at odd angles. In some cases there were only ladders.

The nickname came from their resemblance to uneven stacks of children's blocks pushed together. Each unit contained a living room, bedroom, bathroom, and kitchen and housed around a dozen workers, who were locked in every night, brought out every morning, and packed into trucks to be taken to the fields.

The SUV pulled in front of the apartments, mostly empty, except for a handful of women who were tasked with cleaning.

"Let's go," the driver said.

Odilia followed the driver up a flight of stairs to a third-floor unit. Before she'd escaped, she'd been the only person in the Blocks who had a unit to herself. Her status as Jason's pet granted her this privilege and earned her the enmity of every woman who shared her lot. Following her time in the desert, she was back in a unit surrounded by other women who understood they were to make sure she didn't run away again. They hated her, but at least she wasn't alone anymore. In a life turned upside down, that counted as a win.

———

Following his conversation with Whillans, Luis spent the rest of Saturday preparing for the Sunday service. The familiar ritual of these simple tasks provided the comfort that he needed after the one-two punch of Whillans's news the night before.

Cancer? Possibly only weeks to live? What was God thinking? Pastor Whillans was one of his most faithful servants. Or was this some sort of punishment linked to his relationship with Bridgette Gildea? The Lord as Luis knew him was not petty. No, this was bad luck, pure and simple.

"I'm telling you because I won't be able to tell everyone," Whillans had said. "I need you to watch out for me in case, in my deteriorating state, I should start to unintentionally disclose it."

"But why?"

"Because there are others—yes, even in the church—who would use this to their advantage. They'd remove me before I could finish my work, put me up in some hospice, where I'd die just to avoid everyone's pity. Will you help me?"

When night fell, this was what Luis prayed over most of all. He opened his heart, prepared to listen to God's explanation. Nothing came. The following morning he tried again.

Silence.

He was entering his second hour of prayerful communion when there came a light knock on his door.

"Visitor," Father Territo said through the door in a hushed voice.

Luis said his amens and exited.

Maria waited for him in the courtyard. A concrete statue of Saint Francis stood on a pedestal in a shaded area just off the main path that wound from the rectory to the chapel.

"Ms. Higuera?"

She looked up in confusion, taking a moment to recognize Luis in his Roman collar.

"You really are a priest," she said.

"I am."

"Isn't deception a sin?"

"Of course. But there are instances even in the Bible where it's done in service to a greater cause."

"Uh-huh. Like when?"

"Exodus 1:15–17," Luis offered. "Pharaoh ordered the Hebrew midwives to kill all newborn male babies. They didn't and lied to Pharaoh, for which God blessed them."

Maria took a moment to let this sink in.

"I've had an offer on the farm," she said.

"Are you going to take it?"

"That's just it. It was way too much money, like somebody who knew what was up trying to cover their ass. Pardon my language."

Luis shrugged.

"But I had almost talked myself into it when I decided to take a look at the account statements from Santiago's bank. It was all normal stuff. Like clockwork, you could tell when he paid the workers, when he paid the mortgage, when he bought food and supplies. But there was one transfer between accounts, an error that showed up on a statement only to be corrected on the next one."

"An error?"

"I thought so, too, but my son was helping me. He's a whiz with computers and, well, he did his version of investigating"—she let this hang in the air long enough for Luis to understand she meant hacking—"and discovered that the transfer was legit. It was just for a tremendous amount of money. I know how much he was paying people. This would've paid thousands. No way he had that many people working there. *No. Way.*"

Luis's mind raced. It was a complicated scheme. That much was obvious. Somehow the piece of paper Odilia had brought with her was the key.

"Do you know where your brother had to file employment forms like the one I filled out?" he asked.

"No idea," Maria said. "But I'm pretty sure I could find out. What do you think this is?"

"Right now it could be anything," Luis said. "But so far two people may have died and another been kidnapped to keep it a secret."

Maria glanced to the front of the church. Parishioners were beginning to trickle in for the early service. She watched their progression from the parking lot to the church steps, then turned back to Luis.

"I'm afraid I'll look back on this moment as when I got in over my head," Maria said.

"We may be well past that," Luis said quietly.

Oscar's conscience was bothering him. It had been a week since he'd deposited Luis on a dead man's farm a few miles up the coast, and two days since he'd heard through the grapevine he'd been found out and ejected. This was troubling by itself. If he'd found out, who else might know? There were some hard hitters up that way, likely the same men who'd drawn Luis's attention in the first place. They didn't fuck around worrying about the cops the way Oscar had to. If they didn't like you, you got a bullet to the head and a shallow grave in the desert.

Was that what he'd earned for Luis?

"BMW 7 Series," came a quiet voice over Oscar's phone.

"Pass," Oscar whispered back.

Maybe it wasn't his conscience. Maybe he was just bored.

He was sitting in a tow truck behind a half-built house buried deep in Laurel Canyon. The person on the other end of the line was at a valet station up on the ridge. Parking was a nightmare in the hills, so residents had taken to hiring valets to park their guests' cars when they threw parties. As Laurel Canyon was hardly Bel-Air or Beverly Hills, they usually picked the cheapest valet agency, not knowing they crewed up from a pool of temp labor. On this night Oscar had managed to get one of his own guys on the crew.

"Bentley Mulsanne," the voice whispered.

"That's the one," Oscar said.

Moments later a pair of headlights appeared on a nearby fire road. Oscar hopped out of the cab and met the silver car on the half-poured driveway. A young man climbed out, all nervous energy.

"You remember where the signs are?" Oscar asked.

The boy nodded quickly.

"Down on Brier. By the white two-story place."

A few well-placed counterfeit "No Parking" signs were part of the scam. The valet will have seemingly made a regrettable mistake, and calls to the city tow yards would occupy the car's owner the next few hours. By then the car would be sealed in a cargo container on its way out to sea.

Long gone were the days when stolen vehicles had to be chopped and stripped. Globalization had seen to that. Oscar would have a buyer for the Bentley in Asia before it had even crossed the International Date Line.

"Man, there was a Spyder and an SLS coming up when I got the Bentley," the parker, whose name Oscar thought was Ricardo, said. "I even saw a Vanquish in a driveway on the way over. If we had four tow trucks, we'd have over a million in cars."

"Yeah, but nobody notices one tow truck carrying a fancy car. Four? That shit attracts attention. Then you go to jail."

Kids these days. Too fucking eager.

Ricardo's features softened. He looked just on the border of chastised and humiliated. He might be a kid, but Oscar knew better than to let it go too far to the latter. He took two envelopes from his pocket and handed them to Ricardo.

"These'll be at the shop for you."

Ricardo found stacks of cash in both.

"Why two?"

"One's to pay you for tonight. The other puts you on retainer for a job I've got Tuesday night in Arcadia. You free?"

It didn't look like Ricardo knew precisely what "retainer" meant, but he nodded quickly at his unexpectedly benevolent boss.

Oscar hauled the Bentley to his shop, where an empty cargo container waited. Once the car was inside, one of his boys would run it down to the Port of Long Beach on the back of a tractor-trailer. His thoughts turned to Luis. Why didn't he make his old friend an offer?

Come work for me, bro. You're the only smart person I've ever met. We'll take over this city.

But he knew what it was. This Luis Chavez truly was a changed man. A *holy* man. It was as if he could see right into Oscar, and what he found there hadn't impressed him much. Was that why Oscar drove him to certain death?

Fuck. That.

He pushed all this out of his mind. It was Sunday night, and he wanted to get laid. And not with some local *puta*, either. He wanted one of those gentrified crazy white bitches out looking for strange. They weren't always on the prowl, but he knew where to find them if they were.

But it better not take all night, he thought, checking his watch.

He had a goddamn criminal empire to run.

XVII

"I'll be back by tonight, but I want you to come home right after school. Mrs. Leñero will check in and give me a call. Understood?"

"No prob," Miguel said. "But you've got me worried. Why are you going back up there today? Is this about those guys in the truck?"

"Estate stuff," Maria lied. "I want to be done with this as much as you do."

She kissed him on the forehead on the way to the driveway before doubling back and kissing him on both cheeks and giving him a hug as well. She meant it to be reassuring, but Miguel looked more troubled than before.

"Be safe," he said.

"Of course," she called back.

He's too perceptive for his own good, she thought as she made her way through Monday morning rush hour to St. Augustine's.

But there was something else she'd noticed in her son that weekend. He'd seemed more grown up, but after enduring the murder of his uncle and the possible threats against his mother, what had she expected? He was more protective of her and more confident in his ability to be that protector. She hadn't expected that. It made her feel like a bad mother for making her son be the parent.

Regardless, without his help it would've taken a lot longer for Maria to figure out how her brother's financials worked. It was simple really. He paid them weekly, kept strict records, made the proper deductions, and sent out W-9s at the beginning of the year. Since there was a large and ever-changing pool of workers, keeping it legal could mean submitting employment forms to the county assessor as often as two or three times a month. If there were gaps in Santiago's paperwork for whatever reason, Maria figured the forms on file with the county might provide the most accurate picture.

Truthfully, it wasn't much, but it gave them a place to start.

———

Luis was in the parking lot chatting with a St. John's student when Maria pulled in. He nodded to her, sent the boy on to class, and climbed into the passenger side of the Camry.

"A student of yours?" Maria asked, indicating the boy.

"I actually don't start teaching until the fall," Luis admitted. "He just had a question about the priesthood."

"What kind of question? If you don't mind me asking, of course."

"He's thinking about becoming a priest. He wanted my opinion."

Maria looked surprised. Luis had expected this. In the minds of many, priests were old men. The idea of anyone in this day and age joining the priesthood seemed antiquated, if not downright odd.

"What did you tell him?" she asked.

"I told him to pray, but that it wouldn't be a yes or no answer."

"That's it? Pray?"

"How else do you hear the voice of God?"

"You didn't just ask him why he wanted to be a priest?"

"Answer a question with a question?" Luis joked.

"You know what I mean," said Maria.

"Well, it's not what he asked. Ask them why, and they're opening themselves up to be judged. 'Is my reason good enough? Is it worthy?' And if it's a surface reason, you know them already. They see the respect priests get. They're young men from broken homes looking for fathers. Spend enough time listening for God's voice, and the yearning falls away. That's the only voice you need to hear. Have you ever heard God's voice?"

"I think I did once," Maria admitted. "But that went away with puberty. How do you know whether it's God talking to you and not a figment of your imagination?"

"You have to know what you're listening for, and that takes practice," Luis said, hoping his answer didn't seem too esoteric. "You often pray when you're at your most vulnerable. That's when it's easiest to accept the first reasonable answer that pops in your head. You have to know the difference between what's of the world and what's of God. You have to want to know what he has to say. That's why it's best to pray in silence. He waits for you."

Maria seemed to like his answer.

───

The drive north took two hours. Maria asked about Luis's life before the priesthood and he told her about his mother, where his family had come from, but shied away from anything criminal. She eventually changed the subject to her own son, and this was fine with Luis.

When they reached the county assessor's office, Maria seemed to realize she'd been speaking without break for almost an hour.

"I'm sorry," she said as she pulled into a parking space. "I don't even know what I was talking about."

"A million different things. Your brother and your son mostly."

She eyed him suspiciously, as if he'd used some kind of trick to loosen her tongue. "Find out anything interesting?"

Luis had. Plenty. It was obvious she'd needed someone to talk to for some time.

"You're really good at putting others' needs before your own," he said finally.

Maria fell silent. Luis realized just how judgmental that had sounded.

"I'm sorry," Luis said. "That didn't come out right."

"Yeah, it did," Maria deflected. "I just didn't want to hear it."

The office of the Ventura County assessor was small even as government offices ran. This was, however, in contrast to the power it wielded in the region. The county supervisor, Leon Harradine, determined property values for much of the area's farmland. This decided the amount of property taxes paid by the landowners. As this could mean, in terms of sheer acreage, the difference between millions and tens of millions, Harradine's favor was much sought after.

That it could be bought only made him more popular.

When Maria and Luis entered, the man behind the big desk raised an eyebrow.

"May I help you?"

"I hope so. Are you Leon Harradine?"

After the man admitted he was, Maria explained who she was. Harradine's expression changed.

"I would like to express my and my department's sincerest condolences," he said. "I didn't know your brother, but I understand he was an excellent farmer." As if realizing this was inadequate given the circumstances, he quickly added, "He increased the value of his land."

"Thank you," Maria replied. "We're hoping you can help us with that."

"Anything," he said, opening his hands.

The balding, bespectacled man was dressed for comfort, but it was an expensive shirt and pair of pants. The office was a mess of overflowing file cabinets and banker's boxes, but the desk was a showpiece, a real antique that the assessor kept free from clutter. Luis wondered how much money the little bureaucrat managed to clear each year.

"I'm selling the farm," Maria said.

Harradine seemed relieved.

"For the sake of the sale, we need to know about any outstanding tax debts, any liens. Anything relating to his workers. As you might imagine, we've already had people emerge from the woodwork making claims."

"That's reprehensible," Harradine said. "And to my knowledge, there's nothing to it. His paperwork arrived like clockwork. I can show it to you."

"Would you?"

Harradine rose, scanned the banker's boxes, selected one, and carried it to the desk. Inside were several thick folders marked "Higuera" with a year alongside it. By how readily he was able to retrieve them, they seemed to be a part of the show as well.

"This is what we have," Harradine announced. "You can't leave with it, but I think we can allow you to make copies."

Luis and Maria needed no invitation. They were already flicking through the files, one yellow page after another. Harradine reacted with surprise.

"What are you . . . ?"

"We don't want to waste your time, sir," Maria said. "So we'll just find what we're looking for and be on our way."

This response seemed to befuddle him. He turned to Luis.

"Can I ask what you're doing here, Father?"

"Sixty-four."

"Pardon?"

"According to these forms, Santiago employed sixty-four workers on his farm last year."

"Okay, yes," Harradine said. "If a property is being used for business, that's part of how the taxes are . . ."

"Seventy-one," Maria said, finishing her count. "For the year before."

"Um, yes. That sounds right. His isn't . . ."

He paused, as if considering whether to alter the tense.

". . . isn't the largest farm in the county. There are some workers who come and go."

"A few I could understand," Maria said, then raised a file folder of her own. "But these are his bank statements from his business account. The amount of money that stays in is consistent, but the amount that moves through it is ten to twenty times how much he would've needed to pay these people."

Harradine's jaw dropped. That was the intention. The documents in Maria's file folder were actually dummy bank statements that Miguel had printed off the Internet. They wouldn't have stood up to even the slightest bit of scrutiny. If things went their way, they wouldn't need them to.

"That's . . . I . . . I don't know anything about that," Harradine said.

Luis returned to the folder he'd taken from the banker's box and indicated the stack of yellow pages.

"There's a yellow form for each worker Santiago reported?"

"Yes."

"And you're sure these were the only ones sent to your office?"

"Yes," Harradine insisted.

"Okay, but if you get the yellow copy and Santiago retains the pink, who gets the white?"

Harradine didn't respond immediately. Luis could feel Maria silently panicking but could tell the assessor was only scrambling for the right answer.

"The accounting firm," Harradine finally remembered. "They were sent there."

"Do you know which one?" Maria asked. "There were two."

Luis shot a look over to her. Yes, they'd discussed improvisation, but she'd taken it to the next level. Two sets of paperwork was the oldest scam in the book. Only in this case it was being done with the collusion of government officials at every level, making it practically impossible to prove. There was no smoking gun, no criminal act committed out in the open; there was simply one form saying that a person who had never worked at Santiago's farm was doing exactly that.

Harradine edged Maria aside and flipped through the files in the banker's box. It took him two passes to find what he was looking for.

"This one."

Luis committed the name of the firm and its address to memory.

"Thank you so much for your help," Maria said, picking up her files.

The two were out the door a second later.

"We've got one more shot," Luis said. "Let's make it count."

". . . and in closing, our family would like to again thank Chancellor Dawkins, the staff at UC Davis, the entire University of California system, and the School of Agriculture and Soil Science for this honor," Glenn read. "This is one of the finest institutions of learning in the world. Having a cutting-edge genetics lab will only serve to help carry that reputation into the future."

He paused for applause. If there was one thing Elizabeth Marshak knew how to do, it was write a speech. He glanced over his shoulder to the new wing. There was the Marshak family name spelled out in flat cut metal letters, using the proprietary font of the UC system. Only it was his older brother's name in front of it.

He bristled.

People knew Henry seldom made public appearances. This seemed to make him more of a target for accolades, lifetime achievement awards, and other signs of veneration.

Glenn suspected Henry loved the honors and attention and actively courted them by being elusive. That Glenn had to accept them on his behalf to avoid embarrassment and maintain relationships with important boards and governmental agencies added to Henry's enjoyment—or so he thought. Adding to or perpetuating the Legend of Henry Marshak was Glenn's least favorite activity.

"My brother would love to be here to accept this honor," Glenn said, pausing to acknowledge knowing chuckles from the audience. "But we all know the story of how hard it is to drag the old farmer from his fields. May his diligence and dedication be a lasting inspiration to the students of this university."

Peals of applause came in earnest now. Some stood and the rest followed. Glenn had fought his daughter on the "diligence and dedication" line, even though he knew it struck the right closing beat of humility. He strode off the dais to a barrage of photos, handshakes, claps on the back, and looks of familiarity from people he was sure he'd never seen before. He responded in kind, though all he really wanted was to find his driver and get the hell out of there.

He finally pushed through the throng, the car within sight, when a man of his own age and privileged tax bracket stepped forward, hand extended.

"Donald," Glenn said, shaking his hand. "Does my family have you to thank for sponsoring this honor?"

Donald Roenningke, the semiretired CEO of Crown Foods, shrugged and opened his hands in supplication, which confirmed to Glenn he had nothing to do with it whatsoever.

"Maybe I just wanted to catch you in a festive mood," Donald said with a wry smile.

"I'm assuming this has something to do with our meeting last week?" Glenn asked.

"Oh, you had them quaking in their boots, my son included," Donald said, sighing. "Did it feel good?"

Glenn snorted. *Of course it did.*

"Then you'll be happy to know that we're giving in to most of your demands, *except* the length of the contract. You wanted twenty years before it could be renegotiated? I'll give you ten. That's final."

"You're banking on me not being alive?"

"Yes," Donald said flatly. "Jason's not you. Let him carve out his own legacy."

"Like you're doing for Andrew?" Glenn scolded. "Or is this tough love meant to force him to rise to the occasion, one CEO to another?"

"Maybe it's both."

Glenn smiled but saw that something was still bothering his counterpart.

"What is it?"

"In the spirit of cooperation, there's something I feel I should bring to your attention," Donald said. "We received a packet of information concerning possible criminal activity within your company."

"Now wait a minute—"

"I know, I know," Donald said, raising a hand. "We get things like this all the time. Ninety-nine times out of one hundred there's nothing to it at all. But this came to us over the weekend. It's pretty alarming stuff."

"Alarming how?"

Donald nodded to his driver, who came over with two large padded envelopes. He handed them to Glenn, who eyed them as if he'd been given a dead animal.

"You can see for yourself. The contents suggest you've been using illegal labor in your fields. But instead of a few here and there slipping through the cracks, they show a pattern of illegality, comparing it to an organized crime syndicate, right down to violence and even murder."

"Oh, come *on*," Glenn shot back. "How can you even pay attention to something that preposterous? It's like a tabloid story."

"I agree. When we looked into it ourselves—"

"When you did *what*?"

"When we looked into it *ourselves*," Donald continued, "we came up dry. But our investigation is still open. Unless, of course, you could refute these charges yourself. It would save a lot of time."

"Are you saying the contract hinges on that?"

"I'm saying this is the largest deal my company has ever considered. We can't take chances, even with unlikely fairy tales. Let me know, okay?"

XVIII

Oscar's ringtone wasn't easy to ignore. A popular *narcocorrido* from the ever more popular El Komander, it cut through any conversation with its jaunty lyrics celebrating murder and drug smuggling over a traditional, almost mariachi-style melody. When it broke the silence in the small motel room, Oscar's eyes popped open, and he rolled out of bed to find the phone.

"*Sí?*" he said, plucking the cell from a pile of clothes on the floor.

"Oscar," a familiar voice cooed, equal parts bemusement and condescension. "How's my boy?"

Jesus Christ, Oscar thought. *Not who I thought I'd hear from today.*

"I'm good," Oscar croaked. "How are you?"

"That remains to be seen. It seems a friend of ours has come back to us."

Oscar sat up straight and tried to clear his head. He needed to be in a more lucid frame of mind for this conversation. It occurred to him that the room was empty. He glanced to the bathroom door and saw it open a crack. The shower was running and he could just make out the person inside.

"Oh?" he managed to reply. "Who's that?"

"The young man to whom you gave a ride up into farm country last week."

As Oscar struggled with a response, his eyes fell on the pile of clothes that didn't belong to him. He fixed on a bra, noting its impressive cup size.

Oh yeah, the blond, he remembered.

She'd been in her thirties, with magnificent legs, fantastic tits, a hard, flat stomach, and a tight, round ass—not the most common sight on a white chick, particularly one that had kicked out a couple of kids. He'd thought she'd sneak out after he'd fallen asleep. Not only had she stayed the night, she'd left the bathroom door open.

An invitation if he'd ever seen one.

"Luis," Oscar said, inspired to hurry the conversation. "Yeah, I saw him. Was a real surprise. But you had to know he was here, right?"

"Yes, but you sought him out. Invited him by. Did him a favor. I find that curious."

Great. He's got eyes and ears in my crew. I'll have to deal with that.

"He asked me for help, not the other way around. And I'm not a guy who likes to get his information secondhand. So yeah, I went to see that it was him."

There was a pause.

"Maybe that's true," the voice said. "But we need to keep better tabs on him. It seems like he's up to all sorts of unpriestly activities up there. And you can look in on him in ways I cannot. Understood?"

"Sure," Oscar said.

"Excellent. We'll talk soon?"

Oscar hung up without replying. Any more time on the phone and the woman in the shower might give up on him.

"Important phone call?" she chided when Oscar stepped in behind her.

"I am an important person," he declared.

She laughed. He put his hands on her hips and mouth against her skin where her shoulder met her neck. She moaned obligingly and put one hand on his leg, the other on his erection.

As he kissed her, Oscar realized he'd either forgotten her name or she hadn't even offered it the night before. If he'd thought to, he should've stopped on the way to the shower to search her purse for an ID.

Oh well.

———

The accounting firm was located on the bottom two floors of a modest professional building a stone's throw from several gated communities. The other occupants were two dentists, an optometrist, a lawyer who specialized in small claims, and a tax attorney.

Luis checked the dashboard clock as they pulled into the parking lot. It was a few minutes short of noon.

"Wait," Maria said as Luis reached for the door handle.

"Why?"

"If we get one shot at this," Maria said, eyes on the building's front door, "we have to make it count."

Luis settled back in the passenger seat. He expected Maria to explain, but she said nothing. People began to trickle out a few minutes later, likely on their way to lunch at the fast-food joints nearby.

After another minute Maria opened the car door.

"Let's go."

The inside of the building was functional and anonymous. Any business could move in, establish itself, endure a few downturns, disappear, and be replaced by someone doing the same with minimal cosmetic changes.

Maria moved through the lobby with purpose, Luis hurrying to catch up. The security guards glanced up as she passed but were distracted by Luis's collar. Maria kept walking toward the double doors leading to Suite 100 and entered without knocking.

Three women were arranged behind a single long desk. Two were on the phone. Maria approached the one who wasn't.

"Can I help you?" the young woman asked.

"We're here for the Higuera files," Maria announced.

The woman stared back without recognition. She glanced to the women on either side of her, but they used their calls to keep out of it.

"Did you talk to someone in particular?" the receptionist asked.

Maria held up her file of bank statements.

"We just came from the county assessor's office. We were told the files were here. Santiago Higuera? He was my brother. The one killed in Mexico."

Conversation stopped as everyone froze. Even Luis was taken aback by the starkness of Maria's statement.

"Oh. I'm . . . I'm so sorry," the receptionist stammered. "What can we do for you?"

"My brother was a client of this firm," Maria said. "You kept copies of his employment and tax forms, among other things. We are in the process of donating the property to St. Augustine's Church in Los Angeles."

Luis winced at the lie but said nothing.

"The county assessor assured me the files would be ready to be picked up when I got here from the city. Father Chavez was able to get time away from the parish to help carry them."

The receptionist waited for Maria to continue. When she realized it was her turn to speak, she nodded. "I don't think Janette's left for lunch yet. She'll know what to do."

"She'll know where they are?" Maria insisted.

"She'll know where they are," the receptionist confirmed.

"Great!" Maria enthused. "We'll wait here."

The receptionist rose, seemed to wonder for an instant how it was she came to be hypnotized into this task, then headed back into the office.

Luis eyed Maria with bemusement.

"What?" she asked. "They don't teach you that in the seminary?"

———

Twenty minutes later the receptionist returned. She was trailed by a second woman, as well as two young men pushing handcarts laden with banker's boxes.

"We're pretty sure this is all of it," chimed the receptionist, triumph in her voice.

"How sure?" Maria snapped back.

The receptionist was cowed. The second woman, Janette, stepped forward.

"It's everything that was back there," she said. "We would've liked to make copies, but as you seem to need them now . . ."

Maria ignored the tone and nodded to the young men.

"If you can help us get these to the car, we'll bother you no more."

As Luis watched Janette consider this, even he was impressed with how well Maria had pulled this off.

Ten minutes later they rolled into a supermarket parking lot a few blocks up from the accounting firm. The pair immediately dove into the boxes. Unlike the ones at the county assessor's office, these files were in disarray.

"I can't find anything in here," Maria said. "It's like they just dumped everything in boxes to get rid of us."

"That's exactly what they did," Luis replied, setting one box aside for another. "Doesn't matter. If it's all here, we'll sort it out."

It started small. Luis found a stack of white employee tax forms buried under a stack of returns. They were all marked as having come from the year before. He counted them as he went.

"How many workers did you say were accounted for last year?"

"Seventy-one," Maria remembered. "Why?"

"I'm up to ninety-one."

Maria gasped. Luis realized the thin chance that her brother might not have been involved in some kind of illicit activity had just evaporated.

"What does it mean?" she asked.

"I don't know yet," Luis admitted. "I think we have to keep going. We have to know the whole story."

When they finished going through all the boxes, separating the different forms, they'd counted over seven hundred workers white-sheeted through Santiago's farm that year, over eight hundred the year before, six hundred the year before that, and another seven hundred before that.

What was worse was they all had foreign passport numbers or civil IDs. They'd all signed in their own handwriting. They'd all filled out the requisite biographical information. To dummy up this many fake people would be near-impossible. But if all these people really were somewhere working the fields of the Santa Ynez Valley, where were they?

When Luis finally came across one with Odilia's name, he blanched. "Here it is."

"I don't get it," Maria said. "What's the scheme here? Why would you fake papers? If you're using illegal workers, why would you then register them with the state as employees? It doesn't make sense. How could my brother have died to keep *this* a secret?"

Luis thought he finally knew the answer.

"It's laundering. But instead of money, they're laundering people," he said, paging through a few more of the forms. "If on paper they're paying all this money out through Santiago's farm, then they must have been using him as some kind of front. The government thinks all these people are working there, but they're really somewhere else, likely doing the same job but off the books."

"I don't understand. Why do this?"

"You hear stories like this all the time. Recruiters trawl through Mexico and South America promising jobs up north," Luis explained. "'Don't be like those *pendejos* who hop the border only to spend their lives dodging INS,' they say. 'We'll make it legal by putting you right into a job when you land. You just owe us a small fee. And if you don't have the money now, well, you can work it off when you get there.'"

"That was Santiago," Maria said slowly. "He was so excited. He'd been guaranteed a job. But when he called for me, he didn't want me following in his footsteps. He said, 'I know people now. You don't have to go through what I did.'"

"He already had his own land?" Luis asked.

"Yeah. I was surprised, but this was my big brother. In my eyes there was nothing he couldn't do. How did he get it?"

"That's the rest of the scam," Luis surmised. "He probably worked his ass off for them to pay off the debt. But rather than release him, they proposed a trade. He gets land of his own, but he has to work as a front company for them. But that's the insidious part of the scheme."

He held up all the forms with Santiago's signature on them.

"Whoever's behind it gets all the illegal labor they want," Luis continued. "But if INS or somebody shows up saying this is a big scam, who gets busted? The grower using these hundreds of workers? Or the guy whose name is on all the documents?"

"Jesus Christ," Maria exclaimed. "He was being set up."

"Probably without even knowing it," Luis guessed. "Until Annie Whittaker came along and filled him in. That's when he agreed to expose the whole thing to the district attorney."

"And that's when they killed him."

The pair fell silent for a long moment. But then Luis remembered something Maria had said earlier.

"The buyer for the farm. The one that showed up on your doorstep offering to pay too much. Did they have a name?"

"The Marshaks. Probably the biggest farming concern up there. Why?"

Luis didn't respond, but a theory began percolating in his head.

PART IV

XIX

Jason had been in no mood for a party. His lawyers had called with the bad word from Crown Foods' legal team. It would be another week before a revised offer was ready. Though they'd insisted it was all clerical, experience told Jason this wasn't good. Only days before, the same opposing lawyers had made promises about pulling all-nighters and working the weekend.

One of the Marshak lawyers, a middle-aged man named Burt, was the bearer of all this bad news. "If I had to guess, I'd say it's something new. They finished their final round of due diligence last month. We duly resolved the issues that came up. They weren't holding anything back for contingency's sake."

"But *right now*?" Jason asked. "If it's from an outside source, they must know we're down to the wire. Somebody's trying to sabotage the deal."

The sigh on the other end of the line seemed to confirm this.

"It's a possibility," Burt said. "But that it came up immediately after you rejected their original offer suggests inside knowledge. If you'd signed in the room, this would all be moot. Who really benefits by sitting on the information until it's almost worthless?"

Jason wanted to present at least a few theories of what the "new information" could be before calling Glenn. He thought about it for half an hour or so, trying to come up with a few ideas, but none surfaced. He needn't have bothered.

"I know all about it," Glenn said, cutting him off. "Donald Roenningke just gave me everything they have."

"What is it?"

"That's asking the wrong question," Glenn snarled. "What's more important is to find out who gave it to them."

"If I could take a look, maybe I could—"

"I want to send it to my lawyers first," Glenn countered. "I'll let you know what they find out."

My *lawyers, not* our *lawyers,* Jason thought, knowing Glenn meant his personal team.

"We'll talk at the house later," Glenn said.

"At the house?" Jason asked.

"Constance's party?"

Before Jason could reply, Glenn hung up.

While he loved his cousin and her children, a party to celebrate the oldest's graduation from preschool seemed ridiculous. This was on top of an actual graduation ceremony that morning at the preschool.

He had tried to come up with an excuse, but Glenn's word was final. Which was how Jason found himself two blocks from his uncle's multi-acre estate, dreading the typhoon of children he'd soon be enduring in the old man's terrace and gardens. He looked forward to approaching it with a stiff drink in his hand, then remembered how many professional contacts and colleagues had been invited. If Glenn caught him with a drink in his hand, he'd get another lecture.

A wonderful, calming idea popped in his head like a gift from God. It was accompanied by a pleasant rush of endorphins, and he began to relax. He plucked his cell phone from his pocket and dialed.

"Hey, where are you right now?"

———

A few hundred yards away, Glenn paced through his study, chewing a piece of nicotine gum. He hadn't smoked in decades but kept the gum around for the cravings. He'd found this box in a desk drawer, and though it had expired over three years earlier, he'd popped two pieces into his mouth and followed them up with a glass of scotch.

"Are you all right, Daddy?"

Elizabeth lit into the room in a floral-print dress. Though now in her early forties, to Glenn she didn't look a day older than the incoming college freshman he'd dropped at Boston College two decades earlier. For someone who lived the mostly charmed life of a billionairess, she was by all accounts a good person. The biggest surprise was her success with men, her husband Phillip proving to be a far more solid citizen than Glenn had given him credit for early on.

At times he wondered if his son-in-law would've been a better protégé than Jason. But he was determined the name on the building remain Marshak.

"Daddy?" Elizabeth repeated.

"Fine," Glenn said. "How's the party? Are Constance and her friends having a good time?"

Elizabeth, oblivious to what lay in the two padded envelopes on Glenn's desk, smiled and took her father's hand.

"They're loving it. Everyone's in the garden. Come down."

"Of course," Glenn said, giving his daughter a peck on the cheek. "Five minutes."

Elizabeth smiled again and left. Glenn poured himself another drink.

When he came down half an hour later, he took the outside stairs off the study's balcony, hoping his daughter wouldn't notice how long he'd stayed in after her exit. As he descended, he lurched forward and had to grab the rails to prevent himself from tumbling onto the concrete below. A waiter sprang to his aid, grabbed his arm, and helped him the rest of the way down.

"New shoes," Glenn said by way of explanation.

The house's grounds were arranged so that there was an impressive approach in both the front and back. The house was set back from the street a good thirty yards, cars arriving at a rotunda, where they were met with the home's majestic Mediterranean facade, Spanish-tiled roof, and enough windows to indicate bedrooms in the double digits. But it was on the back patio that jaws really dropped.

The rear of the house emptied out onto a wide veranda that overlooked a series of tiered gardens that stretched out over eight acres. In it were samples of every kind of plant in the Marshak empire: lemon trees, beds of wild strawberries, and rows and rows of grapevines. Beyond several fountains and hidden within an orange grove was an Olympic-sized pool ringed with cabanas. It was the pièce de résistance of the tour, and Glenn delighted in his visitors' awe, even though he hadn't been in the pool for years.

From the rear terrace he couldn't see Constance or her friends. They'd probably tired of the activities closer to the house and ended up by the pool. This was fine by him. Fewer would notice if he slipped away.

The anonymous allegations were distracting him, though not as greatly as a niggling impulse to call Henry. Glenn knew if he got Henry to call up Donald Roenningke, this whole thing would be over. Henry's word was unimpeachable. If he said there was nothing to the charges,

Donald would take it to heart. Signature pages for the Crown Foods contract would be on Glenn's desk by the next day.

But this would require Glenn to admit to his brother that he needed him to sort out a crucial matter for the company that he couldn't do himself.

And Henry would love *that.* He scowled.

There had to be another way. Something he hadn't thought of yet.

"Glenn?"

Someone was trying to flag him down from the side of the house. He considered ignoring them, but the second time they called his name he recognized the voice.

"Glenn," said Jason, jogging over. "There's someone I want you to meet."

Jason stopped short, looking his uncle up and down, and extended a steadying arm.

"Why don't you come inside?" Jason asked, lowering his voice.

"Fuck off," Glenn growled.

When last they'd spoken, his nephew had been frantic over the Crown Foods setback. Now he was upbeat, as if nothing had happened.

"What're you so happy about anyway?" Glenn slurred, aggravated.

He looked past Jason and spotted a young woman in an ill-fitting dress. She hadn't moved from where Jason had left her at the corner of the house.

"What the *fuck*?" Glenn bellowed. "What the holy *fuck*?"

Glenn lumbered toward her. He didn't know her name, but he didn't have to. He'd had more than his share of field girls to know what she was. But bringing her to a party? This was going too far.

"Jason," Glenn said, sobering. "What do you think you're doing bringing that . . . *person* here?"

Jason ran to her side, trying to take control of the situation.

"This is Odilia. She's a friend. A very special one."

Glenn spat in Jason's face with such violence that Odilia flinched. Jason staggered backwards.

"Glenn?"

"Get her out of here!" Glenn seethed, gripping Jason's arm so hard his knuckles whitened.

"But Glenn—"

Glenn twisted his fingers in Jason's flesh.

"If you don't have the mental faculties to understand why bringing her here is a bad idea, take my word for it. Get her out of here right now. And you get out, too."

Jason looked ready to protest when Elizabeth appeared on the veranda. Only then did Glenn notice the other guests and hired help had discreetly moved away.

"Hi, how are you?" Elizabeth said to Odilia.

Odilia smiled back, but Jason already had her by the elbow.

"Let's go."

Jason yanked Odilia toward the house. Elizabeth turned to her father angrily.

"Why did you have to do that?" she asked.

"Are you crazy?" he shot back. "This family has enough free spirits. If Jason doesn't start acting more like the next CEO and less like his father, I just might have to go outside the company to find our next chief executive."

With that, Glenn headed back into the house, wishing for the umpteenth time in his life that Elizabeth had shown any interest at all in the company business.

XX

Bullet holes? A sniper's nest? Laundering illegal workers? Slavery? Crooked cops?

Michael's head hadn't stopped spinning since he'd entered the little café across from the courthouse and Luis started talking.

"Wait, you said you spent the night in Annie's guest room closet?" he asked, trying to slow it down a little.

"I didn't have much of a choice."

"This was in the downstairs bedroom?" Michael prodded.

"Upstairs. The one farthest from the stairs on the left."

Michael nodded. It was a small test but a test nevertheless.

"And the records? You have them?"

"My son printed out the bank error," Maria said, speaking for the first time. "The other records are in my car, both the ones for the people that actually worked at my brother's farm, but also the hundreds of fake ones that were at the accounting firm across town. That's why we're here. We can give them all to you and your team. You can use this, right?"

Michael hadn't expected any of this. He'd initially hoped the priest might come back with something, but he'd mostly forgotten about him after hearing nothing for a week. Then came the e-mail threat with the photos of him and Annie. Any thoughts he'd had of resurrecting the case himself were duly vanquished. Better to let sleeping dogs lie.

But this was even bigger than Annie had hinted. It wasn't just a big case, it was the career maker he'd been looking for. It was clear the targets in the case already had his scent, so he had to keep his distance. Strike only when the opportunity presented itself. Anything else would be career suicide.

And maybe he could just get to the blackmailer before the black-mailer got him . . .

"What about the Marshaks?" he asked. "That's the last piece of the puzzle."

"That's where it gets thin," Luis said, turning to Maria.

"Santiago worked in the Marshak fields before getting his own land, land he bought from the Marshaks," Maria explained. "We located four other small farms in Ventura County with the same pattern of owner-ship. Marshak field hands worked for the Marshaks for several years, then got farms of their own, though it would have seemed out of reach economically."

"And you believe they might have been 'laundering'—to use your word—workers for the Marshaks as well?" Michael asked. "This is a company with literally thousands of workers on the books. You're saying they've got thousands more working some unmarked spur fields away from prying eyes to cut costs?"

"Your theory, not mine," Luis said. "But if they have the support of local law enforcement and the land commissioners, who is going to know the difference between one anonymous hundred-acre square of land and the one across the street? There are miles and miles of fields up there. You keep eighty percent of your business legal, and you're still saving literally tens of millions of dollars, if not more. And if you're not paying them but instead holding these transit debts over their heads, then we're talking about human trafficking and, well, slavery."

It was a provocative word, Michael knew, but provocative words looked great in banner headlines. Still, there was something missing.

"But what about the money? It went into Santiago's account, only to be drawn out a moment later?" Michael asked.

"My son theorized that's why they used Santiago," Maria explained. "If the INS ever discovered one of the illegals working on a Marshak farm, they could turn around and pin it all on Santiago. That their employment forms were signed by Santiago, that money moved through his account to 'pay' them, so that's where the buck stopped. It's genius, really. A new way for a big corporation to use illegal labor but ensure that someone expendable is holding the bag if there is a bust. They were completely insulated."

Michael considered this. That it was the Marshaks was obvious. Who else had the resources to come up with a scam like this? For whom else would the benefit outweigh the risk?

"I hear what you're saying and I want to believe. But what I believe doesn't matter in this case. Other than the fact that the Marshaks offered to buy the land and, as good neighbors, offered assistance in the form of extra workers to help with the harvest, what concrete evidence do you have linking them to these invisible workers?"

Neither Luis nor Maria replied.

"I mean, that's the big point, right? What you've brought me looks like evidence that Santiago Higuera was involved in some sort of tax fraud. Then there's a bank error. Then there's an accounting firm that may or may not have been aware of a fraud that may or may not have existed. There's nothing there to do with the killing of Annie Whittaker. Nothing to do with the kidnapping of Odilia Garanzuay."

"Who else would have the money to run a scheme like this?" Maria interjected. "Or even need that many workers?"

"Do you even know these alleged workers exist? Or could they just be names on a piece of paper for some wider fraud scheme we haven't even thought of?"

"Odilia exists," Luis said quietly.

"That's only one person," Michael said, sitting back in his chair. "You have to think of this the way a lawyer would. That's how it was constructed in the first place. It doesn't matter what you think. It matters what I can prove in court."

The downcast look on Maria's face told Michael that she'd thought this was a slam dunk. That he'd throw himself at their feet in gratitude. Sure, they had discovered perhaps the first actual document worth presenting as a piece of evidence in an eventual case against the Marshaks. But good God, any lawyer worth his salt would discount the pages in a heartbeat as dummied up or the actions of a single actor.

"In fact there's not even anything here that could involve the office of the LA district attorney. Maybe a couple of Ventura County sheriffs. But even then I don't think they'd have enough for a search warrant, much less an arrest."

"You're saying we did this for nothing?" Maria snapped.

"No!" Michael retorted. "Not at all. I am, in fact, inclined to believe your theory. I think you may well have uncovered the major evidence this case will eventually rest on. But you don't know how it stitches together or who to pin it to."

Michael turned to Luis.

"You said you'd be my witness, so *be my witness*. This time in the Marshak fields. Find out where they keep the workers. And if what you heard about the recruitment of the workers is true, I need you to find out how they get them here. Also, find out exactly what they're told will happen to them if they don't do what their bosses say. There's not a judge in the state that'll sign a warrant against a family that powerful or connected unless they have to. But I promise you, if you get that, I can do the rest."

"What about the part that puts this in your jurisdiction?" Luis asked.

"If they were transported through Los Angeles, as Annie hinted, that's for me. If you can prove the Marshaks paid for any of this, that's for me, as their offices and banks are here. And, naturally, if you can prove that they kidnapped Santiago from our safe house here in the city, that's for me, too. I know it's asking a lot, but if there are thousands of people working up there under threat of violence, we can get justice for them and hopefully send a message to others not to do the same."

Michael eyed the pair carefully. It was do or die time, and he was being as blunt and honest as he could. They'd either wilt or rise to the challenge.

"We won't let you down," Luis announced, getting to his feet. "Just make sure you hold up your side of the bargain."

Michael watched them go. Boy, he'd underestimated this priest. Now he just had to make sure he cut off the head before the body had a chance to react.

———

"You're going *back* to the farm?" Miguel asked, his cell on speaker as he continued to type lines of code into his laptop. "I thought you were all done with that."

"Try and sound a little disappointed," Maria said. "I'm dropping off the priest, and I'll be back in the morning."

The priest. When his mother had told him what she was trying to do, he was incredulous. If some cartel types had killed his uncle, they needed Rambo, not some Jesus freak.

"Did you talk to the DA?"

"*Deputy* DA. And we did. It turns out Santiago really was onto something big. I think we can help."

"Be careful," he urged.

When he got off the phone, Miguel allowed himself a little celebration. It had turned out Basmadjian's range of business interests was wider than Miguel had known. Even more problematic, the ways his men had hid his assets and laundered illicit funds through legitimate fronts were so half-assed that the only work he'd managed to do so far was to undo the damage of his predecessors. Having his mother out for another whole night was a big help. Hell, if she stayed away a full twenty-four hours, he might finish the whole thing.

It was as thrilling as it was terrifying. He was a teenager suddenly in charge of laundering close to fifty million dollars. This meant setting up dummy corporations across four states, establishing physical drops or mailing addresses for each, opening countless corporate accounts, and getting access to Basmadjian's own accounts to make it happen. He hadn't expected to be thrown into the deep end so quickly, but they must have wanted to know right away if he had the goods. It was either brilliant or reckless. Which depended on him.

He opened a desk drawer, took out a glass box and papers, and rolled the first of several joints.

—

It was rush hour, so Maria and Luis decided to eat dinner before braving the highway. There was a small Mexican restaurant off MacArthur Park that both knew, so they went there.

Most diners chose to sit at the outdoor tables, but they wanted privacy and asked to be seated inside. The walls were covered with murals, and the waitress sat them under an elaborate fresco of the Virgin of Guadalupe.

Though Luis was in street clothes, Maria still smirked at the waitress's choice.

"Do you think she knew you were a priest even without the collar?"

Luis shrugged. "They always know. I don't know how, but they do."

The waitress returned, and Maria ordered a margarita. Luis stayed with water.

"Do you have a plan?" Maria asked after the waitress left. "Or do you plan to go up there and just what? Put yourself in God's hands and see where he leads you?"

"Does it have to be one thing or the other?" Luis offered.

"Well, as I'm being dragged along with it, I'd love to know what I'm getting myself into."

"Okay," Luis said. "Then I plan to go to where I saw these guys that one night and search from there. There aren't going to be many cars on the road. I'm hoping we get lucky and see something familiar."

"But by 'lucky,' you mean 'hope that God points them out to you.'"

Luis sighed as Maria grinned victoriously.

"As a priest I'm to provide a vessel through which God's will is executed on earth. At the same time, as a man I'm on earth to exercise my own free will. I have to balance that and have faith that I'm on the right path."

Maria laughed as the waitress placed a margarita in front of her.

"That sounds like a very convenient way to have your cake and eat it, too."

Luis smiled. "Maybe it is. I can only tell you what I believe. My faith is everything to me. I'm still learning how to express it, but the feeling is a hundred percent. It allows me so much freedom—yes, freedom—knowing what my purpose is on this earth. I don't have the worries a lot of people do."

Maria surprised herself with a pang of envy. What would it be like to live with that kind of belief? Then her eyes traveled up to the image of Mary above her.

"What?" Luis asked.

"Men can become your equal in the priesthood. But women, like Odilia, you can only save. It's in that way they become objects. I've heard here and there about women who are brought up to the fields.

Some are workers, but others are there just to service the men. I wonder if she was just an object to them, too."

"Odilia?"

Maria nodded. "But I'll bet if you ask those working in the Marshak fields about women, they'll tell you they're sending money back to their sainted mother, to their wives, to a daughter. Sons can make their own way, but women need their men to save them. How much of that mentality must come from the church? Worship a virgin, preach virginity to those holiest among you, and the rest of the world are whores in comparison."

Luis fell silent for so long that Maria thought she'd offended him.

"I know the sins of my church," he began. "They weighed heavily on me as I took steps toward ordination. But it was the men who committed the sins that bothered me almost more than the actions. How could so many across so many centuries corrupt something I saw as so beautiful and binding and human in such grotesque ways? Maybe I'm naïve, but I couldn't believe all had entered the church with nefarious intentions. Was there something inherently corrupting about holding yourself up as the one anointed to save others? When asked to forgive so much sin, did it make it that much easier to surrender to it? Or worse, propagate it?"

"So what made up your mind?" Maria asked.

"I decided that if that was enough to keep me from my vocation, I wouldn't be a very good priest," Luis said. "But I believed and continue to believe in just how much the church's teachings can help people in their everyday lives. The importance of that outstripped everything else."

"But you could do that preaching on a street corner," Maria countered.

"No. I need the fellowship of my brother priests and the structure of the parish to support my soul. If I'm on a corner, it's easier to forget who is meant to be doing the speaking. If I'm one of many in the same clothes and collar in front of the same altar, waking up in the same rectory every day with the same mission, there's strength in that communion."

Maria thought about this for a moment. She took a sip of her margarita, then placed her hand on Luis's.

"What?" Luis asked.

"I might not have much belief in God, but I'm starting to believe in you."

XXI

It was dark by the time they arrived in Camarillo. In that time an idea had occurred to Luis. They wouldn't be able to find the workers, but they might be able to find the overseers. They drove to the grocery and liquor stores nearest the fields and scoured the parking lots. They parked and went into a few but continued to come up dry. They hit convenience stores next, a truck stop, and then simply drove up and down the main drags, checking out the other drivers.

"I think we should head to the farm," Maria said. "We can pick this up again tomorrow."

"I don't know. People know we were at the accounting firm, and they know someone was snooping around Annie Whittaker's house. The longer this goes on, the more likely they're going to figure out what we're up to. We can't risk waiting another night."

Maria drove in silence, Luis going over a map on Maria's iPhone. He opened the window to let in the night breeze, and with it came the familiar scent of the ocean. The air often carried the salty fragrance far inland, and it was something anyone in Los Angeles could pick up from time to time, even if they were well away from the Pacific shore.

But this was different. Underneath the refreshing combination of salt and tide hung fumes that were oily, rotten, and noxious. Something was off.

No, this was not the smell of the wide-open ocean. This was the smell of a seaport and the fume-belching freighters that inhabited it, and it was way out of place.

Luis scanned the area.

"What's that smell?" Maria asked.

"Pull into the truck stop. Go to a pump."

Maria did so. The pair climbed out of the car, the odor much stronger now. Luis glanced around for the source and spied a tractor-trailer taking on diesel a few yards away. The man filling the truck looked like any other trucker in jeans and a flannel shirt. Except for the distinct tattoos running up his neck and down his arms. Luis's eyes traveled to the cargo container on the truck's bed. There was movement, something passing behind one of what looked like a series of holes cut into the container's steel wall.

Aren't shipping containers meant to be airtight and waterproof?

The driver finished pumping and replaced the gas cap. He returned to the cab and opened the door. A second man sat in the passenger seat. Though he only caught a glimpse, Luis recognized him as the man he'd seen in the grocery store the last time he was up here. There was no mistaking his distinctive sharp features and fiery copper eyes.

Holy shit.

Luis exchanged a look with Maria and climbed back into the car.

"They're bringing them in by sea, not over the border," Luis said as Maria keyed the ignition. "That's why Michael couldn't find anything on them."

"Are you sure that's them?" she asked. "Those are the guys who killed my brother?"

"Them or others like them," Luis said. "I think they're ex-military, but I'll bet some of them knew each other even before that."

The tractor-trailer pulled out of the truck stop ahead of Maria. She waited for a couple of cars to go by, then followed at a careful distance.

"They're heading into the foothills," Maria said. "It can't be much longer."

She was right. Five minutes later the truck turned on its right blinker, slowed, and turned off the road into what Luis initially mistook for the middle of a field. A gravel road came into view, and Luis craned his neck to watch the truck amble off into the scrub.

"You think they're coming in through the Port of Long Beach or something?" Maria asked.

Luis's thoughts shot to Oscar and one of the schemes he'd told him about on their drive out, the one with the stolen high-dollar cars going into cargo containers. He prayed he wasn't involved in this.

"Kill the lights and pull over," Luis said.

"Here?"

"Yeah," Luis replied, grabbing his backpack from the backseat.

"No way," Maria exclaimed. "You're just going to follow them?"

"I am," he admitted.

"If they figure out who you are, they might kill you."

"I know. I have something much more important to ask you."

"What's that?" Maria asked.

"Do you believe me now that sometimes the Lord puts things in front of us?"

"Maybe he does," Maria said, pulling to a stop. "Good luck all the same."

"That's a start. See you back in the city."

Luis scrambled out of the car, shot Maria a last grin, and disappeared into the darkness.

___

Luis found the run across open ground exhilarating. He wasn't stupid. He knew he was running toward certain danger, but that wasn't foremost on his mind. For the umpteenth time in his life God had stepped in. He'd asked for God's guidance, and only hours later they'd found what they were looking for.

As he ran, he repeated the same thing in his head over and over:

Thanks be to God . . . Thanks be to God . . . Thanks be to God . . .

The truck had disappeared by the time he'd climbed from Maria's car, but he'd made good time and quickly caught sight of it. He ran parallel to the gravel road, keeping a good fifty yards between it and himself.

The truck slowed, and Luis saw a couple of men at what looked like a checkpoint. He peered into the darkness ahead and saw a barbed wire fence, this one a foot or two taller than the one he'd scaled near the main road. As his eyes became more accustomed to the dark, he was able to make out the thin green wires along the top of it.

Electrified. Damn.

As the guys in the truck chatted with the men at the checkpoint, Luis reached the electrified fence. He was deliberating on the best way to make it over when he spotted notches on a nearby fence post. They were on the side facing him. Easy access. That's when he realized the fence was there to keep something in, not out.

Holding his breath in case he was wrong, Luis jabbed his toe into the first foothold. When a fatal electric current didn't surge through his body, he leapfrogged the rest of the way over.

The truck started up again. Luis had to run to catch up. Less than a minute later he saw that the truck was heading toward what looked like a sprawling, haphazardly constructed apartment complex. The first few cinder-block units on the bottom floor on the west side of the building looked the oldest but also the best constructed. Units had been added on to it all the way to the far end of the concrete foundation that ran along the front. After running out of room, the builders seemed to just pile more of the same-sized units on top of the first level, using building material of lesser and lesser quality. Taken all together they looked like a stack of children's blocks.

The Blocks, Luis realized. He tried to count how many units there were based on front doors and windows but gave up after fifty.

The phantom workers. Here they all are. My Lord.

There were a handful of work lights set up out on the slab. Near them about a dozen men were gathered around tables set with food and drinks. The truck parked alongside the tables, and the driver and the sharp-featured man hopped out.

Luis flattened himself on the ground. He had to come up with a plan. He could stay in the field all night and try to join the workers as they were brought out in the morning, but there were too many variables. He could try and shadow them to the fields the next morning and simply appear in the rows, but that didn't seem like a good idea, either. There had to be a count, and getting onto the Marshak fields couldn't be so easy.

He had one chance. He had to pray they hadn't opened the container at the port. They must have been told how many men were put in the container down in Mexico, but there had to be some margin for error.

Doesn't there?

Two of the men by the tables edged to the rear of the container, followed by the driver. He put his hand on the lever that bolted it shut and gave it a sharp upwards jab. Though the men affected relaxed poses, Luis could see they were all armed, their hands inches from the grips.

"Your journey is over, my friends," the driver said in Zapotec as he opened the container doors. "I am sorry for the hardships you may have endured along the way. But that's all over. If you're here to work, we've got plenty of that. Tonight, however, is to refresh and replenish your spirits. Get some food and drink in you. Then get some rest."

At first there was no response. Luis peered into the dark container and wondered if it had all been an illusion. Then a few men shuffled forward and into the light. They were bleary-eyed and looked sickly. They were joined by a dozen and a half more, all of whom moved awkwardly on legs that probably hadn't touched solid ground for days.

Once they were out of the truck and all eyes were on the newcomers, Luis made his move. He scrambled to his feet and raced to the concrete slab extending from the buildings. He worried the sound of his feet pounding against the flat terrain would alert the men to his presence, but he had only seconds to make the distance.

The field was no problem, and he crossed that in less than forty long strides. Knowing it would make the loudest sound, he leapt across the gravel road without touching so much as a stone. When he was thirty yards from the truck, he thought he saw someone glance his way and he froze.

They turned and he kept moving.

When there was only ten feet between him and the truck, he felt a twinge of doubt. He shook this off and kept going. He reached the cab's front wheel and ducked low.

A terrible thought occurred to him. The overseers might recognize him even in the dim light. Not from the market but the church. He took his hat from his pack and pulled it low over his head. He was rising to come around the truck when he heard a shout.

"Hey! What the hell are you doing over here?" a voice yelled out in Spanish.

Luis turned, trying to look more confused than scared. The speaker, a lithe man with angular features and copper eyes, came around the back of the trailer, hand on a gun in his belt.

"You trying to run away?" the man barked, advancing on Luis. "You think you can pull a fast one?"

"No, boss!" Luis replied in Zapotec. "I'm hungry. And . . ."

The man waited, as if willing to give Luis one more second to plead his case before shooting him dead. One of the others punched him in the back of the head. It was hardly at full strength, but Luis's head shot forward. The gunman took out his pistol.

"What the fuck is all this?"

The men went quiet as the copper-eyed man joined them. He looked from face to face, until he settled on Luis.

"You think you don't have to do what the others do?" he asked calmly.

"I'm sorry, boss!"

"I think he was trying to run away," said the gunman.

"I wasn't!" Luis protested. "I want to work!"

The man pulled his own gun and placed it against Luis's throat.

"You think I won't make an example out of you right now? I'd thank you for the chance."

"I swear! I'm here to work. I don't want to run away. I just wanted a moment to pray. Thank God for getting us here safely."

The man sighed and lowered the gun. He then swung his leg around and kicked Luis under his chin with the heel of his cowboy boot. Luis flew backwards, landing on his ass. He gasped as the air was forced from his lungs and he tasted blood.

After the copper-eyed man moved back to the others, two of the overseers lifted Luis to his feet.

"What he meant to say is that security's a big deal here. We have an understanding with local law enforcement, but you're still in this country illegally. If one of you gets caught out there, everyone can lose their jobs and get kicked back to Mexico the next day. Make sense?"

"Yes, yes," Luis said quickly.

"Good. Now grab yourself a beer or two. You can pray when you get in your room."

———

There were hot dogs, chips, beer, and burritos. The men devoured the convenience-store fare laid out on the tables in about fifteen minutes and were then escorted to the two apartment units they were to share. The other newcomers eyed Luis with hostility and suspicion. They knew he hadn't been in the container with them, but they were too intimidated to say anything. If they started pointing fingers at him, there was no knowing the potential blowback on them.

The Blocks looked deserted. Every door was locked from the outside with a slide bolt as well as a thick metal jamb near the base that was bolted onto the door and then to the ground to prevent it being kicked open from the inside. Every blacked-out window was covered with burglar bars. The fire safety releases were welded shut on the outside. Blackout curtains hung on the inside. Not a single sound emanated from within the apartments.

"Everybody's out the door by six, no exceptions," the overseer said as he let the men into the one-bedroom apartment. "I'd suggest you get up a good half hour before. Shower, get dressed, eat breakfast—you'll find food in the cupboards—but be lined up at the door when we come for you or there'll be trouble. Cool?"

He hadn't said this with any real malice, but the sounds of the door bolting shut, locking, and the jamb dropping onto its strike plate punctuated the remarks.

The men fanned out to inspect their quarters. There were ten of them, five to sleep in the bedroom, five to the living room. There was a single bathroom off the hall, with a sink, toilet, and shower stall. The kitchen had a sink and several cabinets that turned out to be filled with dry cereal, soup, dried fruit, and other snacks, but there was no refrigerator or stove.

"Guess they don't want you burning down the place," one of the men joked.

Luis found a spot in the corner of the living room to lay down his pack. He took off his hat and boots and got ready to go to sleep.

"Who are you?"

He looked up and saw the faces of nine men staring down at him.

"My name is Luis Dedios," he said. "I'm here to work."

"You weren't in Mexico with us, you weren't on the boat with us. So who are you?"

The speaker was a heavyset, gray-bearded man, his voice grave and full of suspicion.

"I heard there was work. So I snuck out here and waited for the next truck."

The old man gestured toward Luis. Three of the others shot forward, two grabbing Luis's arms and pinning him down, while the third tossed his backpack.

"What're you doing?" Luis cried, struggling to free himself.

No one spoke as the contents of his backpack were spread across the floor. No one paid any attention to the clothes, but when a Bible was uncovered, it was passed to the old man.

"This is in English," the old man said, flipping it open. "'Father Chavez?' You stole a Bible off a priest?"

"No," Luis admitted. "I am a priest."

"You?" the old man asked, incredulous.

"Yes. I'm sorry for the deception, but I am here to work," Luis said.

"Ah, I see," the old man scoffed. "A few men doing honest labor, but the church still wants its tithing, no? We have no money here. Look around you."

"I don't want your money," Luis retorted. "And I *am* here to work. If in the course of that I can lessen anyone's burden by providing the sacraments of the church, so be it."

A couple of the men seemed moved by this, but the old man remained nonplussed. He threw the Bible back to Luis.

"In my experience a priest means trouble. If you're here to work, work. But stay out of our affairs, Father."

The men released Luis, and everyone went back to finding a place to sleep. Luis sank onto the wood floor and stared up at the ceiling. He feared the prison-like atmosphere would make it hard to fall asleep, but exhaustion pulled him under a second later.

XXII

There was an accident on the freeway. Maria checked the map app on her phone. Traffic through the hills was stopped in both directions for miles. She was already exhausted and could feel herself nodding off. After the fourth or fifth time jerking awake, she gave in and passed the stopped traffic on the shoulder, took the next exit, and turned around.

She didn't particularly want to spend another night at her brother's farm, but there weren't many alternatives. She could stay on the road for the next three hours and possibly kill herself behind the wheel. Or she could collapse into a bed waiting nearby and hit the road the next morning.

It also meant that she'd be close by in case Luis needed help. He didn't have a phone and had no reason to believe she'd be at Santiago's farm, but he'd certainly proven himself resourceful. If he somehow sent a carrier pigeon to her doorstep with a message, she wouldn't have been surprised.

The drive to the farm took fifteen minutes. The fields were empty when she arrived, though she thought she could make out the glow of cooking fires emanating from the tarp city. She made her way into Santiago's old house, texted Miguel about her detour, and headed to bed.

Though she'd been tired on the road, thoughts poured into her mind. The most rational one told her that she should drive home the next morning, pack Miguel into the car, and drive as far away as possible, maybe to Mexico, maybe all the way to Florida. This competed with, among others, an irrational desire to purchase a weapon, drive to the offices of the Marshak company, and . . . what? Seek out anyone with that last name and punish them for killing her brother? For turning him into some kind of criminal? She couldn't even prove they were involved, so what would be the point?

Out of all these, the one thought that kept returning to the fore was the most simple: she wished her brother were still alive. This was the exact kind of situation he was perfect for. He'd not only know what to do, he'd also make her feel safe.

Luis seemed like a good enough guy, but he'd never be Santiago.

When she heard knocking, she thought it was a dream. It was a tentative, distant sound, like a cat at a stranger's door. When it came again, this time stronger, she woke up enough to check her phone. She'd been asleep for four hours.

The knocking continued louder now. Maria sighed. They weren't going away.

She swung her legs out of bed and reached for her shoes. It suddenly occurred to her that it could be danger. She needed a weapon.

Wait. How do they even know I'm here?

Her car. It was parked right out front.

She made her way to the kitchen but couldn't find a knife. She remembered seeing a broom with a screw-on head and retrieved it from the pantry. She spun the bristle head off with her toe and weighed the improvised club in her hand. It wasn't much, but she could clock a guy pretty good with it.

"I'm coming," she said, hiding her apprehension.

"I'm sorry, Maria," came the voice of Alberto. "One of the irrigation pipes burst. It's flooding the eastern side of the field. We're already losing rows."

What in God's name can I do to help that? Maria wondered, though she was relieved it wasn't something worse.

"How'd it happen?" she asked, throwing open the door. "Can we call somebody?"

She froze. Alberto stood on the doorstep, right eye swollen shut, face caked in dried blood. His other eye was dark and hollow, as if it had burrowed back into his skull after witnessing something unspeakable. He could barely stand.

"I'm sor—" he whispered.

The world burst to light. It was only then, in the split second glow of the muzzle flash, that Maria saw the man standing behind Alberto. Having caught the full force of a shotgun blast to the back, Alberto flew heavenward before his body flopped forward. Maria felt splintered bone and hot shotgun pellets slash into her skin.

She inhaled sharply. A wiry man with a skull-face bandanna covering the lower half of his face ejected the empty casing. He chambered another round, wheeled the barrel around to her, and squeezed the trigger.

Maria had already launched herself backwards, half jumping, half falling through the doorway. She felt the hot wind of the blast pass over her, chewing up the door frame and cabinets, as she landed on her ass. The killer chambered another round and followed her in, only to trip on Alberto's outstretched leg.

"Shit," he muttered.

In those few precious seconds, Maria skittered farther into the dark house. When she reached the hall, she rolled onto her hands and knees and crawled to the bedroom. The shotgun roared again, and the wall above her exploded as if it had been hit by a bomb. She heard another shell snapped into the chamber and wished she'd had the presence of mind to grab the broom handle.

God help me.

It was panic and prayer. She didn't think God would intervene, but what else is there to hope for when you thought yourself seconds from death?

Then something happened. Her body rose to its feet. She picked up the nightstand alongside Santiago's bed and charged to the doorway. As if it were choreographed, she swung the nightstand just as the gunman stepped into the room. It hit with such force that three of the stand's legs cracked off and went flying.

The damage was done.

The assassin's face was caved in. He'd tripped back at an awkward angle. Splinters of wood were embedded in his flesh. He hit the wall and slid to the floor.

Maria didn't wait to find out if he was dead or alive. She grabbed her car keys, picked up the shotgun, and ran toward the front door. As she exited, she aimed the shotgun into the dark and pulled the trigger. She figured anyone expecting the assassin to emerge triumphant would hit the deck.

She unlocked the car and was behind the wheel a second later. The engine turned on immediately and she threw the car in drive. She hit the gas, expecting the car to lurch forward, but heard only the rev of the engine as her flattened tires spun uselessly in the muddy soil.

No!

As she scrambled to find the door handle, a thick cord flew around her neck from the backseat. She managed to get a finger under it before it was pulled taut, but there was no way to stop the makeshift noose from constricting her airway. As it tightened, she flailed wildly, instinctually trying to fight off her unseen attacker.

She kicked the windshield so hard it cracked the safety glass.

Miguel! she thought.

Then nothing.

———

No one woke up Luis. He finally heard the flurry of activity in the room and from the unit directly above and sat up straight. The men had dressed, finished their breakfasts, and lined up by the door. Though they had to have noticed him waking, none met his gaze.

They seemed amused.

Luis could already hear the trucks outside and the doors unlocking down the rows. He tossed his blanket aside, threw on his shoes, and reached for his hat. He had to pee, but that's when the front door opened.

"Everybody out."

Luis laced up his shoes as best he could as the first men hurried outside. The overseer already had his hand on the door to close it.

"Come on, guys," he urged.

A dozen flatbed trucks with extended beds and modified rails waited to take them to the fields. Luis followed the other men onto the truck and took a seat.

"Hold on to something," the man next to him whispered.

Luis curled his arm under the rail as the truck lurched forward, pulling away from the Blocks.

———

Ernesto was losing his patience. How was it that the young officer in the driver's seat of the cruiser had convinced him to come out to Silver Lake an hour before shift to surveil a location? He glanced over at him.

Young officer? More like a kid only a couple of years removed from his first communion.

"I'm sorry, Deputy"—Ernesto stole a glance to the rookie's name tag—"Poole, but I've got to get to roll call."

The cruiser was parked in a spot that overlooked Sunset Boulevard through a gap between houses. It was sufficiently overgrown to provide a bit of camouflage and was a popular vantage point for cops.

"Give me one more minute," Poole pleaded. "It's too weird. I wasn't even sure there was anything to report, but I don't think I'm the right person to make that decision."

Ernesto nodded and sank back in the passenger seat. He'd give him two minutes. Poole would have to understand that what he was asking was . . .

"There!" Poole said.

Poole pointed to a motel down on Sunset as the door to one of its units swung open. As Ernesto watched, local hood Oscar de Icaza stepped out. His hair was wet, as if he'd just showered. He wore clean clothes and didn't carry a bag. He paused to pop a cigarette into his mouth and light it.

"Okay, you've got Oscar de Icaza," Ernesto said. "You see him do something he shouldn't?"

The drapes nearest the door rustled. Someone else was in the room.

"Somebody with him?"

"Watch."

The door opened. Oscar took the cigarette out of his mouth, leaned over, and kissed someone. Ernesto caught a glimpse of a blond Caucasian woman. Oscar smiled and said something else before putting the cigarette back between his lips and moving to his car.

"You want to pick him up for pandering?" Ernesto asked, incredulous. "I appreciate your enthusiasm, but that'll be a hard case to make."

"She's not a prostitute," Poole scowled. "Wait for her to come out."

Ernesto was intrigued enough to wait for the woman to emerge. He was pretty sure de Icaza, while making a show of being a prosperous small businessman, was actually a car thief up to his eyeballs in illegality. If Poole had stumbled across something they could charge him with, it'd be worth it for the search warrant on his business alone.

When she came out, Ernesto was surprised. She was too pretty, too pulled together to be a prostitute, even a high-end one. If there was anything he'd learned in the Sheriff's Department, it was if you thought you were looking at a prostitute, whether a junkie-looking streetwalker or a fashionably dressed escort pumping gas into her VW Bug at eight in the morning, you were probably right.

This wasn't that. The woman climbing into her eighty-thousand-dollar SUV looked more like an upper-class suburban mom, with big blond hair, jeans, and a fashionable blouse.

"They were here all night?"

"No. According to the guy at the desk, they got a room here on Sunday night and didn't leave until the next morning. Then Oscar called around five thirty this morning and said he needed a room again, pronto. That's when she came back, just before dawn."

"You're already working some desk clerk as an informer?" Ernesto asked.

"Well, yeah," Poole affirmed. "The owner's trying to clean out the drugs so he can sell the place. So the clerk calls me when he sees anything suspicious."

Good on you, Ernesto thought, meaning it.

"This qualified?"

"Do you recognize her?" Poole asked.

Ernesto shook his head.

"I figured it was pandering, so I ran her plates."

Poole swiveled the in-car computer screen around to Ernesto.

Fuck. Me.

"Helen Story?"

"Yeah. I found a couple of pictures online to make sure it wasn't just somebody using her car. That was her. I heard the other day you were asking around about some case her husband's involved with, so I thought I should tell you."

A deputy DA's wife sleeping with a crime figure who just happens to be a former cohort of Luis Chavez? Yeah, that's the kind of thing I need to know about.

"Who else knows?" Ernesto asked.

"Just you," Poole said. "I thought you might know him or something."

"I don't. But I need you to keep this under your hat until I do."

Ernesto eyed Poole. The rookie nodded, looking giddy that his instinct to call in the big guns had been right.

Ernesto exited Poole's cruiser and headed to his own. The day hadn't even begun and he already had a bad feeling about where it was headed.

XXIII

The drive from the Blocks to the fields was a short one. They'd gone down the gravel road, passed through some unused pasture, and crossed through another checkpoint where the road became paved. This carried them through a last gate onto an isolated road with no cars or street signs. They continued until the fields on both sides went from scrub brush to cultivated rows of strawberry plants.

The convoy then split apart, each truck heading to a different section. The one where Luis and the newcomers were to work was about in the dead center of the vast plot. The driver hopped out and waved the men onto the field. The sun was just beginning its ascent in the eastern sky.

"Probably the first and only time you'll ever hear this," the man said in Spanish, "but we're all about quantity over quality here. Every berry you see is already sold. If it's fresh and pretty, it'll end up in the supermarket next week. If it's just starting to go, it'll be frozen. If it's shit, it'll be pulped, dried, or juiced. Luckily, that ain't your job to decide. You get them off the plant and into the bins. Call out when you've got a full one, and a new one'll be brought over. We go until an hour before sundown. Keep hydrated, shitter's over there, and we'll bring lunch in a few hours. Go to!"

The men moved right to the rows. There was no lollygagging, no questions, no easing into the work. Luis found a row with an empty bin at the end. He started picking.

This was not what he expected.

No matter where he looked, there was nothing to indicate any connection to the Marshak corporation. Not a logo on the packaging, nothing on the sides of trucks, no uniforms, no signs.

For the next half hour, the flatbed trucks returned to deposit more and more workers to different sections of the fields. He assumed they were from the other trucks he had seen at the Blocks. The sheer size of the workforce was enough for Luis to get a handle on just how vast the fields must be.

Never was a group dropped near his own, however. It was a way of preventing workers from other apartments from intermingling. They couldn't really communicate in the Blocks except when coming or going, and the same went for the fields. Isolating the groups likely cut down on the sharing of controversial ideas.

But do they know they are practically slaves? Luis wondered. They were well fed, well housed—or well-enough housed—they were promised women, they'd been given some arbitrary price they had to work off, and there must be word out there that those who worked hard enough would get paid at some point or even get their own land.

So what happened to those who questioned it? Were they threatened with getting shipped back south of the border? Thrown to local law enforcement? Or did the guns in the waistbands of every overseer do the trick? No questions asked. Keep your head down and keep working and no one gets hurt.

It was madness.

Luis worked in silence for much of the morning. No one spoke to him during the first break or when he called for a new bin. Not that the other workers talked that much either, but there was the occasional utterance of frustration or the joke met with laughter.

Until midmorning.

A shout rang out from a couple of sections over. Luis feared someone had gotten hurt and glanced over. Men stood and pointed.

In the western sky a thick brushstroke of black smoke wisped up into the lower stratosphere. Its connection to the ground below looked severed, the cloud cut free to roam with the wind.

"Small fire," Luis said.

"No way," one of the men closest to him said. "That much smoke? *Big* fire. I bet that's somebody's fields, man."

The speaker watched for a second longer, then went back to work. Luis kept staring, paralyzed. He told himself it was a coincidence, that it couldn't be the Higuera fields. But he found it a thought near-impossible to banish.

———

The fire at the Higuera farm had been burning for hours before Henry Marshak arrived. Three different firehouses had responded to the blaze. The fear was always that the fire could spread at will. Henry had heard about it on the radio, the traffic lady saying it was "under control" but that the wind might carry the smoke up to the highway. When she'd read off the location, Henry had turned around his truck, knowing it could only be the Higuera farm.

"We had a helicopter for a while," the fire chief told Henry after he'd clambered out of his truck. "He directed us to how far it had gone, and we were able to put some corners on it."

"The workers?" Henry asked.

"We checked the gulley where those workers have that tarp city. Everyone had cleared out."

But Henry could tell from the hesitation in the chief's voice he was holding out on him.

"What about the house?" Henry asked.

The chief glanced around, then sighed.

"No confirmation yet, but it's looking like we've got two sets of remains in there. Ventura County sheriffs are taking a look. The fire burned the house down to its foundation. We're thinking it might've started there, took the folks inside by surprise."

Henry didn't believe that. One look into the chief's eyes told him he didn't buy it, either. Henry thanked the chief for the heads-up and moved to the edge of the field. The flames had darkened everything in their path, snaking through the rows like a thresher. But the dark patches closest to the house had burned differently from the rest. A faster burn. That suggested accelerant.

Shit.

Henry watched as a couple of the firefighters dug trenches, throwing dirt on the smoldering remnants. The remaining harvest was lost, but if this had been an accident, a part of Henry could've been happy. Fire was a rejuvenating force after all, injecting soil with a massive amount of nitrogen. When things grew back, the fields' yield would be ten times what it had been before.

But it was the Higuera farm, and given what had already happened here, all Henry felt was guilt.

That this was his fault wasn't a question. He was still playing catch-up, but he was sure of this. It was the how that he hadn't quite sorted, but he was getting close to that, too.

He moved toward the house, where a Ventura County medical examiner's truck was parked. Two yellow sheets marked the location of the two bodies. A sheriff's deputy moved to wave him back, then recognized him. Henry didn't need to go much farther anyway.

He reached the house. He kneeled down and placed his hand flat on the concrete. It still radiated warmth.

"You know who might've been in here?" a uniformed fire marshal, another acquaintance, asked, moving to Henry's side.

"Probably a couple of workers squatting here instead of the arroyo over there."

The fire marshal glanced over to the culvert. When he turned back, Henry was already walking away.

"Take care, Henry," the marshal called.

Henry waved over his shoulder but kept walking.

———

With every snip of the barber's scissors, Whillans had to banish the belief that this would be his last haircut. He stared at himself in the mirror, eyeing the old man's face, where he still thought a young man resided, and wondered if he should've paid more attention to the changes. He recognized himself, because who else would be staring back at him from the mirror? But in truth it was an aged version of who he saw in his mind's eye. When had all these changes happened?

He chuckled at this thought. Then another snip and . . .

Will this truly be my last?

Though he'd promised Bridgette he wouldn't, he'd gone on the Internet to look up what he could expect from this kind of cancer. Everything suggested that it would happen fast. One day he'd be all right, suffering through chemo but on his feet. Then the failing liver would invite the kidneys to fail along with it, and that'd be it. The body couldn't process urine anymore, so jaundice was next. Death arrived in days.

Whillans's doctors could only assure him he'd be pain-free throughout. This meant doping him into oblivion to the point he probably wouldn't even know when he'd entered his final hours. He'd probably pass in his sleep anyway.

Thank you, God, for Bridgette, he prayed for the umpteenth time that day.

He could only imagine what it'd be like if the archdiocese found out. They'd whip into action, throw him in some sort of assisted-living facility, hire round-the-clock care, and get their parishioners to pray. He'd be fed, cleaned, drugged, and have his diapers professionally changed. He'd die surrounded by dutiful strangers.

Besides knowing who he'd want to see and not see, what books he might like read aloud to him, or what his moods might suggest about his condition, Bridgette would be *with him* through this. She'd feel his pain and shoulder some of it herself to ease it. She loved him, and this meant everything.

The barbershop was only three blocks from St. Augustine's, so he walked back after. He had a lot to think about, particularly when it came to the parish. He wanted it to be a smooth, painless transition. It could happen, but he couldn't do it on his own. He'd need help.

He'd just reached St. Augustine's and was thinking he might keep walking when he spotted the large white Cadillac in the parking lot. Though its appearance—or, more importantly, whose appearance it heralded—made him want to not walk but *run* away, never to return, he sighed and made his way to the nave.

Nice to know your sense of humor remains intact, O Lord, Whillans sighed.

He entered through a side door, moved up past the pews and the altar to the administrative wing beyond. Seated in the hall was a fastidious little priest named Uli something, who stood as Whillans approached.

"I'm not the Holy Father, Uli, so you need not stand," Whillans said. "But nice to see you, too."

The priest didn't know what to say to this, so he quickly sat back down, folding his hands in his lap.

He'll be the next archbishop, Whillans chuckled.

The man waiting in Whillans's office was decked out in a full ceremonial cassock, complete with rochet and scarlet chimere. To the pastor, it felt like he'd stumbled onto a Mardi Gras float.

"Ah, Father Whillans," Bishop Osorio said, shoving an iPhone back into his pocket. "You were at the barber?"

"I was."

Osorio made a scolding sound with his teeth.

"I remember when I was in Rome the barbers came to us," Osorio said grandly. "It wasn't vanity."

Of course not.

"The business of the church was all-consuming. There was no time for anything. We worked around the clock at a breakneck pace. That's what killed our beloved Pope John Paul thirty days after his election, not poison or a Mafia hit. The tailors came to us, the cobblers, the laundresses, the florists, the perfumers . . ."

Thank you again, Lord, for sparing me a post in the Eternal City, Whillans thought.

"Sounds spiritually invigorating," he offered. "Now what can I do for you, Bishop Emeritus?"

Osorio wrinkled his brow at "Emeritus" but then eyed Whillans closely.

"It has come to the attention of the diocese that one of your priests has gone, well, *rogue.*"

Osorio's eyes fluttered, as if he couldn't believe it himself.

"Gone rogue?" Whillans asked. "Can we really do that?"

"You don't even want to know who I mean?"

"I assumed that was forthcoming," Whillans replied, refusing to be baited.

"It is Father Chavez," Osorio said. "Which is why the situation is so near to my heart."

"What has he done?"

"You mean other than the incident with the woman the other night?" Osorio asked.

"You mean when he was attacked, trying to prevent her from being kidnapped?"

Osorio waved this away as if they were the same thing.

"If you'll recall, the woman was here against the better judgment of many in the archdiocese. But now he's taken things a step farther."

Whillans could see the bishop was enjoying this, but he knew playing along was the only way he'd get the bishop to finish his story.

"How so?"

"Do you know where he is right now?"

"I relaxed his duties to allow him time to mend."

"Would you believe, up in the Santa Ynez Valley?" Osorio announced. "Harvesting strawberries?"

Whillans froze, limiting his reaction. He didn't want to give Osorio the satisfaction of surprising him.

"Is that a sin?" Whillans asked.

"It is when he's playing detective," Osorio snapped. "He's up there looking for that . . . *woman*. Do you understand? A woman!"

"I hear what you're saying, but I have no reason to believe his interest in Odilia Garanzuay is prurient. No matter what you seem determined to imply."

Osorio raised his hands in horror that anyone might think him capable of such a thought.

"What Father Chavez chooses to do with his time off is up to him," Whillans said. "I have no reason to believe he won't be exemplary in his conduct. He's done nothing to make me question his commitment to God."

This did nothing to mollify Osorio.

"And if he embarrasses the archdiocese?" Osorio said acidly. "There are those who won't blame the novice so much as his parish priest. Think about that the next time you're wondering why you've never been consecrated as a bishop."

"Who is or isn't in favor with the diocese has never been of interest to me. If Father Chavez is following a course he believes in, I think we should give him the benefit of the doubt that he's not doing it outside of God's purview."

Osorio simmered on this before dismissing it with a sad shake of the head.

"Luis Chavez is like the faithful dog searching for a worthy master," Osorio said. "That master is meant to be you. He is too young and inexperienced to fully extrapolate the will of God. Give him too much agency and you will ruin him."

With that, Osorio rose to leave.

"Thank you," Whillans said.

Osorio turned back to him, surprised.

"You're right. I will speak to him."

"We are a clergy of fatherless sons, Gregory," Osorio said in the doorway. "Sometimes the ones who run to us are as damaged as the ones we'll never reach."

Pompous ass.

XXIV

Midway through the day, a pair of overseers came to Luis's row. They'd been the ones driving the trucks full of strawberry bins away throughout the morning, occasionally taking a couple of workers with them. They'd so far left Luis alone, but now they stood over him.

"Hey, don't know if you've noticed, but the guys have taken turns riding to the warehouses with us to cool off," said the taller of the pair, whose accent sounded vaguely Honduran. "You're the only one who hasn't volunteered."

"Warehouses?" Luis asked.

"Yeah, walk-in refrigerators. You get a few minutes of cool breeze on the ride, fifteen minutes of freezer time, then back out in this heat. I mean, we can give somebody else your spot, but fair's fair."

Luis was already on his feet. The Honduran smiled.

"Let's go."

It was a longer drive than Luis expected. From his row he could tell the fields were vast. Passing alongside them on a seemingly endless road, however, made him think there was enough food here to feed the entire country.

The Honduran and his pal—a silent, brooding type with scars on his face—sat up front, while Luis and another newcomer, Rodolfo, were in back with the berries. Though they didn't get much of a breeze, stretching out in the small space behind the containers did wonders for Luis's back.

"Are you really a priest?" Rodolfo asked a few minutes into the journey.

"I am."

"Where'd you grow up?"

"All over. You?"

"Oaxaca," Rodolfo said.

"Where? My mother was from Monjas."

"That's funny. I'm from Ejutla de Crespo."

Luis nodded. It was just up the highway, if he remembered right. They talked for a few minutes longer, and Luis got the whole story. Just as he had suggested to Michael Story, a recruiter had come around Rodolfo's town with stories of jobs up north. Most didn't believe him, until he whipped out his iPhone and showed them pictures.

"He told us that the easiest way to get citizenship was to have a legal job waiting," Rodolfo explained. "He showed us the paperwork and everything. We just got docked a transport fee. We had to find our own way up to the Port of Manzanillo in Colima, but they said they'd take care of the rest. When they saw it was a cargo container on a ship and not some truck, my friends bailed. I got on. I had nothing to lose. When they hear from me, man, they're going to kick themselves."

Luis nodded. He knew what this must look like to someone who'd known nothing but abject poverty.

"You like the States?" Rodolfo asked.

"Like anywhere, it's got the good and the bad."

Rodolfo took a strawberry out of the nearest bin, pulled off the leaves, and popped it into his mouth. "So far it's pretty great."

The truck slowed. Luis saw a cluster of single-story warehouses positioned at the edge of the fields. Each was about the size of half a football field, with over a dozen such buildings arranged in neat rows. On each side were large garage doors, though some had sloped driveways to allow tractor-trailers to be loaded without ramps.

He suddenly got a bad feeling. Had he been so easily talked into riding into an ambush? If they attacked him in the fields, there'd be plenty of witnesses. The warehouses, on the other hand, were isolated and closed off. No one would see and no one would question.

These thoughts pricked at him as the truck came to a stop inside one of the buildings. He stayed behind as Rodolfo and the drivers piled out. Only after his new friend had carted out the first few bins did he stand up.

"Hey, if you want to stay in the hot truck, be my guest," Rodolfo said. "Just don't let the overseers catch you lazing."

Though the boxes of strawberries were heavy, the work felt good. Instead of being bowed over in the fields, Luis carried the crates upright, allowing him to stretch a little more and pull his leg muscles straight as well. It was nowhere near as bad as the first few days in Santiago's fields, but he was still stiff.

The best part about it was that the refrigerators were as promised: *cool.*

"Slow down, Padre!" Rodolfo joked as Luis stacked another three bins atop one another. "You in a hurry to get back to the fields?"

Luis eyed the Honduran overseer, who shrugged. He replaced two of the boxes and walked just one into the fridge this time.

"*Much* better," Rodolfo enthused, doing the same. "Let's stretch this out to an hour. At least."

Luis laughed and took his time.

When the truck was half-empty, he happened to look out toward the road. Bouncing toward the warehouses was a large F-150 pickup pulling a trailer. It was the contents of the trailer that captured his attention. It was a car, one with multiple blue tarps roped onto it. The tarps did a good job of obscuring what lay beneath, but the lower half of the wheels and a sliver of chassis were visible. Its tires were slashed. But as Luis had been in the car less than twenty-four hours before, he knew immediately whose it was.

Maria's.

Everything his vocation had given him was stripped away in an instant: the discipline, the peace, his devotion to God. What stood in its place was the man he'd once been. He wanted to kill someone.

———

Miguel had done it. It had taken all night, but it was done. Sure, he would have to spend the day making calls, returning confirmation e-mails, and faxing—yes, faxing—paperwork to banks and a handful of less reputable institutions, but that was just knocking down the dominoes he'd spent all night lining up.

It hadn't been easy. There were a few things he'd still have to go back and fix. But by and large it was a beautiful machine. Once it was turned on, Basmadjian would look like a moderately successful small businessman who'd invested shrewdly and diversified wisely. There was nothing suspicious about it, nothing implemented that an incredibly well-paid consulting firm wouldn't have recommended as well.

Miguel's only fear was that in his zeal he'd made himself superfluous. This could be ameliorated by stressing his singular ability to maintain the system and how the subtleties of how it all fit together were in his head.

He hoped that would be enough to save his life.

Now he needed fresh air. He'd smoked seven or eight joints over the course of the night and craved convenience-store pizza and Peanut M&M's. He'd already decided not to go to school. He'd find a way to convince his mom it was okay.

He was still seriously stoned on the walk to the convenience store two blocks away. He considered buying a few slices but opted for the whole pizza. Might as well live it up. He filled his arms with candy and energy drinks, dropping them next to the register as the clerk boxed up his breakfast.

When he turned onto his street and saw the squad car parked in front of his house, his first reaction was incredulity. How the hell had they caught him already? Had they seen him leave Basmadjian's place? Had he made some ridiculous rookie mistake that set off alarm bells without him even knowing it? Or worse, had he been so naïve to think the old man wouldn't sell him out the second he was done?

As he got closer, he could see the officers' faces. There was a man and a woman. Both looked drawn, both looked hesitant. The man knocked on the door.

"Hello? Mrs. Higuera? It's the police department. We need to talk to you. There's been a fire. Mrs. Higuera? Are you in there?"

It was the politest tone he'd ever heard from a law enforcement officer. Before he'd even finished the thought, he knew his mother must be dead. The information drained him of thought. He felt as if the earth had suddenly lost its hold on him, gravity weakening to the point that he was neither attached nor bound to anything. It felt empty, like every action he'd ever take again would be meaningless now. He didn't want to know what happened, he didn't want revenge; he simply wanted to blink out from existence as well.

Instead of turning up his sidewalk, he kept walking. He felt the eyes of one of the officers on his back, as if wondering if he might know the person they were looking for. He didn't turn around. He stayed away until long after dark.

Back up in the fields, Luis spent the rest of his day in prayer. Not the kind he'd tutored himself in, but the excoriating, accusatory brand that demanded answers from God. When there was no answer, he taunted God by reeling off the horrible things he would do in his name. This drove him on. His rhythm picked up, and he matched the veteran workers in his harvest. It wasn't conscious. His movements were a reflex as his mind stormed on.

He was just beginning to slow when the trucks came to take them back to the Blocks. As the first to arrive that morning, they were first to leave.

"You guys did great today," one of the overseers said.

Luis wanted to ask the man if maybe he'd killed Maria personally or just watched. He wanted to strip the man's scalp from his skull. He'd seen photos of how warriors used to do it. He was pretty sure he could do the same.

"Padre?"

Luis turned. The old man who'd taken his Bible that morning eyed him with worry.

"You can't look at the overseers like that."

"Like what?"

"Like *that*. You think they can't see?"

Luis saw concern on the man's face but also fear.

"They killed a friend of mine last night," Luis said.

The old man absorbed this for a long moment.

"I'm very sorry."

"You don't seem surprised."

"You hear things, Father," he replied. "It's how they keep everyone in place."

"If you knew this, why did you come?" Luis asked, incredulous.

"You can't escape violence, particularly when it's visited on those who can't fight back. I accept the world as it is and try to make my way through it. Isn't that what God wants?"

"No. God expects us to do something about it."

"You believe that?"

"Yes. It's what he's been telling me to do since the beginning," Luis said, nodding. "I just couldn't hear him."

XXV

On the drive back to the Blocks, Luis formulated his plan. He pictured the apartment in his head, going over it inch by inch. The designers had done their job well. There was no way through the burglar bars, and the only window without them was the small frosted-glass one above the toilet in the bathroom. But this didn't help, as not only had it been installed backwards, to be locked from the outside like the front doors, it was too small to wriggle through.

The only way out was the way they came in.

At first Luis had thought even that was impossible. When he'd been brought in the night before, he'd glimpsed a magnetic sensor for a burglar alarm screwed into the door frame and a second in the door itself. But when he checked it out a second time that morning, he saw no sign that the rest of the system had been installed. He couldn't decide if this was an oversight or if the builders believed the sensor plates were deterrent enough.

Besides, a real alarm would draw attention. It couldn't connect to any legitimate alarm company that might call the cops. But to get through the door itself, he'd have to crack the keyed doorknob with a makeshift skeleton key, then cut through the plywood panel to pull the sliding bolt and lower the kick-proof jamb. Not impossible, just dangerously time consuming.

Most everyone was in bed by nine. To a man they were exhausted, some still sleeping off the journey from Mexico. Luis had to force himself to stay awake for at least another hour before setting to work. He'd said nothing of his plans to anyone but received a few querulous looks when he moved his sleeping place from the living room to the cold kitchen floor.

At ten, some of the men were still stirring, so Luis waited another hour. He recited the Bible to himself as he waited for just the right moment to begin work on the door.

> Joshua 10:6. The Gibeonites then sent word to Joshua in the camp at Gilgal: "Do not abandon your servants. Come up to us quickly and save us! Help us, . . ."

> Joshua 10:7. So Joshua marched up from Gilgal with his entire army, including all the best fighting men.

> Joshua 10:8. The Lord said to Joshua, "Do not be afraid of them; I have given them into your hand. Not one of them will be able to withstand you."

At half past eleven he made his move. He made quick work of the keyed lock with a skeleton key fashioned from wire he'd pulled from a warehouse freezer fan. Using a stem cutter he'd smuggled in from the fields and broken until it resembled a crude box cutter, he stabbed into the door where he estimated the bolt base to be on the other side.

Though the four men sleeping a few feet from where Luis worked hadn't stirred as he unlocked the doorknob, he doubted he'd be as lucky when he began sawing into the wood. He said a prayer, pulled back the cutter, and sawed.

It was easier than he'd envisioned, the wood coming apart like wood shavings as he cut. He could be out in minutes.

"Wha . . . what're you doing?"

It was Rodolfo. Luis was already formulating his response when he saw that everyone in the room was awake.

"What are you doing?" Rodolfo asked, sterner now.

Luis had to say something. As he opened his mouth, another voice cut through the darkness.

"He's doing as God asked him," said the old man, now standing in the bedroom doorway. "And we are going back to sleep, having not seen nor heard anything. Understood?"

No one said anything, for or against. Finally, Rodolfo lowered himself back onto his bedroll and closed his eyes. The others followed suit. The old man eyed Luis as if reconsidering his words. Then he disappeared into the bedroom and closed the door.

Luis resumed his work. This time he cut all the way through the door so he could noiselessly lower the jamb to the ground.

Cool night air rushed in around him as he turned the knob and stepped into the night. He closed it behind him and started running.

———

Luis had never seen the heavens like this. The longer he looked, the more stars he saw, layers revealing layers beyond and layers beyond that. It was a staggering sight, one he wished he could enjoy. After a day of anger it brought him a modicum of peace.

Knowing overseers might be on the road, he stayed close to the foothills. He had no idea how well they guarded the Blocks at night, but as there had been no reaction to the clatter of the lock, security obviously wasn't as tight as he'd imagined. Still, no need to take chances.

Maria.

He couldn't chase her from his mind. He wanted to believe she was alive and tried to convince himself of this. The car meant nothing. That voice in his head that told him the smoke on the horizon was from the Higuera farm was mistaken. He wanted badly to believe.

He estimated he'd been gone from the Blocks for almost forty-five minutes, doing his best to stay in the shadows while following the path he took to the fields each day. When he didn't come upon the warehouses immediately, he worried he was off target.

Even on foot it shouldn't have taken this long.

The stars and the outlines of the mountains to the east were his only guides. He made his best guess and headed in a new direction. When he finally reached one of the fences, he rejoiced and crossed it at a post. The fields couldn't be far now.

Five minutes later he tripped on a cabbage. He'd entered the fields without realizing it. He wondered how close he was to the paved roads.

As if on cue, a pair of headlights appeared in the distance. Luis dove to the ground, flattening himself on the soil between the rows of fledgling cabbage. He waited for the vehicle to turn off, but it continued straight toward him.

He considered hurrying farther into the fields, putting some distance between him and the nearing vehicle, but that was just inviting the headlights to pick up his movement. He was trapped.

He froze, stiff as a corpse. The cabbages, a fall crop, weren't to be harvested for another three months. The plants were barely three inches high. Even prone he was visible.

Lord, let them look the other way.

He pushed his face into the dirt but didn't dare move any other part of his body. If he could have eaten the dirt, he would have. The light was already washing over the cabbage fields. It would be seconds before the pool reached him. He shut his eyes, but the white penetrated his eyelids as if they were clear glass. The sound grew louder.

Luis's thoughts turned to the last moments of his brother's life. Nicolas had been on his way home from seeing Osorio at Sacred Heart Church. He'd gone up the hill on Coronado Street and was crossing to Montana when the two bullets pierced his chest. No one knew if he'd seen the two men sitting in the car he'd just walked past or the one who emerged from the darkness on the other side of the street with the pistol.

The man behind the steering wheel died at the scene. The one in the passenger seat died on the way to Hollywood Presbyterian. The shooter was caught three blocks from the scene and went away for life despite having been a minor when he pulled the trigger. He was killed in prison two years later.

Nicolas had died instantly.

Luis still remembered the day Nicolas said he should stop hanging out with Oscar and his crew. He'd laughed in his face and threatened to beat him to a pulp.

Nicolas, forgive me.

The truck's engine was so loud that Luis had to scream the prayer for absolution in his mind. If this was to be his final thought, so be it. He held on to the image of his brother so tight that he almost cried out.

The sound and the light receded. The truck had never slowed or wavered from its path. Luis waited a moment longer, then resumed his march.

The warehouses glowed in the distance like an earthbound moon. There were a few industrial pole lights, as well as several task lights, rising over their generators to illuminate every corner of the complex, whether anyone was working there or not.

As he neared, he saw a handful of workers loading flats onto tractor-trailers. Still, he'd need an excuse for his presence if questioned.

I fell asleep and everybody was gone. I missed my ride back.

He knew it wouldn't fly if they spoke to any of the drivers, but it was better than nothing.

He kept his head down, his hands in his pockets, and his gait even. When he looked up, his still-adjusting eyes saw everything haloed in oranges and yellows. He didn't even realize he'd passed a group of workers until he'd walked by. He didn't risk a look back.

Every garage and door he passed was locked with a heavy padlock, the service doors with key locks. He had his mangled skeleton key but feared he'd be noticed. He got lucky. A service door was unlocked. He strode in like this had been his destination the whole time.

The lights were off inside, the large space lit only by the red glow of emergency exit signs. The layout was the same as that of the warehouse he'd been in earlier that day. There were four walk-in refrigerators, but they were all off in this building. He moved carefully through the center of the warehouse, larger objects appearing in silhouette. Pallet jacks and storage bins revealed themselves as his eyes adjusted to the shadows, but no sign of Maria's car.

What he did find was a pry bar.

He knew it was risky, but he would only get one shot at this. Lowering the bar to his side, he stepped out of the empty warehouse and walked back to the first locked garage door in the row. He stabbed one end of the pry bar between the shackle and body of the padlock, glanced around, then threw his weight against the other end.

It didn't budge. He changed the angle, manipulating the lock until it was horizontal to the ground. Then he stomped on it. This time the shackle popped right off. He set the pry bar aside and slid back the bolt. The garage door threw up a massive metallic clatter as he lifted it, so Luis only raised it a foot and rolled under.

Though the refrigerators were on in this one, the warehouse was as empty as the first. Luis checked every corner as thoroughly as he could in the dark, then slipped back out. He popped the locks on three more garage doors before hitting pay dirt.

This warehouse was used as storage. Stacks of wooden pallets rose to the ceiling alongside bolts of transparent pallet wrap. Forklifts were plugged in and charging overnight. But Luis's eyes had picked out the size and shape of the car and trailer immediately. The truck that had towed it there was nowhere to be seen.

Luis climbed onto the trailer and tugged at the ropes holding the tarps in place. They didn't budge. He tried tearing the tarp from around the base of the car, but it held fast.

As he made his way around the car, looking for any spot where the tarp might have met a sharp edge, his foot crunched down on something small and hard. It crumbled under his shoe. He bent and picked a pebble of safety glass out of the tread.

He ran his fingers along the driver-side windows. Both were solid. He checked the back windshield, then moved to the front. His fingers found something sharp. Carefully, he traced the edges of a baseball-sized hole in the windshield, finding the tarp thinner from wearing against the broken glass. He tried to tear it with his fingers. When that didn't work, he leaned all the way over and tore into it with his teeth. When he worked open a large enough gap, he dug his fingers in and pulled it apart. The material unzipped down to the hood and up to the roof, stopped only by the ropes.

He didn't need more.

Though Maria's body wasn't inside, it was clear she'd spent the last moments of her life there. Even in the dim light he could see that the driver's seat was bent backwards at a terrible angle and the headrest was missing. The steering wheel looked like it had been kicked off its column. The dashboard was shattered, and someone had torn the cover off the center console.

With their fingernails, Luis realized.

There was no mistaking the moment of great violence that had happened here. Luis said a prayer for Maria even as he watched her last terrifying moments in his mind's eye. He wanted to tell her how sorry he was for dragging her into this. That he would bring her killers to justice. That her death wouldn't be in vain any more than her brother's had been.

But his words felt empty. Really, what could he promise that didn't sound like a lie?

He pushed himself off the car and contemplated his next move. He'd take the information back to Michael Story, but what if the car was gone when he got back? Would Story just tell him again how sorry he was but his hands were tied?

Damned to know the truth but unable to prove it: the fate of priests.

Something moved. Luis froze. The warehouse lights came on and the copper-eyed man who'd assaulted him beside the tractor-trailer his first night at the Blocks stepped forward.

"My God, look at you, Father," the man snarled. "What is it the Bible says? 'The day of the Lord will come like a thief in the night'? What would your God think about you breaking in like this?"

"Who do you think led me here?" Luis shot back.

"Tough words for a dead man," the overseer said, producing a rubber police baton. "And if you think I have any qualms about killing a priest, don't worry. Given the number of people I've killed up to this point, I doubt I could be any deeper in the Lord's black books than I already am."

XXVI

The beating was short. Luis had endured much worse. It was half over before he realized that the man the men called Matachín and his boys were going at him at half strength. They obviously didn't want to turn the unmarked warehouses into a crime scene.

"That's enough," Matachín said finally, Luis in a bloody heap at his feet. "Throw him in the back of my truck."

Luis barely felt it when they lifted him off the ground. They carried him to the back of the truck like a load of tools or, worse, like he was already dead. He wasn't in bad enough shape to go into shock, but he could feel himself shutting down.

"We heard you were some hard-ass gangbanger back in the day, Padre," Matachín said, climbing into the truck bed beside him. "You should've known to stay away."

Luis said nothing. Matachín rapped twice on the back window of the cab. The truck, followed by a second one, pulled away from the warehouses onto a dirt road.

"The crazy thing is I didn't recognize you last night. I guess when I saw you at the church and then behind the Whittaker woman's house,

I was looking at you through night-vision specs. But when Maria Higuera's car was seen near the Blocks last night, it wasn't hard to guess why. Figured if we pulled her car past the fields a couple of times, you'd emerge from the woodwork, too."

"You killed her?" Luis croaked, eyeing the pistol in his attacker's belt. It was some kind of mod with a long barrel. The kind one could use for long-distance shooting. Like from a ridge all the way to a front driveway.

Matachín said nothing. He jabbed lightly at Luis's face with his boot.

"Why don't we be quiet for a while?"

It wasn't a request.

"Where's Odilia?"

Matachín eyed him as if deciding whether to answer. He shrugged.

"She was just a few doors down from yours and up a flight of stairs. Your God didn't bother telling you any of that? You ever think he just likes fucking with people?"

Matachín lit a cigarette and looked out into the darkness as if bored with it all. Any thought Luis might have harbored of this being an interrogation he'd walk away from evaporated. They'd done this a dozen times: snatched someone, thrown them in a truck, driven them to the middle of nowhere, and put a bullet in their head. They'd put more thought into what to eat for breakfast.

"You're Chavez, like Chavez Ravine?"

"Chavez like nothing. Like Rodriguez. Like Smith."

"My grandparents were up in there," Matachín said, exhaling smoke. "They had a house in La Loma. You know the story?"

Luis did but wanted the man to keep talking, so feigned ignorance.

"Chavez Ravine was that chunk of East LA by Echo Park. Three neighborhoods—La Loma, Palo Verde, and La Bishop. Mostly poor Mexicans, all in these run-down, dirt-floor houses going up the sides of the ravine. Some *güero* from the city came along and told them if they vacated they'd get first dibs on a new housing development going up there. My grandparents, God love 'em, packed their shit and left like everybody else. A few weeks later the city razed the barrio. Weeks go by, then months. No one's saying anything. No one's building. Where are the developments? 'Guess what, *papi* and *mamá*? The city's changed their mind. Dodgers are coming out from Brooklyn and they need a stadium.' Guess where they found the land?"

Matachín took a last puff of his cigarette, lit a second one with the tip, and tossed the first out of the truck.

"I guess the only difference now is that companies and the city"—he indicated to himself and then over to Luis—"use us against each other now."

Luis thought about this for a long moment and nodded. Then he added, "My brother was killed up near there."

"No shit?" Matachín said. "Telling you. It's bad news for everybody." Matachín went quiet for a while after this.

Luis knew the overseers wouldn't do their dirty work close to home, but it seemed like hours had passed. He stared up at the stars, idly wondering if anyone was staring back.

They moved from a gravel road to one of packed earth. Though on his back, Luis could tell from the lack of trees and the dust kicked up by the truck that they had left the farmable land behind. This was the desert.

"Almost there," Matachín said idly, lighting a third cigarette.

The truck slowed as it bumped onto an incline. Luis slid toward the tailgate before Matachín stopped his progress with his boot. They wound up a hill. Luis saw boulders and cacti off the driver's side of the truck. His heart rate, which he'd struggled to contain, accelerated.

He banished a thought of Nicolas. When he'd conjured him before, it was because he needed his forgiveness. He didn't want to think of his brother as a witness to this.

The incline flattened out, and the trucks came to a stop. Matachín dropped the tailgate and hopped out, barely looking at his captive. It was as if he knew Luis wouldn't run. Not now. He grabbed Luis under both arms and dragged him out of the truck bed.

"Walk on your own," he said.

Luis looked around. There was an old fire tower in front of the trucks, as well as a shack tucked into the nearby rocks. Beyond that an endless stretch of darkness. He could only get a sense of how high up they were from where the star field met the land on the horizon. He glanced to the top of the hill, where it formed a dome like a basilica.

The other men stayed behind Matachín as he guided Luis toward the base of the fire tower. Someone had dug a large hole. Luis realized what it was meant to contain.

"I guess you have no reason to fear what comes next," Matachín commented.

Luis's leg was in motion before Matachín finished his sentence. With his right foot planted firmly in the soil, he fired the heel of his left into the overseer's left kneecap with tremendous force. It snapped like a dry branch. Matachín fell forward as Luis turned around and grabbed the pistol from the crippled man's waistband. Luis made note of its overlong barrel. This weapon was designed for distance.

Luis only needed it to shoot a target two feet away.

The first round tore through Matachín's heart, the second his face. The men behind him reacted quickly, but Luis was faster. He shot a second man in the hip, a third in the arm. By the time answering rounds were flying back at him, Luis was rolling to the hip-shot man and grabbing his gun. He shot a fourth in the gut, raised the second pistol, and aimed in the direction of the three still standing.

"Take one truck and go!" he shouted. "I won't fire."

The arm-shot man managed to shoot back at him, but Luis shot him twice in the chest. One of the remaining gunslingers tried to aim, but Luis sent a bullet into his throat. As the man sank to his knees, blood sheeting out of the wound, the will to fight ebbed from the others. Luis scanned the remaining men until he settled on the only one whose eyes weren't clouded with rage and adrenaline.

A look of mutual self-preservation passed between them. They could either die in seconds or reach a silent accord.

"Let's get out of here," the gunman barked at his comrades, lowering his gun.

"He'll shoot us!"

"I won't," Luis said, trying to sound steady even as he kept his guns trained on the overseers. "Get the wounded into the truck and get the fuck out of here. I won't shoot."

It was over. As Luis shielded himself behind a boulder, the survivors hauled their friends into the bed of the second truck as efficiently as they could. When they stepped toward Matachín, however, Luis waved them off.

"Not him."

No one batted an eye. A few seconds later they were gone.

After counting out four full minutes, Luis moved to Matachín's body. Blood gurgled from a hole in his jaw as his eyes rolled around, unable to fix on anything. His skin had paled and his limbs had gone limp.

"Gnh . . . gnh . . . ," the overseer muttered.

Luis's anger was gone. He knelt beside the man and took his hand.

"O Lord Jesus Christ, most merciful Lord of Earth, we ask that you receive this man into your arms . . ."

Matachín's sightless eyes struggled to locate him as Luis continued the last rites.

"Do you have anything to confess?"

Matachín whispered something into Luis's ear, but he couldn't make out the words. He absolved the dying man of his earthly crimes, recited the prayer of universal thanksgiving, and moved on to the final benediction.

"And thus do I commend thee to you, O Lord, in everlasting peace. A-men."

He crossed himself and took the overseer's hand, but it was cold. He waited until his beating heart had stilled before going through his pockets. Finding a small key, he went to the shack and tried it on the padlock. It snapped open. He dragged the dead man's body into it and locked it back up.

He returned to the truck that had brought him here, slid behind the wheel, and began the long trek back to civilization.

———

When his ringing cell woke him at four in the morning, Michael assumed it was bad news. Good waits for first light. Bad can't wait to unburden itself.

"Hello?" he said.

"The car they killed Maria Higuera in is at an unmarked warehouse facility out in Ventura County. I can give you the coordinates."

Jesus Christ, Michael realized. *The priest.*

"Maria is dead?" he asked, sitting up straight. "The fire was all over the Internet. But the reports said the bodies found in the shack were both male."

"They buried her elsewhere. I know where."

"The Marshaks?"

"No, the army of former gangbangers the Marshaks use to keep their workers in line."

"You can tie them together?"

"No, but I can give you the end of the thread that unravels the whole thing, starting with Annie's killer and the possible murder weapon. I can also give you the guy who gave the order."

A chill ran up Michael's spine, but of excitement, not fear. If he wanted headlines, this would do it.

"Where are you now?"

"I don't want to say. I'll have the physical evidence delivered to your office in the next few hours. But right now you've got to get to that car. I'm also sending you coordinates for two other locations you're going to want to add to your raids this morning."

"*Raids?* What am I looking for?" Michael asked, grabbing a paper and pen.

For the next ten minutes Luis told him everything he knew, from the workers that didn't exist to the way they were brought up from Mexico. When he said that he was in the truck the killers drove, Michael had him pull the registration and read off the license plate. Luis complied, and the stack of actionable information Michael had in front of him grew higher. He considered who he'd have to call first. It would take every favor he'd ever earned to secure the warrants he needed. They'd need strike teams and marshals in multiple locations across two counties. If Luis was wrong about even one detail, this would blow up in Michael's face.

If he was right, however . . .

"Okay," Michael said as Luis finished up. "We can tie the land to the Marshaks and probably more once we get people to talk. But who's on top? Doesn't sound like Glenn Marshak was out there directing things."

"I don't know," Luis admitted. "But that's what I hope to find out."

Luis hung up. Michael stared at the cell as if wondering if what he just heard was a dream. He sensed someone's eyes at the back of his head. He turned to find Helen eyeing him curiously.

"What was all that?" she asked, bewildered.

"Remember this moment when we're packing up."

"What?" Helen scoffed. "Where are we going? The DA's office?"

"Governor's mansion," Michael replied. "We're about to be the top story of every news channel, paper, and website in the world."

PART V

rightly that it involved illegal labor but couldn't guess in which industry. The INS and the FBI were alone in using the words "human trafficking." Only when an agent was told that no, they would not be coordinating with Ventura County law enforcement, did she inform her colleagues that something widespread was afoot.

The Los Angeles district attorney's and US attorney's offices were the only ones that had all the information. The latter was looped in after Justice filed an immediate inquiry with DA Rebenold. When this was ignored, a call from the US attorney general to her personal cell phone came in.

Arrangements to share information and resources were made quickly.

———

At his home in Conejo Valley, Jason Marshak slept in, but it was a troubled sleep. He could scarcely close his eyes without seeing Odilia. It was the same image on repeat, the resignation on her face as they left his uncle's house. She'd looked like a beaten dog, and it was his fault. He told her it would be different once the Crown contract was signed and he was in charge. Glenn would have to understand that his role would be diminished, as Jason would be leading the company into the future. But just like that, he'd shown her how short a leash Glenn had him on.

He should've defended Odilia. Told Glenn that it was his company now and there was nothing he could do about it. Instead, he'd taken her by the arm and raced out like an embarrassed schoolboy. Her disappointment in him burned as hot and raw as it had in the moment.

Once upon a time he'd been able to stomach the reality that he had to share her with several men. If he showed favoritism, took her out of the Blocks too early, she wouldn't respect his authority. She wouldn't be grateful enough to him, her savior. But all that was over now. Santiago

Higuera had believed he loved her more than Jason did, and a part of Odilia had bought into that for whatever reason.

Santiago had probably been a good liar.

But Odilia was a changed person after she'd come back from the desert. She'd learned her lesson. Still, he couldn't let a Santiago happen again. He had to make things right before he went crazy. Anything else prolonged the pain. He knew she was hurting, too. This made it all the more urgent.

He threw back the covers and made a beeline for the shower. He masturbated, thinking only of his Odilia. When he got out, he got dressed, grabbed his keys, and hurried out of the house.

He was energized, thinking of the look on her face when he told her how much he loved her. This time he'd back it up by carrying her away from the Blocks, never to return. He'd even take a few days off. Sure, things were hectic at the office these days and he had multiple meetings with Glenn on the books, but he so seldom took days off, they'd have to respect this.

"I love you," he practiced as he drove. "I *love* you. I love *you*."

He played with the emphasis. He didn't want to be over the top, too flowery or romantic. He wanted sincerity, gravity. There had to be an emphasis on how much the word meant to him and how voicing it was not something he took lightly.

As dawn broke, he turned off the main road and bounced onto the gravel path toward the Blocks. It was a beautiful day. Daydreaming into the cloudless sky, he didn't see the INS trucks until he was twenty yards away.

His immediate impulse was to turn around, but they'd already seen him. *What is this?* He knew everybody at the INS. This couldn't be a real sting, right? The money had gone out the door, and the paperwork was as good as gold. Maybe one of his workers had gotten away and they were returning him.

Shit, I hope they don't expect a reward, he thought.

He pasted a curious look on his face and rolled down the window.

"One of my neighbors darn near panicked seeing you rolling in here with all these trucks, so I told her I'd check it out," he said, pouring on the rube. "Some kind of hazardous material leak or something?"

The INS agent didn't crack a smile.

"Sir, we need you to turn around and return to the main road."

They didn't recognize him. *Oh shit.* They didn't recognize him.

"That bad, huh?" Jason asked, keeping it light.

Before the man could repeat his order, Jason waved a hand.

"I'm going, I'm going."

He pulled a few feet up, executed a quick turn, and was gone before anyone would have time to run his plates.

"What you've done is beyond words," Basmadjian said, sipping his morning OJ from a coffee cup. "I understand maybe not all of it, but I've had friends of ours in the legal field take a look. When even they're impressed, I know I'm onto something. So, thank you."

Miguel nodded, taking the stack of cash from the table and shoving it in his pocket. He only half heard the words. Basmadjian angered.

"You don't like praise?" the old man asked.

"I'm sorry," Miguel said, feigning gratitude. "I'm happy you're satisfied. I wanted to do a good job, but part of that was making sure everything fit together as neatly as possible. If changes need to be made, the system can be upgraded with minimal teardown."

Basmadjian eyed Miguel for a long moment. Then to Miguel's surprise, the old man placed his hand on his.

"I am aware of your family's trouble. I have informed those who need to know that not only are you uninvolved, I have personally guaranteed your safety."

"Do you know who killed my mother?"

"Not the name, no," Basmadjian said softly. "But I have learned that the man who oversaw her killing was already dispatched as well. This was the same person who oversaw the killing of your uncle."

"Who's left?"

Basmadjian pulled away his hand, eyeing Miguel as if he should know better than to ask.

"We can't have vendettas here. There are rules."

"What about cops?" Miguel asked, keeping his gaze steady.

Basmadjian raised an eyebrow. Miguel slid his phone across the table. On the display were photos of two Los Angeles County sheriff's deputies, one white, one Asian.

"I pulled the GPS records from various law enforcement motor pools," Miguel said, voice crackling with anger. "I also found out where the safe houses used by the DA's office are. Their vehicle was parked out front of one of these addresses for less than five minutes around the exact time my uncle disappeared. Judging from their tax records and bank statements, I'm pretty sure they were involved."

"What are you asking me?"

Miguel said nothing. If the old man didn't know, Miguel wasn't going to spell it out for him.

"I asked you a question, Miguel."

"I know what I'm asking. And I know you'll do it."

"Why is that?"

"Because it would put me in your debt."

"Deep in my debt," Basmadjian stressed. "*Permanently* in my debt. You need to ask yourself if this is worth that. You don't get to ask many favors of me."

"I knew what I was asking. And if I didn't think I'd earned it, I wouldn't have asked."

Basmadjian snorted.

"I'm not joking," Miguel pressed, trying to sound older than he was.

"I know you're not," Basmadjian said, handing back the phone. "If that's what you want, it will be handled. Don't think on it again."

Miguel rose to exit, but Basmadjian raised a finger.

"This time I *require* your gratitude," Basmadjian said.

"Thank you," Miguel said, though he felt worse than before he'd walked in the door.

———

Henry thought he had a better sense of the town. He'd grown up here, could remember the construction of every major building. But as he stared at a post office that he'd thought was the police station, he knew he was lost.

"Dammit," he said, sighing.

"Help you with something, old-timer?"

Realizing he might've spoken louder than he'd meant to, Henry turned apologetically to a grinning old man in a postal uniform, who'd sidled up next to him.

"Who are you calling old-timer, old-timer?" Henry said. "Blake, right?"

"Wow! Good memory there, Marshak," the postman nodded.

"Yeah, except for police stations. I thought that was right here."

"Well, you're half-right," the postman said. "About once a week I find a contemporary out here doing the same thing as you. The station moved back in nineteen eighty-*eight*."

The postman pointed across the street to a large building Henry had mistaken for a trade school.

"Ah. Thank you kindly."

Henry moved his truck from the post office parking lot to a curb across the street. Behind the front desk in the station's lobby sat a middle-aged man with a sergeant's stripes on his bicep. He looked too overweight for street duty.

"Morning," Henry said, finding his usual cheerfulness left behind in his truck.

"Can I help you?" the desk sergeant replied, giving Henry an officious stare. "Unfortunately, yes," Henry said, nodding and moving close. "I'm here about the murders of Anne Whittaker, Santiago Higuera, and his sister, Maria Higuera."

The sergeant's features froze, though his hand traveled to something Henry couldn't see under the desk.

"Right now Maria Higuera is simply missing. Do you know otherwise?"

"She's dead, Officer," Henry explained. "I'm the one who killed her and the others. Do you have somebody I can talk to?"

Everything happened quickly after that.

XXVIII

Maria Higuera's car was still smoldering in the fields when the first federal agents came upon it. Due to the haphazard way it'd been torched, a theory quickly circulated that the perpetrators knew law enforcement was onto them. Still roped to the trailer, the car had been abandoned in the middle of a field of bell pepper plants just off the main road and set alight. Deep ruts in the soil and chewed-up foliage marked the path of the truck that hauled it.

They'd done a fairly professional job with the burn, lighting up the interior instead of the exterior and breaking the windows to provide plenty of oxygen. They'd poured lighter fluid across the seats and dashboard as well, leaving the empty canister to burn up inside the car.

Even then the vehicle's make, model, and color were still identifiable as matching those of Maria Higuera's Camry.

"If they were in that big a hurry, then they might have forgotten to destroy the security footage from the warehouse cameras," Michael told the warehouse team leader over his cell phone. "See if you can pull it and send it over to me this morning."

Michael hung up. He was in a convoy of four highway patrol cruisers and two SUVs bearing the door sigils of the Marshals Service en route to the Marshaks' corporate campus in the Santa Ynez foothills a few miles from the unmarked warehouses. The road was flanked by fields, workers already pulling up the day's harvest. Unlike the anonymous fields Luis had described to him, you couldn't go a hundred yards without seeing the Marshak name on a water tank or truck.

When all the arrests were done and the trial under way, Michael hoped he would at least come away with a sense of why a company as prominent as the Marshaks' would embrace illegality in such a broad and reckless fashion. As he was learning, corporate slavery in America was nothing new. It was believed many food companies benefited from the wide-scale use of illegal workers in the Florida sugarcane fields, where conditions were even worse than here. But these corporations insulated themselves behind endless fronts and shell companies to establish unimpeachable, plausible deniability.

The Marshaks seemed to have ramped up their foray into human trafficking with the zeal of a convert and the forethought of a child. It didn't make sense.

The convoy entered the parking lot of the Marshak campus, its yucca- and cacti-lined sidewalks still wet from the morning sprinklers. Michael called DA Rebenold's cell to get an update.

"Everyone's in position at the offices and accounting firms," she told him. "INS and the marshals are in the foothills around the housing complex but won't move in without our say-so."

"The team at the warehouse is almost there as well. They found the Higuera car burning out in the fields."

"Jesus Christ. What about the desert location? La Calavera?"

"Still en route. They're out of cell range right now, but they've got a helicopter with them, so we should hear something soon."

Michael checked his watch. It was 7:48.

"Okay. Give the word and I'll pass it," she said.

"Let's do it."

When Michael emerged from the lead Tahoe, a curious security guard met him at the front door of the Marshaks' admin building. He glanced from Michael to the row of vehicles and back again.

"Good morning," Michael said. "I'm Los Angeles Deputy DA Michael Story. We have warrants to search and seize company documents, computers, and hard drives. The FBI will be here soon to set up a command post to facilitate this. We're going to need help turning away workers and sealing the building."

The guard gave Michael the kind of look that suggested he'd long believed a visit like this was in the cards.

———

Glenn watched as Donald Roenningke's eyes traveled between a page in his right hand and an image on his phone in his left. He compared their salient points with care, eyes flicking back and forth. He looked like a professor trying to determine which of two pupils might have cheated on the final. On the other side of the table, Glenn ate his breakfast in peace, as if the billion-dollar deal hanging in the balance was the farthest thing from his mind.

They were seated in the Bella Vista restaurant in the Santa Barbara Four Seasons, overlooking the ocean. Though its breakfast buffet was one of the highest rated in the country, Glenn had ordered from the menu to keep their ups and downs to a minimum. He wanted Donald's focus. He wanted him to know just how misinformed he'd been about his company.

His counterpart finally lowered the pages.

"I owe you an apology," Donald said finally. "Of course, I'll need my legal team to go over this, but as a lawyer myself—"

"As a lawyer yourself, you know what you're looking at," Glenn interjected.

"Yes. I should've known better. It's not the first time we've been approached by fraudsters looking to disrupt deals, but it's still embarrassing that I gave it credence over not only your word but that of my own due-diligence team. For that I apologize."

Glenn shrugged as if Donald had done little more than lose a borrowed pen.

"They're getting good, these 'fraudsters,' to use your word," Glenn said. "They used to have a reason: a disgruntled employee, a competitor. Now you've got folks just doing it to see if they can get away with it."

"Well, forgive me all the same," Donald stressed. "How about we extend the terms another year to make it up to you?"

Glenn laughed.

"So we can't renegotiate once we've surpassed our performance milestones for another twelve months? That is a definite no. Nice one, though."

"Can't fault a guy for trying," Donald said, palms up. "At least let me buy you breakfast."

"That I can agree to," Glenn said, though he hadn't seen a bill in this place for years.

Their cell phones rang in unison.

"We're popular," Glenn announced, fishing his cell from his pocket. "Hello?"

"Where are you?" came a worried voice.

It was Jack Iskander, senior partner at Baringer & Iskander, who had been one of the Marshaks' primary counsels for thirty years.

"Jack! You'll be happy to hear I'm sitting with Donald right now concluding our business—"

"You're in Santa Barbara?" Jack interrupted.

"I am," Glenn replied, seething that it had not been acknowledged that he had earned a victory Jack and his team should've delivered. "But maybe you didn't hear me. I'm with Donald Roenningke, from Crown Foods."

Glenn glanced over to catch Donald's reaction to his show of bombast, only to see that he looked furious.

"Donald?"

"Fuck you, Glenn," Donald said as he rose and walked toward the door.

"What the hell . . . ? Jack, Donald just stormed out of here."

"He probably got the same news I did. Something big is going down. There are warrants being served at all of your office locations, warehouses, and accounting firms. They've even come here."

Warrants? Against my company?

"What on earth for? What are the charges?" Glenn roared, ignoring the sidelong glances of his fellow diners.

"We don't know."

"Don't they have to say on the warrant?"

"They're vague. They do cite an unimpeachable informant, but they seem to be casting a wide net in hopes of shaking new witnesses and evidence out of the tree."

"Bullshit!" Glenn spat, slapping his hand on the table. "Who's behind this? Is this the same people who tried to screw up the Crown deal? Or is some jumped-up politician who couldn't get his name in the paper trying to use mine?"

Glenn's teeth were clenched so tight his jaw popped.

"We have to get out in front of this," Jack said, trying on a calming tone. "You need to start thinking of ways to deflect this from your personal portfolio."

Glenn went still. *Nothing about containment? Nothing about riding it out? Was his lawyer actually talking exit strategy already?*

"Are you serious?"

"I've never seen anything like this," Jack admitted. "People are already lining up on the sidelines to watch. No one thinks the DA would make such a move without something to back it up."

Where there's smoke there's fire, Glenn thought.

"But none of it's true," Glenn offered.

"You've been around long enough to know that doesn't matter. I've been putting calls in to judges we've known for years. They're not calling back. Apparently Crown got a stack of witness testimonials and stills purporting to show undocumented workers in your fields and warehouses—that was the shot across the bow. What it looks like the DA's got is the broadside, financials purporting to show that this was some kind of widespread and carefully organized effort with players on both sides of the border."

"Are you . . . ?" Glenn stammered. "That's insane! I marched with Cesar Chavez! I signed the first deal with his United Farm Workers in this state!"

"Look, we've been tipped that the DA is giving a press conference in forty-five minutes. We'll know more then. I need you to get down here as quickly as you can."

Even as his pulse returned to normal, Glenn still couldn't believe what he was hearing.

"I'm on my way," he said wearily. "One question: Where's Jason?"

———

No one in the Blocks knew what to do when the INS vans pulled up. The trucks hadn't come for them that morning, so the residents were already on edge. As the vans idled out front, everyone gathered their things and waited, but the agents didn't emerge. Instead, they eyed the apartments, talked into their phones, talked amongst themselves, and made more calls.

Odilia watched all this from her window. She refused to let herself be hopeful. Deportation took time, but maybe this was the first step.

An hour after they arrived, two men got out of the first van.

This is it, Odilia thought.

Then they just lit cigarettes, stared at the makeshift apartments, as if having no idea a thousand people were looking back at them, and laughed about something. When the smokes were done, they got back in their air-conditioned vehicles.

Military vehicles arrived about fifteen minutes later, two dozen trucks with a handful of national guardsmen in each. They pulled up in front of the apartments, and a man in an officer's uniform hopped out to consult with the INS agents. After a ten-minute back and forth, the officer gave a lazy wave to his men, and they poured out of their vehicles and lined up to be directed by the INS agents.

In another unit, someone screamed as if believing a massacre was imminent. Behind her, Odilia heard crying and hushed voices. Another woman, an apparent veteran of such events, told the women what phrases to use in order to get moved to the safer, more responsive medical wing of the facilities they'd be taken to. Things like "sudden and acute" and "sharp pain."

"But they keep track of who comes in more than once," she admonished. "So use them sparingly."

Someone passed the window and knocked on the door.

"Are you able to open this door?" came a voice speaking American-accented Spanish.

"It's locked from the outside," Odilia replied. "What's going on?"

"This is *not* a raid. We have been informed of your status and been in contact with the government of Mexico as to your treatment here in the States. We're here to get you out of this situation."

It wasn't the best-rehearsed speech Odilia had ever heard, but it said all the right things. She couldn't imagine how this had happened, until a realization spread over her.

The priest. It was the priest.

Tears swelled into her eyes. He'd done it. Somehow he'd done it.

The door handle and bolt were unlocked, but it took the INS agents a few tries to remove the jamb. When it was finally down, the door swung wide. The agent stared in at the twelve women for a moment before waving over a female guardsman, a Latina with Carrizales on her name tape. She eyed the women with undisguised horror.

"How many of you are there in here?" she asked.

"Twelve," Odilia replied. "There are five or six women's units, but I'm not sure which are which."

"Can you provide information about the fields where you worked?"

"We didn't work in the fields."

A look of tragic understanding passed between the agent and Odilia.

"We'll get you some help. Don't worry."

"Thank you."

"Don't mention it," Carrizales said. "I'm only sorry we weren't here earlier."

XXIX

Michael rode the rush all morning long. He'd never felt anything like it. The victories piling up at his feet were almost too much. Every phone call, every text, every e-mail was a new document found or connection made. They found building contracts related to the Blocks, leases for the unmarked warehouses, and even customs information relating to cargo containers brought in through the Port of Long Beach.

If they'd had to go in blind, it would have taken months if not years to get a foothold. But thanks to Luis, it took hours. All the more shocking was the key evidence that had gotten the ball rolling. Not the murder weapon, not the location of the fields, not even where Luis believed Maria and possibly others were buried. No, it was the registration of the truck that provided the financial road map once they gained access to the Marshak Corporation's financials. It was a company truck, but not one that belonged to the Marshaks. Not directly anyway. Rather, it was owned by a holding company with a single officer, Jason Marshak. The holding company received substantial financial transfers from the Marshak Corporation, money that inevitably disappeared, albeit on dates a clever Treasury liaison linked to various construction projects relating to the Blocks. These payments went back ten years. Once this was uncovered, the rest unraveled neatly.

Never let it be said criminals were smart.

Of everything he'd recovered himself, Michael's saddest discovery from the files at the main campus related to the laundering of the workers through Santiago's farm and five other alleged landowners' farms. "Alleged" because even as the Marshaks went through the motions of transferring ownership to these trusted former field hands, there were any number of clauses that would allow them to yank it back out from under them. They couldn't sell it to a third party, they couldn't grow anything that the Marshaks couldn't sell, and they couldn't add on to the parcel. For all intents and purposes the laborers and, to a lesser degree, the landowners were indeed slaves, but by the letter of the law, it was perfectly legal.

What quickly became clear was that few in the company actually knew about the conspiracy. The overseers, whose pay was handled by the same shell company that owned the truck Zarate drove, were free to hire who they wanted. No one at the Marshak company would know they were on the payroll. The irony was if more people—specifically, more accountants or lawyers—had known about the illegal side of the business, Michael's job might've been more difficult. Without much effort, they could've covered their tracks more efficiently.

Guess Marshak didn't trust his own lawyers not to rat him out, Michael thought. *Maybe there's hope for the human race after all.*

And in the mix of all of this, he kept waiting for the other shoe to drop. For the blackmailer with the photos of him and Annie to forward that story to the *Los Angeles Times*, to his superior, or even to Helen. But it never came. He knew he wasn't so lucky that the whole thing would vanish. He was now hoping the blackmailer, realizing how stacked the deck was against him, might be holding on to the pictures to use as leverage in a potential plea down the line.

That Michael could handle.

The phone rang. It was Rebenold for the tenth time that hour alone.

"You're about to hear from the state highway patrol. They found remains."

"Zarate?"

"Yes, but even more after they searched the area with metal detectors. They believe the first one they pulled out of the ground is Maria Higuera. There are more coming."

Though he'd assumed this would be the case, it still hit Michael like a hammer blow. She'd been in front of him only days before. He'd been the one who'd sent her up there. Now, like Annie and Santiago, she was dead.

And he would reap the benefits.

"When the press gets word of the recovered remains, this becomes something else entirely," Rebenold cautioned Michael. "As it involves foreign nationals and a major American corporation, it'll be front-page news around the world. We have to be extremely sensitive."

"Of course."

He got off the phone and sat back in his chair. He'd taken over one of the Marshak conference rooms, which was now an obstacle course of boxes and files. A steady stream of assistants and clerks navigated their way over to him, but he asked that everyone set up elsewhere. He didn't want the background noise.

But now the silence was almost too much.

His cell rang. Rebenold again.

"Turn on the news," she said.

Michael looked for a remote for the television on the wall and couldn't find one. He opened his laptop and went to the website for the local ABC affiliate. There was a press conference going on, but he couldn't tell where. It was in front of a courthouse, but it wasn't LA, and the man identified as a police chief was no one he recognized.

"What is this?" Michael asked.

"Henry Marshak just turned himself in for the murders of Annie Whittaker, Santiago Higuera, and Maria Higuera."

Oh, today is just going to be full of surprises, isn't it? Michael thought.

———

The roundup of the Marshak field workers was unprecedented in scale. INS had been told to expect large numbers, but they thought this meant a couple hundred people. When they discovered it was clearly many more than this, they called in members of the Air National Guard to help.

If this had been a typical scenario, a clusterfuck would have been inevitable. Getting local government agencies to allocate hard-won resources for something previously unbudgeted for was difficult to impossible. But in the face of what appeared to be a grotesque violation of human rights directly under their noses, a rare moment of unity coalesced.

Trucks were mobilized; local businesses contributed emergency supplies, from food to toiletries to clothing; and hangars at Santa Ynez Airport were repurposed to house the workers. Cots were laid out and fans arranged at the doors to deal with the stifling heat. Temporary barricades kept the workers corralled and far off the runways.

Though there were far more men than women—Odilia guessed it was about one hundred to one—no one had to be told that the women needed to be housed separately. Few had any doubt what the women had gone through was far worse than the men. The male workers were treated as victims, too, but law enforcement determined the men had been allowed to use the women as unpaid prostitutes. Once they realized that, they couldn't help regarding them as criminals. Several of the male workers had actually looked away in shame when their female counterparts were brought from their apartments. This was the first time many of them had seen the women in the daylight.

There was a prevailing sense of uncertainty among the workers. No one knew how long they would be in custody. Some feared they'd be jailed, despite the agents' assurances. Virtually all believed they'd seen the last of the Blocks, though they hadn't been privy to the inner workings of the Marshak clan the way Odilia had. She'd seen how the laws of the land didn't apply to them.

Santiago told her they'd be heroes, that everyone who'd been wronged by this evil family would rally to them. That they'd start a new life together and raise a family. That he would care for her forever.

And, of course, he told her how different he was from Jason Marshak.

But just like all the others, he'd picked her out because she was pretty. After he'd had his way with her a few times, he decided he would save her. When she was in the metal shack on La Calavera, memories of Santiago kept returning to her no matter how much she'd vowed to never think of him again. She hoped, now that she was away from the Blocks, that all of this pain would finally be allowed to fade.

When they arrived at the hangar, each woman was given two towels, a blanket, two bottles of water, and three military MREs. They were told to pick a cot, shower if they wanted to, and that hot meals would be arriving soon.

As others took cots closest to the temporary showers or food lines, Odilia selected a cot closest to the back doors. Hot as it was, she knew they wouldn't close them at night, and she wanted to sleep as close to the stars as she could.

———

Glenn was halfway to Los Angeles when he learned his brother had confessed to triple murder. It was Jack who let him know, the lawyer sounding now a decade older than he had an hour before.

"This is the last day you need something like this thrown onto the fire," he said with a sigh, "but I can't imagine any day that news like this would be welcome. Additionally, I'm sorry to ask you over the phone, but I need to know how you want me to proceed."

Glenn searched his mind for an answer but found none. He wondered if this was what it felt like to have a stroke. He had never felt less in control in his life, as if he was hurtling down a ski slope, unable to turn or arrest his progress. There'd be a crash soon. What scared him most was not knowing the extent of the damage. It was sure to be a permanent injury, but maybe he'd still be able to walk away with some of his dignity intact.

"Did he call you?" Glenn asked.

"He did, but only to say he'd only talk to you."

"Oh for Christ's sake."

"I agree. I think that would be a terrible idea."

Glenn hung up and told the driver to turn around. His eyes flitted around the back of the SUV, as if the answer were waiting there to be found. He wondered if Henry had heard about the raids and suffered some kind of mental break. He needed to be hospitalized, not arraigned. He reached for his phone to inform Jack of this assessment but then paused.

Is there a solution here? he wondered. *Could they just dump all this at Henry's feet and call it a day?*

He pondered this for the rest of the drive. If there was some kind of crime uncovered within the company, the coincidence of his brother turning himself in for murders—plural—he obviously didn't commit just might spin things in the right direction. Henry had been plagued by guilt and this was the result, full stop.

When they arrived at the police station, the television press was already out in force. They reacted to Glenn getting out of the SUV like iron filings to a magnet.

"Mr. Marshak! Can we speak to you?" they said, hurrying over with cameramen in tow. "Can you comment on your brother's statement?"

He considered saying something off the cuff, then realized he needed to look like a man already in mourning.

"Not . . . not right now," he offered, voice shaking.

A man in jeans and a button-up shirt emerged from the station to escort him in.

"I'm Detective Heidecker. Next time, give us a heads-up when you arrive and we'll let you in the back door."

Glenn nodded and shot a look back. Henry's truck was parked at the curb a few yards away. If the folks in the news vans flanking it had any idea whose it was, he was sure they'd have a camera on it.

"He drove himself," Glenn said.

"What's that, sir?" the detective asked.

"Nothing," Glenn replied. The image of Henry calmly parking and walking in didn't square with the raving madman Glenn had conjured.

Rather than a cell or conference room, Glenn was led to the station's break room. There he found Henry sitting at a card table, legs stretched underneath. The only things indicating he was there in any official capacity were the handcuffs on his wrists. He grinned up at Glenn, as if having finally been discovered at the end of a long round of hide-and-seek.

"How are you, Glenn?"

Glenn couldn't look at him. His eyes flitted to a pair of police officer's union posters on the wall and then to packets of coffee creamer spilled onto the counter next to an ancient coffeemaker. If his brother expected him to play along with his mania, he had another thing coming.

"I want you to know I didn't plan it to happen this way," Henry went on. "I had no idea the district attorney's office was making its move today. I had a feeling they knew something, but today suggests they knew quite a bit more than I thought."

Glenn had prepared himself for crazy conspiracy theories, incoherent raving, or perhaps even jealousy and bile. This rational, almost conciliatory Henry suggested calculation. He'd thought about this ahead of time and was in perfect control of his faculties when he stepped into the police station.

"What did you tell them?" Glenn asked, his voice a rasp.

"That I was responsible for the murders of three people."

"Ah, so you were being a colossal semantic asshole. You knew exactly how they'd react. That is, before our lawyers explained to the police that you meant it in some sort of metaphorical sense."

Henry scowled.

"Not quite. I informed them that people in our employ committed the murders and that they did so at our request. I explained how they were paid and where the killings took place. I also said that I'd aid any investigation into our company. If the LA district attorney had simply waited a few hours, they wouldn't have needed all those warrants."

"But *why*, Henry?" Glenn asked, practically shouting.

"Do you remember when I came to you about Santiago Higuera?"

"Yes," Glenn said, lowering his voice. "You showed me an article about a murder and asked me if we'd done it."

"That's it. I should have been more clear with you then. Instead of asking you if we'd done it, I should've just come right out and told you that we had."

"Are you *crazy*? We haven't killed anyone! We're a Fortune 500 company, for God's sake."

"I couldn't have said it better myself. We are no longer responsible for the actions of merely ourselves but an entire corporation. So yes, let me assure you, we did kill someone, and I believe we've killed more."

Glenn was flabbergasted. He simply couldn't understand why these things were coming out of his brother's mouth.

"I'm not sure I want to hear this," Glenn said, resigned.

"Because you already knew?"

This pissed Glenn off. He shot up from his chair so fast, even Henry looked spooked.

"You want to play the Mad Hatter and flush your reputation down the toilet, be my guest," he snarled. "Just don't expect me to stand by and let you bring the rest of us down with you."

The boyishness left Henry's face. Everything about him seemed to recede, beginning with his eyes. Glenn waited for him to say anything else, then turned for the door.

"She tried to see you, you know."

"Who?" Glenn shot back.

"Anne Whittaker," Henry said quietly. "Several times. She told me at first it was 'merely impossible' to get ahold of you, but when she pressed the matter and included evidence of our practices in her queries, the pushback from our lawyers was such that she feared for her safety. Her words. 'Feared for my safety.'"

"Our lawyers?"

"Apparently it's standard operating procedure. We brazen our way through, and our law firm does the same. Most of the time it works. But it had the opposite effect on Anne Whittaker. The more recalcitrant we were, the calmer and more steadfast she became."

"I don't even know what you're talking about," Glenn said, meaning it. "Are you just inventing stuff now? What do you mean, 'she told you'?"

"She came to me after she tried our lawyers," Henry explained. "It turns out I'm more accessible than you are if you know where to look. Santiago did, and he told her. She showed up at one of the test vineyards with her satchel full of files."

"And you couldn't have just sent her away?"

"I took her to lunch," Henry said. "At first I thought she was a kook. But I've always had a soft spot for kooks. If she'd come up with some mad conspiracy theory she was about to unleash into the world, I thought we should know about it ahead of time. When I saw what she had, I understood that however unlikely it seemed, it was more than that. I told her I'd look into it myself, but she said she couldn't wait long. When she was killed in her driveway a couple of weeks later, I really wanted to believe the police that it was a carjacker."

"What'd you do?" Glenn asked, already knowing the answer.

"I'm one man, and an old one at that. This was a job for professionals, who'd know a lot better than I how to decipher her findings."

"Then you sent these cooked-up files of hers to Crown Foods' lawyers," Glenn declared, furious at himself for not recognizing his brother's mental instability earlier. "Why didn't you just ask me if it was true?"

"So, you didn't know," Henry said quietly. "I was afraid that might be the case. I thought you must suspect something. Maybe you just turned a blind eye. But completely in the dark? There's culpability there, too."

Glenn got to his feet and moved to the door.

"The next time you hear from me will be through our lawyers," Glenn said quietly. "You've made your bed. Now lie in it."

Glenn waited for his brother to respond. Henry simply stared back, a look of pity on his face. Glenn scoffed and left.

XXX

Odilia was hard at work passing out hot food when she heard her name.

"Odilia Garanzuay? Are you here? Odilia Garanzuay?"

She glanced up in surprise. After deciding to reveal to the soldiers guarding the women's hangar that she was trilingual, she'd become indispensable as a translator. She'd resolved conflicts, dealt with medical emergencies ("sudden and acute," "sharp pain"), and passed out supplies. When a Spanish-speaking FBI agent came to let them know they would be interviewed by agents individually starting the next day, it was Odilia who'd stood next to him, translating this into Zapotec.

She hadn't told anyone her last name.

"Odilia Garanzuay?"

A number of the women in the hangar, particularly those who found her new prominence as offensive as her special status in the Blocks, were looking her way. She couldn't feign ignorance much longer. She turned to the agent who'd appeared at one of the barricades and raised a hand.

"I'm Odilia."

As he led her out of the hangar, she assumed it was for some new official task they'd decided to entrust her with. Her only fear was that being recognized as someone who could liaise between law enforcement and the workers would prolong her stay.

Marching onto the tarmac, however, a premonitory chill ran up her spine. The agent hadn't bothered to introduce himself. He wore a dark suit and sunglasses like the others but no name badge. He didn't speak, preferring to hurry along, as if this was an unwelcome task he wanted to get over with.

They passed the mobile command center set up by the terminal and then the employee parking lot, where the number of law enforcement vehicles seemed to triple by the hour. The signage indicated they were heading for the regular parking lot beyond the arrivals gate. As it had been closed off earlier in the day, with flights to the airport being diverted to LAX and Santa Barbara Municipal Airport, it was empty.

Except for a single black SUV.

"Oh God," Odilia whispered aloud.

The agent made no indication he'd heard her, except to pick up the pace. The driver-side door opened and Jason stepped out, a big smile on his face. He waved to her.

"No," Odilia repeated, stopping in her tracks. *"No."*

The agent turned to her, exasperated.

"This is your ticket out of here. What the fuck do you think you're doing?"

Odilia felt like throwing up.

"Odilia!" Jason called out. "It's over! Let's go home."

"No!"

The agent grabbed her arm and squeezed, as if redressing a petulant child. He pulled her forward, but Odilia planted her feet.

"Trust me," the agent hissed. "Anywhere is better than this place."

"No!" Odilia screamed.

The agent was angry now. Odilia turned to Jason. His confusion was turning to fury. This was the side of him he thought he was so good at hiding from her. This was the real man, ugly and cruel, that was right under the surface. Odilia knew him for what he was. He was the person who'd sentenced her to a week of roasting alive in a shack and expected to be thanked for letting her live.

When the agent gave her another tug, she screamed louder. This time someone listened.

"What's going on here?" came a voice behind them.

The agent turned. An Air National Guard officer, a captain, was coming up behind them. The agent sneered at Odilia as if this was somehow her doing.

"We've been authorized to expedite Miss Garanzuay into the care of private legal counsel," the agent explained to the officer. "It's an extrajudicial matter relevant to the case at hand."

Odilia knew that this should be the end of it. But then she saw the young Latina guardsman, Carrizales, standing just behind the captain. Her eyes weren't on Odilia or the agent but on the SUV parked behind them.

"We've been ordered not to let a single witness leave the premises until they've been processed," the captain said. "No exceptions."

"In this case I've been given a court order that supersedes that from a county judge," the agent replied, triumphantly pulling a folded piece of paper from his pocket.

The captain didn't take it.

"Sir, this airport is under military jurisdiction," the captain explained. "That cut through the red tape for the FAA to close the runways. So at present nothing supersedes our authority. You'll have to address this with the chain of command."

The agent faltered, one stone wall of bureaucratic bullshit toppling in the face of another. He released Odilia's arm.

"Please escort this woman back to the hangar," the captain ordered Carrizales.

As they walked back, Odilia tried to thank the young woman but couldn't through her tears.

"You'll be okay," Carrizales whispered.

For the first time, Odilia had hope that this was true.

———

As Jason watched Odilia walk away, he thought his head would split open. If he'd had a gun in his glove box like he'd meant to, he'd have used it. Whether on Odilia, the agent, the officer, the soldier, or himself he had no idea.

It made no sense. The agent had a court order. Did they have any clue how many hoops he'd had to jump through to secure *that*? What did they want from him? *Blood?*

It was madness. It was like setting up a row of dominoes and having them fall up. He had to get away from there. He got back behind the wheel and peeled out of the parking spot. As he negotiated the barricades and lampposts, he fought the urge to plow into them at high speed. He wanted to die.

What kind of woman would do this to a man? Is my love so worthless?

When he reached the highway, the urge to die grew stronger. He glanced to his phone and saw a number of new messages from the Marshak company lawyers. As it began to ring yet again—this time a call from his uncle's cell phone—he realized he didn't care one bit what happened to the company. Had he ever cared? Had it ever been anything other than an inherited responsibility that gave him nothing but pain?

Worse, by sheer quirk of fate it had given him Odilia. But as if realizing its mistake, it was now taking her away.

He decided to let fate continue to have its way with him. He accelerated past one hundred miles per hour. If he hit someone or someone hit him, if the vehicle swerved off the road or hit a barrier, he'd be at peace with this. It was in the universe's hands.

He relaxed. It was nice to let someone else be in charge for a change.

———

The LA district attorney's office resembled an ant hill set ablaze. People were coming and going so fast that Luis saw a steady stream of employees and visitors alike eschewing the elevators for the stairs. He waited for the elevator.

On any other day a man dressed as a day laborer whose face betrayed a recent beating would've raised any number of eyebrows. Today people didn't have the time. The chaos of the Marshak raids had everyone focused on whatever was in front of them. The periphery was just that.

Luis signed in as a messenger and was pointed in the direction of Michael's office. Though Michael was gone, one of the office's pool assistants nodded to the envelope in his hand.

"Michael's out of the office today, but I can sign for that."

"Thank you. He's expecting it. The key is for a bike locker at the Red Line stop at Grand Park. You should probably get somebody over there right away."

"What's in the locker?" the assistant asked.

"Michael knows. I couldn't bring it into the building."

The assistant hesitated, as if running through the few things that couldn't be brought in.

"Sir?" she said with sudden urgency. "What's your name?"

"Luis Chavez."

"You're the priest," she exclaimed. "My God, you're the priest. The bike locker has the . . . um, weapon?"

"It does."

"Okay. I'll retrieve it myself and get an officer to escort me back up. Thank you. Michael said it might not be the easiest thing to take possession of. You seem to have come up with a good solution."

Luis said nothing.

"Oh, and I have a message from Michael. If you came in, I was supposed to tell you that they found Odilia Garanzuay. She's alive and safe."

Luis closed his eyes and said a prayer of thanks. When he opened them, he saw that the assistant inexplicably had tears in her eyes.

"I know a little of what you've gone through the past couple of weeks. We're grateful."

"Thanks," Luis said, collecting himself.

"Do you want to wait? I can call Michael and see if he's going to be back anytime soon."

"No, thank you," Luis said. "I just want to go home."

The package Luis had left at Michael's office contained the registration to Jesús Zarate's truck, the truck's keys, and the ticket he'd taken from the machine when he'd parked it in the public garage under the Walt Disney Concert Hall. He'd marked the level and space on it with a pen.

He'd also left the keys to the public storage unit in Chinatown, where he and Maria had off-loaded the boxes from Santiago Higuera's accounting firm to place in safekeeping. Their decision not to keep them at Maria's house or even Santiago's farmhouse had proven wise.

Carless, Luis took the bus back to St. Augustine's. He still had much to do, but he had to pray, he had to rest within its walls.

When he reached the parish, St. John's was letting out. Having endured a number of horrified looks at his appearance on the bus, Luis ducked his head to avoid notice. A few boys saw him anyway, reacting to his battered face with a mix of shock and bemusement. Though others might've seen his unscathed knuckles as an indication of who won the fight, the boys at St. John's saw only that Luis was still standing.

When he entered Whillans's office, the pastor eyed Luis's injuries but didn't comment.

"A lot of interesting stories coming over the radio today," he said. "Raids on offices and farms. A thousand undocumented workers discovered in squalid conditions, held against their will. Bodies found. One of the founders turning himself in and admitting to murder."

"Yeah," Luis said.

Whillans came around his desk and embraced Luis.

"That's good work, Father," Whillans said quietly. "I'm a fool for doubting you, and it won't happen again."

When Whillans moved away, Luis saw the hitch in his gait.

"How are you feeling?"

"Oh this?" the pastor said, tapping his leg. "Tripped on the rug by the altar. Don't tell me I have to worry about you overanalyzing my movements for signs of my impending demise. I've already got enough of that in Bridgette."

Luis's face flushed red. Whillans raised a hand.

"Sorry."

"No, I'm sorry. Who am I to judge?"

Whillans hesitated, as if searching the statement for malice, but seemed to find none.

"Exactly right. By the way I'm glad you're here. It's done."

"What is?"

"I've gotten the archdiocese to approve your promotion to assistant pastor, Father Chavez," Whillans explained. "While several voiced reservation, a few loudly, I've retained the necessary sway to get at least this done."

"I don't understand," Luis protested. "What about Father Holmes?"

Father Holmes was the current assistant pastor, as well as the priest with the most seniority in the parish.

"Hadn't you heard? Father Holmes is leaving us. A seminary in Georgia needed a rector. He has family there, including an older and infirm sister. He wanted to go."

"And Father Stott-Murray?" Luis asked, referring to an ambitious priest who served as choirmaster at St. John's.

"Of the many sins of the clergy, being unable to cloak one's ambition is the most easily and most often punished," Whillans replied. "Are we done, or do you need to go down the list of every other priest at our parish first?"

Luis did not.

"Then it's settled. We'll meet next week to go over your new tasks. First order of business will be for you to go to the archdiocese with me to meet the bishops you haven't met yet, but also the archbishop."

Luis hated that this glimpse of power sent a thrill up his spine. Whillans noticed the sour look on his face and laughed.

"If we didn't glorify the earthly office, why would our parishioners? And there are good men in the archdiocese. It's just your job to discover who. What do they say? 'Not all who rise do so for love of the pearl of great price, and those that do aren't always the enemy.' There are many things asked of God's priesthood. If only one type of man was called, we wouldn't get much done."

Whillans eyed Luis closely.

"You have a question?"

"Is this because I know about Bridgette?" Luis asked.

"I wish you didn't think me capable of such a cynical move, but maybe I deserve that," Whillans sighed. "The answer is no. In truth I initially fled from this decision because not only are you a good priest, you're a good man. Any minute you're made to spend on parish bureaucracy rather than ministering to the congregants is a minute wasted. But in the coming months I'll need to lean on my assistant pastor more and more. I have to trust that person and—"

"Okay," Luis interrupted.

The pastor extended a hand to him. Luis shook it.

There was a knock on the door, and Erna poked her head in.

"There's a police officer here to see Father Chavez. He said you called him."

When she saw Luis's battered face, she shrank in horror.

"Oh my!"

The police officer waiting in the nave turned out to be Ernesto.

"We tracked Jason Marshak's phone to LAX using a Stinger," Ernesto explained. "He got out of his vehicle but never entered the gate. We're operating on the theory that he saw the heavy police presence and figured it was for him."

"So, where'd he go?"

"The surveillance cameras show him leaving his car behind to get in the taxi line. He left his cell phone on a bench and disappeared. Any clue where he'd go?"

Luis thought for a moment before nodding.

"I've got a pretty good idea."

XXXI

"Worst-case scenario, you resign but maintain your innocence. The company is sold with the understanding that you will have no involvement with it again, in name or not. No stocks, no board seat emeritus, no consulting on the transition."

The speaker was a crisis manager named Brenda, allegedly one of the best in the world, video-conferenced in from her office in London. Jack had explained to Glenn that getting her to ring on such short notice, particularly given that it was so early in the morning there, was a coup.

Glenn didn't quite buy this, given that she could practically name her price.

"You would also have to divest yourself of any investments related to the company, its subsidiaries, or anything else tangentially related," she continued. "You'd also sign an NDA that would prevent you from speaking to the media about any aspect of the deal or about the company going forward, no matter what form it takes. You would also offer to sign a noncompete contract that would prevent you from ever working in this field again."

How did it come to this so quickly? Glenn wondered.

He sipped from a glass of scotch as he sat in his home office, half paying attention to the faces on the computer screen. They weren't talking about some pop star who'd run over a fan or an athlete busted for drugs. This was a company that had taken a century to build. That it could crumble in an afternoon was somewhere between tragic and surreal.

"Does that make sense, Glenn?" Jack asked, still in his office.

"Are we at worst-case scenario?" Glenn asked.

No one said anything. Brenda gave them another second before jumping in.

"If you wish to maximize your potential profits, then yes, that is where we are," she said gravely. "Every passing day, you hurt your position. Divest and sell now, separate the charges against the company from any that might be brought against your family, and your losses will be minimal and solely financial. You won't see the inside of a courtroom."

"But it'd be an admission of guilt," Glenn countered. "I'd be a sacrificial lamb."

The *no shit* look on Brenda's face made him wonder if she'd forgotten it was a video chat. That made him smile.

"It's contrition," Brenda said. "It's the captain of the ship accepting the blame even before it's been assigned. We'd then go to work in the press reiterating that you hadn't been charged with a thing, but that didn't matter to you. What you cared most about was your reputation and your workers. By putting the company in someone else's hands, the story dies faster. No one writes hit-whoring op-eds every few weeks calling for your resignation. Think of the press like a predatory animal. It savors the hunt and kills its own food. It loses interest when a scapegoat arrives on a silver platter, and it moves on."

Glenn supposed it all made sense. She even knew to make it sound like he could wring a small victory out of it. There was just one more point to address.

"What about Jason? Will he be able to stay on?"

The silence that followed was heavy with incredulity that Glenn hadn't figured this out for himself.

"Same deal as you," Brenda said evenly. "No involvement whatsoever."

"No, that's unacceptable," Glenn protested. "A lifetime noncompete for me is no big deal at my age. But this is all Jason knows. He's not the boss here. Why does he have to fall on his sword? I'd think he'd be valuable during any transition, particularly given his relationship with vendors and suppliers."

"I'm not saying it's the easiest thing to accept, but his financial compensation would be as significant as your own."

Glenn stood to make a point, then saw the video screen was framed up on his midsection. He sat back down.

"Hold on a minute. Are you saying it's the name? The *name* is tainted? In one day?!"

"That is what I'm saying," Brenda replied, now agitated. "But you can't look at it like it's something gone in a day. The allegations suggest a pattern dating back at least ten years."

"They're *allegations*!" Glenn roared. "There haven't even been charges, much less anything proven!"

"Right, but you said reputation. Your brother slash cofounder confessed to a triple homicide on the very day your company was raided by law enforcement and over a thousand undocumented forced laborers freed. Headlines like 'Marshak Workers Freed' are already popping up around the world. Not 'farm workers,' not 'undocumented workers,' but 'Marshak workers.' It is the shorthand, it is the perception, true or not. There was no *Valdez*; it was *Exxon Valdez*. This was another hundred-year-old company that had already had to change its name from Standard Oil to Esso to hide negative connotations. These things have permanent consequences in the public sphere."

"What about putting it all on Henry?" Glenn said, reaching. "He's already confessed. Let him do something to benefit the family for a change."

"Doesn't pass the smell test, Glenn," Jack chimed in. "We've looked at all angles and there's nothing there. Everyone knows he hasn't been part of the day-to-day operations for years. It has to be you. If anything, Henry set the stage for you to come in and say that you're 'needed at home.' It'll be sympathetic. Could even help Jason."

Glenn emptied his glass. He needed a refill, and the bar was on the other side of the room.

"Give me the night to think about it."

He heard three or four intakes of breath, the lawyer readying to unleash the many reasons why it had to be tonight as he hit the button to disconnect the call. He smiled at the idea of annoying Brenda and her colleagues, unable to walk away from the big-fish commission, but not knowing if it was theirs or not.

He rose, snagged his glass, and made for the bottles.

"That didn't sound promising."

Glenn dropped the glass. It bounced twice on the Persian rug, splashing out its contents, before clunking into the baseboard.

"Sorry," Jason said, stepping in from the doorway. "Where's Charlene?"

Glenn wasn't sure how long Jason had been standing there. He recovered and picked up the glass.

"Catalina. She got on the last ferry. The Seidels are there for a wedding. They booked her a room at the bed-and-breakfast where they're staying. They thought she could use some privacy."

"So, it's just you tonight?"

"Well, me and my new best friends in the press. You must have passed the news vans as you came in."

Jason shook his head and glanced out the window.

"No. I parked on the fire road behind the pool house and came in through the garden."

Glenn shoveled the loose ice cubes into the tumbler and made a mental note to tell the housekeeper about a possible stain on the rug. He considered a small pour but then filled it to the top despite the consequences that would arrive in the morning. He'd need all the liquid courage he could summon for the chat he now had to have with Jason.

"So, how much did you hear?" Glenn asked. "I would've looped you in to the call, but you were pretty hard to get ahold of today."

"I heard enough to know it's serious," Jason said. "What're we going to do, Glenn?"

"*We?* I don't know what *we* are going to do, Jason. Before deciding that, I think I'd like to know what you have done. They're trying to throw the whole family to the wolves. That's not something I can allow to happen. But it sounds like you've been, well, what's the word? *Ambitious?*"

For a moment it looked like his nephew might disappoint him with a denial or a lie. His instinct was self-preservation after all. But this receded quickly as the young man's face became serious and drawn.

"How'd you find out?"

"I didn't," Glenn said. "From what little I know about the investigation thus far, you're the only one with the necessary access other than your father and myself. And Henry—well, he was never one to cut corners."

"Ah, I should've known my sin was getting caught, not committing the act in the first place," Jason sneered. "That's really your response?"

Glenn eyed his drink dully. Somehow the conversation had gotten off on the wrong foot. His company was collapsing all around him. He knew he should be furious, at least indignant. But there was a part of him, however fatalistic, that felt he'd been proven right. Jason was incapable of leading the company. Glenn was the only man for the job. It could never survive without his guiding hand.

"No, Jason, it's not that," he said, fighting to articulate his thought. "You're family. You screwed up. Now you're here for forgiveness, and I'm here to tell you that you don't even have to ask."

Jason let out a peal of laughter.

"Forgiveness? Do you know what it was like hearing you in that meeting with Crown, railing against them for running businesses into the ground with impossible demands? I almost broke up laughing."

"What?" Glenn asked. "I'm not sure I'm following . . ."

"You've made my life hell," Jason continued. "When I went to college, the last thing I wanted to do was come back and work in the family business. But you said I'd be groomed, that they needed the next generation of Marshaks, that one day I'd run the whole thing. I said yes and sealed my fate."

Glenn sipped his drink. He'd witnessed the father's tantrum that morning at a police station, so why not the son's tonight? *But what a ridiculous display,* he thought.

"But once I made real inroads and people started to take me seriously, you recognized that your own position was in jeopardy. Everyone talking about pushing you aside and letting the new blood run the show."

"No one was talking about that," Glenn said, chuckling.

"Oh, you'd be surprised," Jason shot back. "To prevent it, you put the most impossible tasks in front of me. Streamline this, raise-the-quotas that. Increase profits, lower the overhead. You just wanted me to prove myself unworthy. So maybe I did have to cut corners. Maybe I did have to look to a different labor pool and play a little rougher to keep those rules in place. But I raised those quotas and increased our profits more than you ever could. And there's nothing harder to argue against than success. I earned my place at the table. I didn't get it simply because of my name."

"Is that what you think?" Glenn barked, furious at having his methods questioned in such a way. "It seems your earning of a place at the table is losing us the whole company! There's your legacy. Congratulations. Now, do what you came to do."

Jason twisted his face. Glenn nodded to a mirror on the far wall, where the gun tucked into the back of Jason's pants was reflected.

"You fucking child," Glenn continued. "A child blames others, never himself."

"Then maybe I am more your son than Henry's," Jason said, pulling the weapon and crossing the room to place the barrel on Glenn's chest.

Glenn didn't flinch. He'd had a few guns pulled on him in the early days, usually by mobbed-up liquor distributors. He'd come to realize if they didn't shoot in the first second, they weren't actually angry enough. It was all threat, no bite. He raised his glass to his lips and finished his drink. Jason pulled the hammer back and tightened his grip on the handle.

"Jason?"

Glenn glanced to the doorway as the young woman from the party appeared behind Jason. She was flanked by a priest.

"What are you doing here?" he exclaimed.

"I came to see you," she said. "We ended things badly. I wanted a chance to fix that."

"Who is this?" Glenn demanded.

"This is Odilia, the girl you said I couldn't have, Uncle," Jason said. "The one you humiliated in front of the family."

Glenn said nothing. Jason turned to Luis.

"You brought her here?"

"I did," Luis began. "But before she'll talk to you, you need to put the gun down. You didn't really come here to kill your uncle. We know that."

"How do you know that?"

"If you had, he'd be dead by now," Luis explained. "You just wanted him to understand why you wanted him to die. He gets that now."

"You think so?" Jason asked cavalierly. "To me he just looks like a drunk version of the asshole he always is. You think he's come to a great new understanding?"

"I think you tried your best, and a bullet isn't going to change that," Luis offered. "But if you don't put your gun down, we've got two sheriff's deputies with us who have guns of their own trained on you right now. I asked them to allow me and Odilia a chance to talk to you first. You don't have much time. Do you understand?"

Glenn scanned the room but saw no deputy. It was a good bluff, but he didn't think Jason would go for it, either. "Fuck you."

Jason went to raise the gun, but Odilia moved toward him and put her hand on his.

"Jason, it's over. Please. Put the gun down, or they'll kill you."

"I'd think you'd like that," Jason snapped.

"Not true," Odilia replied evenly. "Hasn't there been enough violence? Annie? Santiago? The others?"

Jason held her gaze for a long moment. She stared right back at him.

"Will you stay with me?" he asked.

"Of course."

"Through whatever happens next?"

"Jason. Please do what they say. Then we'll talk."

A part of him seemed to relax, the tension leaving his body. Slowly he put his arms around Odilia, and she reciprocated. He held her for a moment tight to his chest, then raised the gun to the back of her head.

"This was all for you," he said quietly.

The shot was so loud that its echo sounded like two more. The body wavered, as if unable to decide if it should fall or remain standing. It selected the former and toppled to the ground in a heap.

"Jesus Christ."

The words came from Glenn, who stared at his fallen nephew in shock. Odilia, who had blood splattered up both arms and across her chest and face, eyed Jason's corpse with revulsion. The shattered balcony door, through which the fatal round had been fired, opened and two sheriff's deputies hurried in. The lead deputy kicked Jason's gun aside and knelt next to the body to check the pulse.

"I've got nothing. Help me roll him over."

The two deputies rolled Jason onto his back, but it was clear he was gone. The bullet had entered his torso just under his left armpit and likely pierced the heart. Death was instantaneous.

"Padre?" The deputy gestured to him.

Luis knelt to deliver the last rites, but Glenn waved him away.

"We never bought into any of that malarkey. Save your breath."

Luis waited for Glenn to change his mind, but the older man forcibly pushed him aside.

"I said something to you," Glenn snarled. "Get away from him."

The deputy gripped Luis's shoulder and led him away. Glenn stared down at Jason's lifeless body, unable to comprehend how it had come to this. Maybe his nephew was right. This was his doing. Everything that had happened, everything soon to come, a result of his hubris.

It wasn't Jason who was right about me, Glenn thought. *It was Henry.*

The other deputy, the younger one, helped Odilia wipe the blood off her clothes.

"I'm sorry. We had to shoot him when we did."

"He was right, you know," Odilia remarked. "I did want him dead."

No one knew what to say to this. Luis glanced over to Glenn, who ran his fingers through his nephew's hair.

"He wasn't a bad boy," Glenn declared. "Can you tell your god that?"

"Yes," Luis said, turning back to Odilia.

"Will you pray for him?"

"I will."

"You'll pray for me as well, Father?"

Glenn placed Jason's pistol in his mouth and pulled the trigger.

XXXII

No one criticized Deputies Quintanilla or Poole for failing to recover Jason Marshak's weapon during the confrontation. After all, they'd only stepped aside to call for backup after shooting an admitted killer who'd been holding the soon-to-be suicide hostage. Who could have predicted the old man actually wanted to die?

"Jesus Christ," Michael said when called in the motel room he'd taken in Camarillo. "Who shot who again?"

"A Los Angeles County sheriff's deputy shot Jason. Glenn Marshak then picked up his nephew's gun and shot himself."

"What was the deputy's name?"

"Ernesto Quintanilla."

"Were there any other witnesses aside from law enforcement?"

"We're getting conflicting reports. Some say they were acting on a tip. Others say there was someone else in the room, possibly someone who worked at the residence. They have a description."

"Anybody see a priest?"

There was a pause.

"A priest was on scene, but we assumed he came when the ambulance did. Everyone in the press vans heard the gunshots. It was a zoo."

"I'll be right over."

He hung up and sank back onto the bed. He'd known this motel was close by, as it was one he and Annie frequented. He didn't know if they'd ever been in this room, but the layout and décor were about the same in each. He closed his eyes in hopes of catching one of those memories, finding quiet moments rather than racier ones. Annie propping her head up on one arm as they talked through the afternoon. Annie pacing around on her cell phone. Annie strolling to the bathroom naked to retrieve a towel.

Upon revisiting this last one, Michael felt physical agony at not being able to rise and wrap his arms around her waist.

It hit him all over again in a wave. He'd come to terms with the fact that he'd never see her again, much less make love to her. But it was the thought that he'd never share the same physical space with her that was so overwhelming. He wanted to feel her presence in the room, the subconscious recognition of scent, sound, or simply the feeling of the air pushed aside as she moved past. That her soul had been extinguished and all that remained of her was rotting in a cemetery never to return was too much for him. He'd never feel whole again.

He tried to picture her but realized he was remembering images from the deleted photographs, not ones pulled from his mind. She was gone.

———

A few miles away Henry Marshak was suffering through a night of restless thoughts as well, albeit for different reasons. The few times he drifted off to fitful sleep, with only a thin blanket to cover his old man's body, upon waking it still took him a minute or two to realize where he was and how he got there.

There had been some debate the previous evening as to whether they could keep him in the cells or if a cot in the break room might be more appropriate for a man of his age. A judge was consulted, but out-of-the-ordinary accommodations were disallowed. The fear was that they could be seen as granting him special status due to his name, not his age, and this could affect the eventual trial. This was discussed with Henry. He told them he needed no such special provisions, as it couldn't be so different from sleeping out in the cold desert, which he did on occasion.

He soon learned just how wrong he had been.

In the desert he was free. In the cell, every detail was arranged to remind prisoners that free was the last thing they were. Every surface was cold and hard. It was loud. Lights passed by the window repeatedly. Guards went up and down the hall all night. Rest, much less sleep, was impossible.

When morning light streamed in through the windows, Henry was bleary-eyed with exhaustion. He was hungry and needed to pee but knew it would take a good quarter hour of gentle movement and stretching before he'd be able to stand.

As he rotated his ankles and wrists, he heard sounds coming from elsewhere in the station.

The morning shift, he surmised.

The officers he'd spoken to during the night when they came to check on him, a ritual he interpreted as a quasi deathwatch, were amiable enough, but some looked at him in a way he wasn't used to. They took him at his word that he'd killed innocent people and, if not that, that he'd ordered killing. For no reason he could think of, Henry hadn't prepared himself to be treated like a criminal. Maybe he was the old fool his brother so often accused him of being.

But the officer who came in that morning wasn't chatty. He looked at Henry with pity, not enmity. He brought breakfast but didn't say more than was necessary.

Around eight the detective from the previous day came for him, unlocking the cell and indicating for him to follow. Henry offered up his wrists to be cuffed, but the detective shook his head.

"Just come with me, please."

Henry was brought to the break room, where he found a man in a rumpled suit waiting for him. Judging from the fellow's eyes, he'd filled his tank with nothing but coffee that morning.

"Good morning, Mr. Marshak. I'm Deputy District Attorney Michael Story. There's fresh coffee if you want some."

"Thank you."

Michael poured him a cup and placed it on the table. Henry let it cool and waited for the bad news.

"There was an incident last night at your brother's house," Michael began. "Your son arrived with a gun around midnight and threatened to kill his uncle, your brother. Los Angeles County sheriff's deputies, in the area due to the case, arrived and, seeing that Glenn Marshak was in imminent danger, shot . . ."

He hesitated just long enough for Henry to fill in the words: "your son."

". . . shot Jason Marshak one time. The bullet pierced his heart and killed him."

"Oh my Lord," Henry said, ducking his head as his vision blurred. "He died?"

"Yes, sir."

"My God. That's—"

"That's not all, sir," Michael continued. "Your brother, despondent we believe, picked up Jason's gun when the deputies called for an ambulance and took his own life."

Henry couldn't breathe. His heart grew so heavy he thought he might pass out.

"He's gone?"

"Yes, sir. Of course, with any incident like this, an investigation into the officers' accounting of events has already been opened."

"I doubt that's necessary," Henry said, a million miles away. "What was your name again?"

"Michael Story. I'm a deputy district attorney in Los Angeles."

Recognition flashed behind Henry's eyes.

"Of course. Anne Whittaker mentioned you."

It was Michael's turn to look surprised.

"She was very complimentary," Henry said, his voice barely a whisper. "Did the deputies hear anything Jason or my brother might've been speaking about?"

"That's why I'm here," Michael explained. "Before he died, Jason seems to have acknowledged his role in, if not outright confessed to, the same crimes as you have. But unlike with you, we've amassed a great deal of corroborating evidence and even a witness that claims the actual killer was Jesús 'El Matachín' Zarate, who worked as a field boss in one of your spur fields."

"That's what you're calling the illegal ones?"

"Yes, sir."

"Where is Zarate now?"

"He was killed in a gun battle two nights ago. We've discovered a great number of communications between Jason and this Matachín going back years. We've found no such records from your phone."

Henry paused to blow on his coffee. He took a few long sips as he considered his response. When the cup was half-empty, he set it down.

"I should talk to my lawyer."

"You should," Michael said. "But for the time being we feel that there is not enough evidence with which to detain or charge you. We've been in touch with your niece . . ."

"Oh God. How is she holding up?"

"She's strong," Michael said. "We informed her about your impending release and asked her if she knew somebody who could pick you up. She's waiting out front."

Henry felt lost. He finished his coffee and sat still for a few minutes. When he looked up and saw Michael, he'd almost forgotten the deputy DA was still there.

"I can go?"

"You can. We'll be in touch as the cases progress."

Henry rose unsteadily, gripping the chair as he did. Michael rushed to help him, but Henry shook him off.

"I'm all right," Henry said. "And thank you for your courtesy. I don't envy you the cleanup job in this case."

When Henry stepped out of the building and into a sea of news cameras a few minutes later, he felt as if his body were being consumed by fire. The guilt he felt over Santiago's, Maria's, and Annie's murders burned stronger than ever. But it was compounded now with the realization that his actions had sent his own brother and son to their deaths as well. That justice, an abstract notion that in this case applied to hundreds of faceless people, had been done was cold comfort.

He gazed past the squawking newsmen and found Elizabeth's cold, red-rimmed eyes staring back at him in judgment. *Why couldn't you just . . . ?* they said.

He wished he could turn around and retreat back into his cell, realizing the one he'd created for himself in his own mind was far, far worse.

———

Miguel had never been inside a church, at least not one this grand. His mother hadn't been a big believer in religion, but that didn't mean his curiosity hadn't led him through the doors of a couple of neighborhood churches here and there. He liked how quiet they were and was attracted to their air of mystery.

Not enough to attend services, of course. They were like museums—something to admire from afar. If he hadn't been invited today, an invitation he'd been suspicious of enough almost to ignore, he might never have entered one again.

St. Augustine's wasn't like anything he'd seen before. Instead of a single building, this was an entire campus stretching halfway down a city block. He wondered how many people came in and out of the facility over a week. He then wondered how much money it cleared in the same amount of time.

Having arrived by bus, he joined the throng heading into the nave for Sunday services. Vendors had set up tables in the parking lot and along the sidewalk and were selling religious icons, bottles of water, clothes, and even fruit to people on the way in. One man had several ties hanging over his arm and multiple hats on his head. Miguel didn't own a tie, much less a suit. He'd put on his best button-up shirt and slacks, but even then felt outdone by some congregants arriving in fancy pressed blue jeans, cowboy shirts, hats, and polished belt buckles.

No matter what the dress, everyone's mood entering the church was sober and respectful. Miguel took a seat near the back and waited for the service to begin.

During the hymns he rose but made no effort to sing. During the prayers he bowed his head. During the sermon he half listened. During communion he rose and left. He was halfway down the front steps when someone called him by his uncle's name.

"Mr. Higuera?"

A priest in a black full cassock and Roman collar came up the sidewalk. He was Hispanic and looked young, way too young for the office he represented.

"Are you Luis Chavez?" Miguel asked.

"Yes," the priest said, extending a hand. "I'm terribly sorry for your recent losses."

Miguel shook the stranger's hand warily.

"Walk with me a moment," Luis said.

He led Miguel around the side of the church. They said nothing as they went, the sound of the organ echoing out to them as the congregants moved to the altar a row at a time. When they reached a courtyard with a concrete bench and a statue of Saint Francis, Luis indicated for Miguel to sit.

"This is where your mother and I sat when she came to see me. I didn't know her for long, but she was a very brave, very wonderful woman."

Miguel scoffed. "When my uncle got himself killed, she should have run in the other direction," he said. "Instead, she did the same thing expecting a different result, which a bumper sticker'll tell you is the definition of insanity. Now she's dead. Is that brave? Or stupid?"

"Have you been reading any of the stories about the Marshak workers? She did that. She saved those people."

Miguel looked away, shaking his head. "I know I'm supposed to be in awe of this 'sacrifice,' but forgive me, Father, for wishing it had been somebody other than my whole family who had to pay so that the cops were forced to do what they should've been doing this whole time."

"I hear you," Luis said. "My older brother was killed when I was your age. And all the platitudes in the world about 'God calling my brother home' or 'Heaven needing another angel to do God's work' sounded like so much bullshit to me. Now that I'm a priest I believe in that interpretation of God's role in our lives even less."

"You said on the phone you had an offer that could make my life a lot easier," Miguel said. "That it wasn't charity and it wasn't bullshit. That's why I'm here, though so far all I'm hearing is the latter. If you have something to say, say it. Otherwise, I'm out of here."

"I heard a story that the two deputy sheriffs who kidnapped your uncle from the DA's safe house turned themselves in," Luis began. "I heard they'd been beaten and threatened beforehand."

"So?" Miguel said with a shrug.

"The rumor is that this came at the hands of a gangster out in Glendale, Dzadour Basmadjian. The same guy you work for."

"Whoa. I don't know *what* you're talking about, but man . . . ," he protested, getting to his feet.

Luis went still and did nothing to stop him. Miguel huffed and considered taking off but then sat back down.

"I don't know what you're talking about."

"Whatever the case, if Basmadjian was your employer, I'd imagine he has offered to help you out with some kind of guardianship or relocation," Luis continued. "But that would make you his slave."

Miguel went very still. He was all ears now.

"What I wanted to offer you was to become a ward of the church. Your mother rented the house you're in, but the archdiocese would purchase it outright. You'd live there rent-free until your eighteenth birthday. Anything school related, anything to do with the legal system, anything official, and you've got the church backing you up instead of a man with a dozen targets painted on his back. This, a guy who may or may not one day decide he has no further use for you."

"Let me guess. On the condition I stop working for the old man."

"Did I say that?" Luis asked. "Also, I rang up Johnny Mata. He owns a couple of car dealerships in the Valley. I told him about your skills. He said you're a little young to be full-time but that he was looking for a new IT guy for his shop in Van Nuys. It wouldn't be as much money as Basmadjian's paying you, but it'd be legit."

Miguel thought about this. What did he want to have to do with some car salesman, much less the church? He saw certain advantages, sure, but he just didn't trust this priest.

"What do you get out of it?" Miguel asked. "Does it assuage your guilt for the part you played? That you're alive and she's dead? Or are you just one of those priests that likes guys my age?"

"Oh, I've got a job you'd have to do for me," Luis said. "It'd be weekly, and yeah, it'd be contingent on that. But once you've had time to mull this over, I think you'll see how minor it is compared to what I offered."

"And it is?"

"We have an elderly parishioner who can't make it in to services anymore," Luis explained. "Very nice, very religious old guy. More importantly, he's a guy in need. I go by twice a week to offer him the sacraments of communion and confession. But my responsibilities here at the parish just increased for the foreseeable future. I need someone to look in on him from time to time. Is this something I can ask of you?"

Miguel hesitated. It wasn't what he expected. Yeah, he'd have to think about it.

"Let me get back to you."

EPILOGUE

It was a gorgeous Memorial Day weekend. Wilshire was closed between MacArthur and Lafayette Parks, a small carnival parked in the street complete with rides, a midway, and all kinds of food. A concert shell had been erected at the south end of MacArthur Park Lake. Several people had already laid out blankets, set up tents, and fired up barbecues as they waited for the first bands, which were to start around noon.

Though it was early, peddlers already moved through the area as well, selling everything from ice cream to toys to fresh corn on the cob cooked in a steel vat of boiling water mounted in a shopping cart. Butter and bags of toppings hung off the sides of the cart as steam filled its wake.

In Lafayette Park a crowd gathered around the outside of a large soccer field. There were six rows of bleachers, but they'd been filled for half an hour. The match was a local club game between a team wearing the red-and-white-striped home jerseys of the Guadalajara Chivas (Nanny Goats) and the blue and red away colors of the Veracruz Tiburones Rojos (Red Sharks).

Not that the fans or players were from Guadalajara or Veracruz, the uniforms selected mainly because they were easy to find at any local sporting goods store. Still, there were a few diehards on both sides who'd only play if they could wear their home colors.

A referee sat on the corner of the lowest riser and drank from a bottle of water as the players warmed up. He checked his watch, drank, and checked his watch again. A few rows behind him, Michael checked his watch as well.

In the weeks after the Marshak raids, Michael had barely been home. He felt tremendous guilt every time he pulled into the driveway and saw that the lights were already off in the children's rooms. He'd see them in the morning before school, but he was sometimes out the door before they'd even reached the breakfast table. At least summer was almost here, and in theory, he'd see them more.

Thank goodness for Helen, he thought.

She'd more than stepped up, even as her own business increasingly took her away at odd hours, necessitating babysitters. When this was all over, he'd have to do something big to make it up to her.

This was why he was perturbed. He'd wanted to spend time with his family. Sure, he'd have had to put in a couple of hours with the staffers at the courthouse anyway, but that wouldn't have been much. He'd have had the rest of the afternoon off.

But given what he owed Father Chavez, he'd agreed to meet.

"Sorry I'm late."

Michael turned as Luis appeared alongside the bleachers. In his collar he certainly stood out, but no one seemed to notice.

"How're things at the parish?" Michael asked, hopping down.

"Usual chaos. Had to baptize a baby at Good Samaritan late last night, as they were afraid she wouldn't make it. When I went back this morning, the doctors had revised their opinions. She might be out of the hospital by the end of the week."

"What was it?"

"Autoimmune encephalitis. The baby's immune system was creating antibodies to fight an imaginary tumor. It's often fatal."

"Wow. If I was in your shoes, I don't know if I could've handled that."

"Well, God helps," Luis admitted.

"Of course. '*In persona Christi capitis,*'" Michael quoted. "You are the Lord's vessel. I think I was better with that stuff when I was a kid."

"What about your family?"

"My wife's not religious, and we don't take our kids to church," Michael said, surprising himself by feeling guilty. "When my oldest started kindergarten, she had a classmate who had spent the summer at Bible camp or something. This kid returned full of stories, ready to convert the rest of the class."

Luis laughed.

"They always start with the kids."

"I know!" Michael exclaimed. "She came home asking me all about Noah's Ark and God and floods. I had to make a choice. Get into the conversation about other people believing different things or just do what parents have done for years and say, 'Oh yeah—God. Guy who lives in the sky, sees you when you're naughty, like Santa Claus, so don't act up!'"

"Which did you choose?"

"I compared it to myths and fairy tales she knew: Hercules, Hansel and Gretel, My Little Pony. I explained why people all throughout history have always created fables as lessons and cautionary tales. It was easier than just saying, 'Here's a law. Follow it and don't ask questions.'"

Luis nodded as if this were what he preached, too. Hoping to get on with it, Michael changed the subject.

"I don't know how much you've heard, but the state set up a commission to help accelerate the Marshak workers' applications for legal status. It required emergency legislative authorization, but we called in a lot of favors."

"I'd heard some of that," Luis said. "What about the ones who just want to go home? Like Odilia."

"Working out the kinks with their respective national governments, but it's going to happen, too," Michael replied. "In fact, the Mexican government has been helping us with the preliminary identifications of the bodies we found out by Maria Higuera's grave, as well as with rounding up the various overseers and recruiters who made it under the border. What we're weak on are the cases against law enforcement collusion. It looks like the arrangements between the Marshaks and the cops and local officials were as pervasive as they were informal. No magic ledger or list of names has come up. Did you ever figure out Odilia's story?"

"Yeah," Luis admitted. "Turns out she was taken from her home when she was still a kid. That's how this kind of trafficking works now. They told her parents she'd be working in the north, but really she was in a camp just south of the border being trained. It used to be that sex traffickers looked for girls that were twelve or thirteen. Not anymore. They want them as young as eight or nine to get them trained in these tent cities down south. They just set them up outside an auto plant or other kind of factory. Once they've been brainwashed into believing that's all they've got going for them in life, it's safe to send them to the States."

Michael couldn't quite believe his ears. "Can't we help them?"

"That's the other problem. Prostitution's the easiest crime here. So if the girls are found, they tend to get arrested. They never really know who was behind it, so they can't even identify their trafficker, much less reliably testify against them in court. They're the ones that get lost in situations like these."

"Well, I'll bet Odilia Garanzuay is glad she met you, then," Michael stated. He searched his memory for anything else. "Was there something more to the case you wanted to hear about . . . ?"

"There's you," Luis interrupted.

The statement was made without malice, but it hung heavy in the air.

"What do you mean?" Michael asked, genuinely unsure.

"*Your* arrangement with the Marshaks, Jason in particular," Luis said. "I know it predates your first meeting with Annie Whittaker. But I also know to your credit you realized you were on the wrong side of things and cut off contact. That's when Jason tried to blackmail you."

Michael's eyes went hot. He had no idea how the priest could know about this. The introduction by Judson to 'an influential someone looking to make a friend in the DA's office'? The occasional drop-in by the junior Marshak when he was in downtown LA? He didn't think Judson would give him away out of revenge. There was no upside for someone so attuned to which way the political winds were blowing at any given time.

Then he realized: the blackmailer. Though they'd recovered Jason's laptop from his apartment, allowing Michael to not only discover the identity of his blackmailer but to delete the evidence right away, the possibility existed that he'd made a copy or told someone else.

That someone else was Odilia.

"Don't worry, I don't have proof," Luis said, raising his hands. "And as you're the one overseeing access to Jason's phone and bank records, I don't see that changing."

Michael shook his head, as if trying to dislodge something caught in his hair.

"I don't know what to say. I have no idea what would give you that idea."

"Let's say you were approached at some point by a middle man who said they had a wealthy friend looking for some 'advice'—nothing illegal, mind you—from the DA's office. It was presented like a consulting position. There were a few questions easily enough answered, and some money changed hands but not much. If there had been more, a part of you, however small, might've felt compelled to formally report it to your superiors as you're meant to do with potential conflicts."

"Father, I really don't know where you're getti—"

"When Annie Whittaker first approached you, you didn't even think about it," Luis continued. "You gave him the heads-up that some do-gooder was patrolling his fields and could possibly stir up a headline or two. He reciprocated with the same kind of simple 'Thanks!' and asked to be kept informed if she turned up anything else. Which you did."

Michael went still. He was no longer interested in hearing what the priest had to say. His gaze traveled to the soccer field, where a Chivas midfielder was dribbling the gold and white ball toward the opposing goal.

"At some point you stopped. You suddenly realized that what Annie was telling you was true and that your partner, Jason, was a very bad guy. So you cut things off. I choose to believe that version because the alternative, that you were selling her out while you were sleeping with her, is too much. Particularly after he started trying to blackmail you with that information."

The Chivas player lined up a shot and fired it toward the goal. The goalie leaped and batted it away.

"As you said, you can't prove any of this," Michael said dully.

"In your line of work it's all about what you can prove," Luis said. "In mine all that matters is belief. If you'd just looked me in the eye and said it wasn't true, maybe I would've been gullible enough to have believed you. You're good with words. Your job is about convincing people. But it remains a mystery how the sheriff's deputies knew Santiago would be at that address at that exact time. Especially if you'd stopped feeding Jason information by then."

On the field the referee blew the whistle, but Michael couldn't tell which side was at fault.

Fuck you, priest.

That's when he noticed Luis's hand outstretched in front of him to shake. He didn't take it, keeping his eyes on the field as a Red Sharks forward hurried over for a corner kick.

"Maybe next time," Luis said, dropping his hand. "But let me put this in your mind. I think—I believe—Annie knew, but she went along with it anyway, hoping it'd turn out different. She had Odilia sitting right in front of her telling her stories of motel trysts and powerful men who made all kinds of promises. How could she not draw parallels?"

Michael turned back to Luis.

"I loved her," he said quietly. "I really did."

"Then you're already in hell. Look for me if you're ever ready to come out."

Michael opened his mouth, but no words came out. Luis nodded and walked away.

———

It had taken Luis the better part of an hour to find Nicolas's grave. His mother had been buried alongside his brother in the same cemetery, so he thought he'd have an easier time. But it was night, and in the darkness he couldn't make out enough of the landmarks he'd used to find it in the past. He tried to triangulate the location off the surrounding hills, but without a moon, the silhouettes blended in with the night sky.

At least he'd remembered which gate along the back row was broken, allowing visitors in after dark.

He'd finally happened upon the pair by accident. He was moving methodically from row to row, trying to read the names on tombstones in the dim light. He wasn't having much luck until he recognized the shape of one headstone as the kind his mother had. This made it easier. Four rows later he was standing over her and her other son.

"Hello," Luis whispered, lowering himself to his knees.

When he prayed anywhere else, he prayed to God. But when he was at Nicolas's grave, he prayed to his brother. He knew this was not only apostasy but ridiculous, but he found it a way to place his brother's voice in his head. Not his *actual* voice, but its memory. This always brought back so much else.

He didn't have a conversation in mind tonight, though. After all he'd been through, he wanted silence, but silence in Nicolas's presence. He wanted to remember what it felt like when he still had a brother.

He'd arrived just past ten. It was getting on toward two when he heard the voice.

"Luis? Hey, man, where are you?"

For a moment he couldn't place the voice. When he opened his eyes and rose to his feet, he saw Oscar loping toward him with a six-pack of beer, two bottles already missing.

"Oscar," he said. "What're you doing here?"

"Looking for you, man," the gangster said, holding out a beer for Luis to take.

Luis considered leaving it in Oscar's hand but realized he really wanted it. *Just one,* he thought, taking the proffered bottle and keying off the cap. Oscar sank onto the ground above Nicolas's grave and popped the cap on his own bottle. Luis noticed that his hair was askew and his face slicked with sweat.

"Where are you coming from?" Luis asked, unable to banish the innuendo from his voice.

"Where do you think?" Oscar scoffed.

"What's her name?"

Oscar said nothing for a moment. Then shrugged. "Can't tell you that."

"You don't know, or you don't want to say?" Luis asked.

Oscar shrugged again.

"Sounds like love," Luis said.

"It wasn't, then it was, then I found out a little about her, then it was complicated, and I thought we'd have to go our separate ways. But then we both realized neither of us want to."

Luis didn't know what to make of this, so he quietly sipped his beer. He wondered if Oscar's "work" had ever led to anyone winding up here.

"I'm proud of you, Luis," Oscar said quietly. "You did something good out there."

"It was God, Oscar," Luis replied. "I was just his instrument."

Luis felt Oscar's eyes peering at him through the darkness. When he tried to meet his gaze, all he saw were two tiny pinpricks of light at the center of twin black orbs. It was like looking into the face of a spider. He turned away.

"What's crazy is that you believe that," Oscar said.

"You don't believe in God?" Luis asked.

"I didn't say that. I just don't think God gives a good goddamn what we do. He's not trying to tell me how to live my life."

Luis shot back the rest of his beer. Oscar offered him another, but he shook his head.

"Yes, he is," Luis said. "Just because you're not listening, doesn't mean he's not there trying to get through to you."

"You think?"

"I know."

Oscar chuckled. Luis reached out and took his hand. Oscar froze.

"Pray with me," Luis said. "Just pray with me."

Oscar seemed so thrown by Luis's hand on his that he didn't respond at first.

"Pray with you?"

"Yeah, Sunday school style. On your knees, head bowed, eyes closed. Pray with me."

Oscar moved as if to leave, but Luis tightened his grip. When Oscar tried to bounce to his feet, Luis kept him anchored.

"Thought we weren't going to do any of this 'change your ways' shit," Oscar tried.

"I'm not asking you to pray for yourself," Luis said. "I'm asking you to pray for me."

Luis felt the tension leave Oscar's hand. He still seemed confused but now amiable.

"How do we do that?"

"Get on your knees, bow your head, and close your eyes."

Oscar did as he was told.

"Now, without speaking, imagine that you are before God and you are alone with God."

There was a long pause. Then finally, "Okay."

"Now let him ask you a question. When he does, you answer in whatever way you'd like. And I'll do the same."

Luis watched as Oscar's features relaxed. His breathing remained steady as his shoulders rose and fell. He closed his eyes now and found his brother still there waiting for him. He tried to see if he looked proud of him, angry about his tactics, or conflicted about what had happened. He waited to see if he would say anything. He waited until Oscar had fallen asleep, until the sun began to rise in the east, and until the morning dew rose on the grass around him.

And when it was too late to wait anymore and he had to get back to St. Augustine's to change clothes before heading over to teach at St. John's, he heard the tiniest voice whisper:

Wait just a little longer . . .

ACKNOWLEDGMENTS

The author would like to acknowledge the contributions of the many talented people who took this book apart and put it back together in a clearer, more readable form each time, including Lisa French, Charlotte Herscher, Kjersti Egerdahl, Marcus Trower, and Will Tyler. Also, his agent, Laura Dail, who had faith in the piece since day one and who encouraged the early and most significant cuts (and a thank-you to Sarah Mlynowski for slipping it to Laura in the first place). Finally, he would like to acknowledge the contribution of filmmaker and frequent collaborator Morna Ciraki, with whom he spent hours discussing this story, as he does just about every writing project.

ABOUT THE AUTHOR

Photo © 2015 Morna Ciraki

A Texas native, Mark Wheaton studied English at the University of Texas at Austin and playwriting at Indiana University. In addition to writing novels, he has worked as a journalist, screenwriter, comic-book creator, and video game scribe. He lives in Los Angeles.